CRITICAL PRAISE FOR *SONG OF KALI*

"The best first novel in the genre I can remember."

— Dean R. Koontz

"*SONG OF KALI* is as harrowing and ghoulish as anyone could wish. Simmons makes the stuff of nightmare very real indeed."

— *Locus*

AND FOR DAN SIMMONS

"Earth, air, fire, and water: Dan Simmons. Justly, in awe, we watch him, and marvel."

— Harlan Ellison

"You should be reading Dan Simmons."

— *Denver Post*

"Simmons is not only good, he's versatile."

— *Isaac Asimov's Science Fiction Magazine*

"Simmons is emerging as one of the most flexible and talented writers to enter the field."

— *Science Fiction Chronicle*

"Challenges appear to be what Dan Simmons is all about."

— *Locus*

DAN SIMMONS

SONG OF KALI

TOR HORROR
A TOM DOHERTY ASSOCIATES BOOK
NEW YORK

NOTE: If you purchased this book without a cover you should be aware that this book is stolen property. It was reported as "unsold and destroyed" to the publisher, and neither the author nor the publisher has received any payment for this "stripped book."

This is a work of fiction. All the characters and events portrayed in this book are fictitious, and any resemblance to real people or events is purely coincidental.

SONG OF KALI

Reprinted by arrangement with Bluejay Books

A Tor Book
Published by Tom Doherty Associates, Inc.
49 West 24th Street
New York, N.Y. 10010

Cover art by Gary Smith

ISBN: 0-812-51592-7

Library of Congress Catalog Card Number: 85-15649

First Tor printing: November 1986

Printed in the United States of America

0 9 8 7 6 5 4 3 2

For HARLAN ELLISON,
who has heard the song,
And for KAREN and JANE,
who are my other voices.

". . . there is a darkness. It is
for everyone . . . Only some Greeks
and admirers of theirs, in their
liquid noon, where the friendship
of beauty to human things was perfect,
thought they were clearly divided
from this darkness. And these
Greeks too were in it. But still
they are the admiration of the
rest of the mud-sprung, famine-
knifed, street-pounding, war-
rattled, difficult, painstaking,
kicked in the belly, grief and
cartilage mankind, the multitude,
some under a coal-sucking Vesuvius
of chaos smoke, some inside a
heaving Calcutta midnight, who
very well know where they are."

—Saul Bellow

"Why, this is Hell; nor am I
out of it."

—Christopher Marlowe

Some places are too evil to be allowed to exist. Some *cities* are too wicked to be suffered. Calcutta is such a place. Before Calcutta I would have laughed at such an idea. Before Calcutta I did not believe in evil—certainly not as a force separate from the actions of men. Before Calcutta I was a fool.

After the Romans had conquered the city of Carthage, they killed the men, sold the women and children into slavery, pulled down the great buildings, broke up the stones, burned the rubble, and salted the earth so that nothing would ever grow there again. That is not enough for Calcutta. Calcutta should be *expunged*.

Before Calcutta I took part in marches against nuclear weapons. Now I dream of nuclear mushroom clouds rising above a city. I see buildings melting into lakes of glass. I see paved streets flowing like rivers of lava and real rivers boiling away in great gouts of steam. I see human figures dancing like burning insects, like obscene praying mantises sputtering and bursting against a fiery red background of total destruction.

The city is Calcutta. The dreams are not unpleasant.

Some places are too evil to be allowed to exist.

Chapter One

"Today everything happens in Calcutta . . .
Who should I blame?"

—Sankha Ghosh

"Don't go, Bobby," said my friend. "It's not worth it."

It was June of 1977, and I had come down to New York from New Hampshire in order to finalize the details of the Calcutta trip with my editor at *Harper's*. Afterward I decided to drop in to see my friend Abe Bronstein. The modest uptown office building that housed our little literary magazine, *Other Voices*, looked less than impressive after several hours of looking down on Madison Avenue from the rarefied heights of the suites at *Harper's*.

Abe was in his cluttered office, alone, working on the autumn issue of *Voices*. The windows were open, but the air in the room was as stale and moist as the dead cigar that Abe was chewing on. "Don't go to Calcutta, Bobby," Abe said again. "Let someone else do it."

"Abe, it's all set," I said. "We're leaving next week." I hesitated a moment. "They're paying very well and covering all expenses," I added.

"Hnnn," said Abe. He shifted the cigar to the other side of his mouth and frowned at a stack of manuscripts in front of him. From looking at this sweaty, disheveled little man—more the picture of an overworked bookie than anything else—one would never have guessed that he edited one of the more respected "little magazines" in the country. In 1977, *Other Voices* hadn't eclipsed the old *Kenyon Review* or caused *The Hudson Review* undue worry about competition, but we were getting our quarterly issues out to subscribers; five stories that had first appeared in *Voices* had been chosen for the O'Henry Award anthologies; and Joyce Carol Oates had donated a story to our tenth-anniversary issue. At various times I had been *Other Voices* assistant editor, poetry editor, and unpaid proofreader. Now, after a year off to think and write in the New Hampshire hills and with a newly issued book of verse to my credit, I was merely a valued contributor. But I still thought of *Voices* as *our* magazine. And I still thought of Abe Bronstein as a close friend.

"Why the hell are they sending *you,* Bobby?" asked Abe. "Why doesn't *Harper's* send one of its big guns if this is so important that they're going to cover expenses?"

Abe had a point. Not many people had heard of Robert C. Luczak in 1977, despite the fact that *Winter Spirits* had received half a column of review in the *Times*. Still, I hoped that what people—especially the few hundred people who counted—*had* heard was promising. "*Harper's* thought of me because of that piece I did in *Voices* last year," I said. "You know, the one on Bengali poetry. You said I spent too much time on Rabindranath Tagore."

"Yeah, I remember," said Abe. "I'm surprised that those clowns at *Harper's* knew who Tagore was."

"Chet Morrow called me," I said. "He said that he had been impressed with the piece." I neglected to tell Abe that Morrow had forgotten Tagore's name.

"Chet Morrow?" grunted Abe. "Isn't he busy doing novelizations of TV series?"

"He's filling in as temporary assistant editor at *Harper's*," I said. "He wants the Calcutta article in by the October issue."

Abe shook his head. "What about Amrita and little Elizabeth Regina . . ."

"Victoria," I said. Abe knew the baby's name. When I had first told him the name we'd chosen for our daughter, Abe had suggested that it was a pretty damn Waspy title for the offspring of an Indian princess and a Chicago pollock. The man was the epitome of sensitivity. Abe, although well over fifty, still lived with his mother in Bronxville. He was totally absorbed in putting out *Voices* and seemed indifferent to anything or anyone that didn't directly apply to that end. One winter the heat had gone out in the office, and he had spent the better part of January here working in his wool coat before getting around to having it fixed. Most of Abe's interactions with people these days tended to be over the phone or through letters, but that didn't make the tone of his comments any less acerbic. I began to see why no one had taken my place as either assistant editor or poetry editor. "Her name's Victoria," I said again.

"Whatever. How does Amrita feel about you going off and

deserting her and the kid? How old's the baby, anyway? Couple months?"

"Seven months old," I said.

"Lousy time to go off to India and leave them," said Abe.

"Amrita's going too," I said. "And Victoria. I convinced Morrow that Amrita could translate the Bengali for me." This was not quite the truth. It had been Morrow who suggested that Amrita go with me. In fact, it was probably Amrita's name that had gotten me the assignment. *Harper's* had contacted three authorities on Bengali literature, two of them Indian writers living in the States, before calling me. All three had turned down the assignment, but the last man they contacted had mentioned Amrita—despite her field being mathematics, not writing—and Morrow had followed up on it. "She *does* speak Bengali, doesn't she?" Morrow had asked over the phone. "Sure," I'd said. Actually, Amita spoke Hindi, Marathi, Tamil, and a little Punjabi as well as German, Russian, and English, but not Bengali. *Close enough,* I'd thought.

"Amrita wants to go?" asked Abe.

"She's looking forward to it," I said. "She hasn't been back to India since her father moved the family to England when she was seven. She's also looking forward to our spending some time in London on the way to India so her parents can meet Victoria." This last part was true. Amrita had not wanted to go to Calcutta with the baby until I convinced her that it was important to my career. The stopover in London had been the deciding factor for her.

"Okay," grunted Abe. "Go to Calcutta." His tone of voice let me know precisely what he thought of the idea.

"Tell me why you don't want me to," I said.

"Later," said Abe. "Right now tell me about this Das thing Morrow's talking about. And I'd like to know why you want me to save half of next spring's issue of *Voices* for more Das stuff. I hate reprints, and there can't be ten lines of his verse that hasn't been printed and reprinted *ad nauseum*."

"Das, yes," I said. "But not reprints. New things."

"Tell me," said Abe.

I told him.

"I'm going to Calcutta to find the poet M. Das," I said. "Find him, talk to him, and bring back some samples of his new work for publication."

Abe stared at me. "Uh-uh," he said. "No way. M. Das is dead. He died six or seven years ago. In 1970, I think."

"July of 1969," I said. I could not keep a trace of smugness out of my voice. "He disappeared in July of 1969 while on his way back from his father's funeral, cremation actually, in a village in East Pakistan—Bangladesh now—and everyone assumed he was murdered."

"Yeah, I remember," said Abe. "I stayed with you and Amrita for a couple of days in your Boston apartment when the New England Poets' Alliance held that commemorative reading for him. You read some of Tagore's stuff, and excerpts from Das's epic poems about what'shername, the nun—Mother Teresa."

"And two of my Chicago Cycle pieces were dedicated to him," I said. "But I guess we were all a bit premature. Das seems to have resurfaced in Calcutta, or at least some of his new poetry and correspondence has. *Harper's* got some samples through an agency they work with there, and people who knew Das say that he definitely wrote these new things.

But nobody's seen the man himself. *Harper's* wants me to try to get some of his new work, but the slant of the article is going to be 'The Search for M. Das,' that kind of crap. Now here's the good news. *Harper's* gets first refusal on any of the poetry I get rights to, but we can print the rest in *Other Voices*."

"Sloppy seconds," grumbled Abe and chewed on his cigar. This was the kind of enthusiastic gratitude I'd grown used to during my years with Bronstein. I said nothing, and eventually he spoke again. "So where the hell's Das been for eight years, Bobby?"

I shrugged and tossed him a photocopied page that Morrow had given me. Abe inspected it, held it at arm's length, turned it sideways like a centerfold, and tossed it back. "I give up," he said. "What the shit is it?"

"That's the fragment of a new poem that Das is supposed to have written within the past couple of years."

"What's it in, Hindi?"

"No, Sanskrit and Bengali, mostly. Here's the English translation." I handed over the other photocopy.

Abe's sweaty brow furrowed as he read. "Sweet Christ, Bobby, is this what I'm holding the spring issue for? This is about some dame scewing doggie-style while drinking the blood of a headless man. Or did I miss something?"

"Nope. That's about it. Of course there are only a few stanzas in that fragment," I said. "And it's a rough translation."

"I thought Das's work was lyrical and sentimental. Sort of the way you described Tagore's stuff in your article."

"He was. He is. Not sentimental but *optimistic*." It was the same phrase I'd used many times to defend Tagore. Hell, it was the same phrase I'd used to defend my own work.

"Uh-huh," said Abe. "Optimistic. I like this optimistic part here—'*Kama Rati kamé / viparita karé rati*.' According to the translator's copy it means—'Maddened by lust, Kama and Rati fuck like dogs.' Sweet. It has a distinctive lilt to it, Bobby. Sort of early Robert Frost-ish."

"It's part of a traditional Bengali song," I said. "Notice how Das had embedded the rhythm of it in the general passage. He shifts from classical Vedic form to folk-Bengali and then back to Vedic. It's a complicated stylistic treatment, even allowing for translation." I shut up. I was just repeating what Morrow had told me, and he had been repeating what one of his "experts" had said. It was very hot in the little room. Through the open windows came the lulling sound of traffic and the somehow reassuring cry of a distant siren. "You're right," I said. "It doesn't sound like Das at all. It's almost impossible to believe that this is from the same man who wrote the Mother Teresa epic. My guess is that Das isn't alive and that this is some sort of scam. I don't know, Abe."

Abe pushed back in his swivel chair, and I thought for a second that he actually was going to remove the cigar stub from his mouth. Instead he scowled, rotated the cigar left and then right, leaned back in his chair, and clasped his stubby fingers behind his neck. "Bobby, did I ever tell you about the time I was in Calcutta?"

"No." I blinked in surprise. Abe had traveled widely as a wire-service reporter before he wrote his first novel, but he rarely talked about those days. After he had accepted my Tagore piece, he idly mentioned that he once had spent nine months with Lord Mountbatten in Burma. His stories about his wire-service days were rare but invariably enjoyable. "Was it during the war?" I asked.

"No. Right after. During the Hindu-Muslim partition riots in '47. Britain was pulling out, carving India into two countries and leaving the two religious groups to slaughter eath other. That was all before your time, wasn't it Roberto?"

"I've read about it, Abe. So you went to Calcutta to report the riots?"

"Nope. People didn't want to read about any more fighting right then. I went to Calcutta because Gandhi . . . Mohandas, not Indira . . . Gandhi was going there and we were covering *him*. Man of Peace, Saint in a Loincloth, the whole *schtick*. Anyway, I was in Calcutta for about three months." Abe paused and ran a hand through his thinning hair. He seemed at a loss for words. I'd never seen Abe hesitate a second in using language—written, spoken, or shouted. "Bobby," he said at last, "do you know what the word *miasma* means?"

"A poisonous atmosphere," I said. It nettled me to be quizzed. "As from a swamp. Or any noxious influence. Probably comes from the Greek *miainein,* meaning 'to pollute.'"

"Yeah," said Abe and rotated his cigar again. He took no notice of my little performance. Abe Bronstein *expected* his former poetry editor to know his Greek. "Well, the only word that could describe Calcutta to me then . . . or now . . . was miasma. I can't even hear one word without thinking of the other."

"It was built on a swamp," I said, still irritated. I wasn't used to hearing this kind of garbage from Abe. It was like having your reliable old plumber suddenly break into a discourse on astrology. "And we'll be going there during the monsoon season, which isn't the most pleasant time of the year, I guess. But I don't think—"

"I wasn't talking about the weather," said Abe. "Although it's the hottest, most humid, most miserable goddamn hellhole I've ever been in. Worse than Burma in '43. Worse than Singapore in typhoon weather. Jesus, it's worse than Washington in August. No, Bobby, I'm talking about *the place*, goddammit. There was something . . . something miasmal about that city. I've never been in a place that seemed as mean or shitty, and I've spent time in some of the great sewer cities of the world. Calcutta *scared* me, Bobby."

I nodded. The heat had caused a headache to start throbbing behind my eyes. "Abe, you've just spent time in the wrong cities," I said lightly. "Try spending a summer in North Philadelphia or on the Southside of Chicago where I grew up. That'll make Calcutta look like Fun City."

"Yeah," said Abe. He wasn't looking at me anymore. "Well, it wasn't just the city. I wanted out of Calcutta so my bureau chief—a poor *schmuck* who died of cirrhosis of the liver a couple of years later . . . this jerk gives me an assignment to cover a bridge dedication way out in the boonies of Bengal somewhere. I mean, there wasn't even a railroad line there yet, just this damn bridge connecting one patch of jungle to another across a river about two hundred yards wide and three inches deep. But the bridge had been built with some of the first postwar aid money sent from the States, so I had to go cover the dedication." Abe paused and looked out the window. From somewhere down the street came angry shouts in Spanish. Abe did not seem to hear them. "So anyway, it was pretty dull. The engineers and construction crew had already left, and the dedication was the usual mixture of politics and religion that you always get in India. It was too late to start back by jeep that evening—I was in no hurry to get back to Calcutta, anyway—so I stayed in a little guest house on the edge of the village. It was probably left over from British inspection tours during the Raj. But it was so damn hot that night—one of those times when the sweat won't even drip, it just beads on your skin and hangs in the air—and the mosquitoes were driving me crazy; so sometime after midnight I got up and walked down to the bridge. I smoked a cigarette and headed back. If it hadn't been for the moon I wouldn't have seen it."

Abe took the cigar out of his mouth. He grimaced as if it tasted as foul as it looked. "The kid couldn't have been much more than ten, maybe younger," he said. "He'd been impaled on some iron reinforcement rods sticking up out of the cement abutment on the west side of the bridge. You could tell that he hadn't died right away; that he'd struggled for some time after the rods went through him—"

"He'd been climbing on the new bridge?" I said.

"Yeah, that's what I thought," said Abe. "And that's what the local authorities said at the inquest. But for the life of me I couldn't figure out how he'd managed to hit those rods. . . . He would've had to have jumped way out from the high girders. Then, a couple of weeks later, right before Gandhi broke his fast and the rioting stopped back in Calcutta, I went over to the British consulate there to dig out a copy of Kipling's story 'The Bridge Builders.' You've read it, haven't you?"

"No," I said. I couldn't stand Kipling's prose or poetry.

"You should," said Abe. "Kipling's short fiction is quite good."

"So what's the story?" I asked.

"Well, the story hinges around the fact that at the end of every bridge-building, Bengalis used to have an elaborate religious ceremony."

"That's not unusual, is it?" I said, half guessing the punch line of all of this.

"Not at all," said Abe. "Every event in India calls for some sort of religious ceremony. It's just the way the Bengalis went about it that caused Kipling to write the story." Abe put the cigar back in his mouth and spoke through gritted teeth. "At the end of each bridge construction, they offered up a human sacrifice."

"Right," I said. "Great." I gathered up my photocopies, stuffed them in my briefcase, and rose to leave. "If you remember any more Kipling tales, Abe, be sure to give us a call. Amrita'll get a big kick out of them."

Abe stood up and leaned on his desk. His blunt fingers pressed down on stacks of manuscripts. "Hell, Bobby, I'd just prefer that you weren't going into that—"

"Miasma," I said.

Abe nodded.

"I'll stay away from new bridges," I said while walking toward the door.

"At least think again about taking Amrita and the baby."

"We're going," I said. "The reservations have been made. We've had our shots. The only question now is whether you want to see Das's stuff if it *is* Das and if I can secure publication rights. What do you say, Abe?"

Abe nodded again. He threw his cigar into a cluttered ashtray.

"I'll send you a postcard from poolside at the Calcutta Oberoi Grand Hotel," I said, opening the door.

My last sight of Abe was of him standing there with his arm and hand extended, either in a half-wave or some mute gesture of tired resignation.

Chapter Two

"Would you like to know Calcutta?
Then be prepared to forget her."
—Sushil Roy

On the night before we were to leave, I sat on the front porch with Amrita as she nursed Victoria. Fireflies winked their cryptic messages against the dark line of trees. Crickets, tree frogs, and a few night birds wove a tapestry of nocturnal background noise. Our house was only a few miles from Exeter, New Hampshire, but at times it was so quiet there that we could have been on another world. I had appreciated that solitude during my winter of writing, but I realized now that I was restless; that it was partly those very months of isolation that were making me itch to travel, to see strange places, faces. "You're sure you want to go?" I asked. My voice sounded too loud in the night.

Amrita looked up as the baby finished nursing. The dim

light from the window illuminated Amrita's strong cheekbones and soft brown skin. Her dark eyes seemed luminous. Sometimes she was so beautiful that I physically ached at the thought we might not have met, married, had our child together. She lifted Victoria slightly, and I caught a glimpse of a soft curve of breast and raised nipple before her blouse was back in place. "I don't mind going," said Amrita. "It will be nice to see Mother and Father again."

"But India," I said. "Calcutta. Do you want to go there?"

"I don't mind, if I can be of help," she said. She put a folded, clean diaper on my shoulder and handed Victoria to me. I rubbed the baby's back, feeling her warmth, smelling the milk and baby smell of her.

"You're sure it won't be a problem with your work?" I asked. Victoria wiggled in my grasp, reaching a chubby hand toward my nose. I blew on her palm and she giggled and then burped.

"It won't be a problem," said Amrita, although I knew it would be. She was to start teaching a new graduate-level math course at Boston University after Labor Day, and I knew how much preparation lay ahead of her.

"Are you looking forward to seeing India again?" I asked. Victoria had moved her head closer to my cheek and was happily drooling on my collar.

"I'm curious to see how it compares with what I remember," said Amrita. Her voice was soft, modulated by her three years at Cambridge, but never clipped in the flat British manner. Listening to Amrita was like being stroked by a firm but well-oiled palm.

Amrita had been seven years old when her father moved his engineering firm from New Delhi to London. The memories of

India that she had shared with me supported the stereotype of a culture rampant with noise, confusion, and caste discrimination. Nothing could have been more alien to Amrita's own character; she was the physical essence of quiet dignity, she despised noise and clutter of any sort, she was appalled by injustice, and her mind had been disciplined by the well-ordered rhythms of linguistics and mathematics.

Amrita had once described her home in Delhi and the apartment in Bombay where she and her sisters had spent summers with her uncle: bare walls encrusted with grime and ancient handprints, open windows, rough sheets, lizards scrabbling across the walls at night, the cluttered cheapness of everything. Our home near Exeter was as clean and open as a Scandinavian designer's dreams, all gleaming bare wood, comfortable modular seating, immaculately white walls, and works of art illuminated by recessed lighting.

It had been Amrita's money that made both the house and our little art collection possible: her "dowry," she jokingly used to call it. I had protested at first. In 1969, the first year of our marriage, I declared an annual income of $5,732. I had quit my teaching job at Wellesley College and was writing and editing full-time. We lived in Boston, in an apartment where even the rats had to walk stoop-shouldered. I didn't care. I was willing to suffer indefinitely for my art. Amrita was not. She never argued; she agreed with the principle behind my protests over the use of her trust fund; but in 1972 she made the down payment on the house and four acres and bought the first of our nine paintings, a small oil sketch by Jamie Wyeth.

"She's asleep," said Amrita. "You can quit rocking."

I looked down and saw that she was right. Victoria was fast

asleep, mouth open, fists half-clenched. Her breath came soft and quick against my neck. I continued rocking.

"Shall we take her in?" asked Amrita. "It's getting cool."

"In a minute," I said. My handspan was broader than the baby's back.

I was thirty-five when Victoria was born; Amrita was thirty-one. For years I had told anyone who wanted to listen—and a few who didn't—all about my feelings concerning the foolishness of bringing children into the world. I spoke of overpopulation, of the unfairness of subjecting youngsters to the horrors of the Twentieth Century, and the folly of people having unwanted children. Again, Amrita never argued with me—although with her training in formal logic I suspect that she could have laid waste to all of my arguments in two minutes—but sometime in early 1976, about the time of our state's primary, Amrita unilaterally went off the pill. It was on January 22, 1977, two days after Jimmy Carter walked back to the White House from his Inauguration, that our daughter Victoria was born.

I never would have chosen the name "Victoria" but was secretly delighted by it. Amrita first suggested it one hot day in July, and we treated it as a joke. It seemed that one of her earliest memories was of arriving by train at Victoria Station in Bombay. That huge edifice—one of the remnants of the British Raj, which evidently still defines India—had always filled Amrita with a sense of awe. Since that time, the name Victoria had evoked an echo of beauty, elegance, and mystery in her. So at first we joked about naming the baby Victoria, but by Christmas of 1976 we knew that no other name would fit our child if it was a girl.

Before Victoria was born, I used to grumble about couples

we knew who had been lobotomized by the birth of their children. Perfectly intelligent people with whom we'd enjoyed countless debates over politics, prose, the death of the theater, or the decline of poetry now burbled at us about their little boy's first tooth or spent hours sharing the engrossing details of little Heather's first day at preschool. I swore that I would never fall prey to that.

But it was *different* with our child. Victoria's development was worthy of serious study by anyone. I found myself totally fascinated by earliest noises and most awkward movements. Even the repellant act of changing diapers could be delightful when my child—*my child*—would wave her pudgy arms and look up at me in what I took to be loving appreciation at the thought of her father, *a published poet*, carrying out such mundane tasks for her. When, at seven weeks, she blessed us with her first real smile one morning, I immediately called Abe Bronstein to share the good news. Abe, who was as well known for never rising before ten-thirty in the morning as he was for his sense of good prose, congratulated me and gently pointed out that I had called at 5:45 A.M.

Now that Victoria was seven months old, it was even more obvious that she was a gifted child. She had learned to play "So big!" almost a month earlier and had mastered "Peeka-boo!" weeks before that. She was creeping at six and a half months—a sure sign of high intelligence, despite Amrita's comments to the contrary—and it didn't bother me at all that Victoria's attempts at locomotion invariably moved her backwards. Each day now her language abilities became stronger, and although I hadn't been able to pick *dada* or *mama* out of the babble of syllables (even when I played back my tapes at half-speed), Amrita assured me, with only a slight smile, that she had heard several complete Russian or German words and once an entire sentence in Hindi. Meanwhile, I read to Victoria every evening, alternating Mother Goose with Wordsworth, Keats, and carefully chosen excerpts from Pound's "Cantos." She showed a preference for Pound.

"Shall we go to bed?" asked Amrita. "We need to get an early start tomorrow."

Something in Amrita's voice caught my attention. There were times when she asked, "Shall we go to bed?" and there were times when she said *Shall we go to bed*? This had been one of the latter.

I carried Victoria up to her crib and tucked her in. I stood and watched a minute as she lay there on her stomach under the light quilt, surrounded by her stuffed animals, her head against the bumper pad. The moonlight lay across her like a benediction.

In a while I went downstairs, locked the house, turned off the lights, and came back upstairs to where Amrita was waiting in bed.

Later, in the last seconds of our lovemaking, I turned to look at her face as if seeking the answer to unasked questions there, but a cloud had crossed the moon and everything was lost in the sudden darkness.

Chapter Three

"At midnight, this city is Disneyland."
—Subrata Chakravarty

We flew into Calcutta at midnight, coming in from the south, over the Bay of Bengal.

"My God," I whispered. Amrita leaned across me to peer out the window.

On the advice of her parents, we had flown BOAC into Bombay to go through customs there. That had worked fine, but the connecting Air India flight to Calcutta had been delayed for three hours due to mechanical problems. We finally were allowed to board, only to sit at the terminal for another hour with no lights or air conditioning because the external generators had been detached. A businessman in the row ahead of us said that the Bombay-Calcutta flight had been late every day for three weeks because of a feud between the pilot and flight engineer.

Once airborne, we were routed far south of our path because of severe thunderstorms. Victoria had fussed much of the evening, but now she was sleeping in her mother's arms.

"My God," I said again. Calcutta was stretched out below, over 250 square miles of city, a galaxy of lights after the absolute blackness of cloud tops and the Bay of Bengal. I had flown into many cities at night, but none like this. Instead of the usual geometries of electric lights, Calcutta at midnight was ablaze with countless lanterns, open fires, and a strange, soft glow—an almost fungal phosphorescence—that oozed from a thousand unseen sources. Instead of the predictable urban progression of straight lines—streets, highways, parking lots—Calcutta's myriad of fires seemed scattered and chaotic, a jumbled constellation broken only by the dark curve of the river. I imagined that this was what London or Berlin must have looked like—burning—to awed bomber crews during the war.

Then the wheels touched down, the terrible humidity invaded the cool cabin, and we were out in and part of the shuffling crowd making its way toward Baggage Claims. The terminal was small and filthy. Despite the late hour, sweating mobs were jostling and shouting all around us.

"Wasn't someone supposed to meet us?" asked Amrita.

"Yeah." I had rescued the four bags from the broken conveyor belt, and we stood by them as the crowd ebbed and flowed against us. There was a sense of hysteria in the pulses of white-shirted, saried humanity in the little building. "Morrow had a contact with the Bengali Writers' Union. Some fellow named Michael Leonard Chatterjee was supposed to give us a ride to the hotel, but we're hours late. He probably went home. I'll try to get a cab."

One glance at the doorway jammed with shoving, shouting men made me stay standing by the bags.

"Mr. and Mrs. Luczak. Robert Luczak?"

"*Loo-zack*," I said, automatically correcting the pronunciation. "Yes, I'm Robert Luczak." I looked at the man who had shoved his way up to us. He was tall and skinny, wearing dirty brown trousers and a white shirt that looked gray and grimy in the green fluorescent lighting. His face was relatively young—late twenties, perhaps—and clean-shaven, but his black hair stood out in great electric tufts and his dark, piercing eyes gave an impression of such intensity that it bordered on a sense of restrained violence. His eyebrows were dark brush strokes that almost met above a falcon's predatory beak. I took half a step back and dropped a suitcase to free my right hand. "Mr. Chatterjee?"

"No, I have not seen Mr. Chatterjee," he replied shrilly. "I am M. T. Krishna." At first, through the noise and heavy singsong dialect, I heard it as "empty Krishna."

I extended my hand, but Krishna had turned and was leading the way outside. He used his right arm to shove people aside. "This way, please. Quickly, quickly."

I nodded at Amrita and lifted three of the bags. Incredibly, Victoria had continued to sleep through the heat and bedlam. "Are you with the Writers' Union?" I asked.

"No, no, no." Krishna did not turn his head as he spoke. "I am a part-time teacher, you see. I have contacts with the U.S. Education Foundation in India. My supervisor, Mr. Shah, was contacted by his very good and longtime friend, Mr. Abraham Bronstein of New York City, who asked me to extend this kindness. Quickly."

Outside, the air seemed even heavier and more moist than in the steaming terminal. Searchlights illuminated a silver sign above the terminal doors. "Dum-Dum Airport," I read aloud.

"Yes, yes. It is here they made the bullets until they were outlawed after World War Number One," said Krishna. "This way, please."

Suddenly we were surrounded by a dozen porters clamoring to carry our few bags. The men were reed-thin, bare-legged, draped in brown rags. One was missing an arm. Another looked as if he had been in a terrible fire: his chin was welded to his chest by great wattles of scar tissue. Evidently he could not speak, but urgent sounds gurgled up from his ruined throat.

"Give them the luggage," snapped Krishna. He gestured imperiously as the porters scrambled over one another to get at the bags.

We had to walk only sixty feet or so along the curved drive. The air was weighted with moisture, as dark and heavy as a soaked army blanket. For a dizzy second I thought it was snowing, as the air appeared to be swirling with white flecks; then I realized that there were a million insects dancing in the beams of the terminal spotlights. Krishna gestured to the porters, pointed to a vehicle, and I stopped in surprise. "A bus?" I said, although the blue-and-white van was more of a jitney than a full-fledged bus. The legend USEFI was printed along its side.

"Yes, yes, yes. It was the only transport available. Quickly now."

One of the porters, agile as a monkey, clambered up the back of the bus to the roof. Our four bags were handed up and secured to the luggage rack. As they tied down a strip of black plastic over the luggage, I wondered idly why we couldn't have taken them in the bus. Shrugging, I fumbled out two five-rupee notes to tip the porters. Krishna took them out of my hand, gave one back.

"No. It is too much," he said. I shrugged again and helped Amrita to get aboard. Victoria had finally awakened at the shouting of the agitated porters and was adding her shrill cry to the general confusion. We nodded at the sleepy driver and took the second seat on the right. At the door, Krishna was arguing with three of the porters who had carried our bags. Amrita did not understand all of the cascade of Bengali, but she picked up enough to tell me that the porters were upset because they could not divide five rupees three ways. They demanded another rupee. Krishna shouted something and went to close the door of the bus. The oldest porter, his face a maze of deep gullies forested with white stubble, stepped forward and blocked the folding door with his body. Other porters drifted over from their place near the terminal doors. Shouts turned to screams.

"For Chrissake," I said to Krishna, "here, give them a few more rupees. Let's get out of here."

"No!" Krishna's gaze swept my direction, and the violence there was no longer restrained. It held the gleeful look one sees on the faces of men at a blood sport. "It is too much," he said firmly.

There was a mob of porters at the door now. Suddenly hands began slapping against the side of the bus. The driver sat up and adjusted his cap nervously. The old man in the doorway had stepped up onto the lowest step as if to enter, but Krishna put three fingers against the bare chest and pushed firmly. The old man fell backward onto the sea of brown-garbed forms.

Gnarled fingers suddenly gripped the partially opened window next to Amrita, and the porter with the burned face pulled himself up as if he were on a chinning bar. Inches from us, his mouth worked frantically, and we could see that he had no tongue. Saliva spattered the dust-streaked window.

"Goddammit, Krishna!" I rose to give the porters the money. At that moment three policemen appeared out of the shadows. They wore white helmets, Sam Browne belts, and khaki shorts. Two of them carried *lathi* sticks—the Indian version of a cop's nightstick—three feet of heavy wood with an iron core in the business end.

The mob of porters continued shouting, but melted back to let the police advance. The scarred face dropped away from Amrita's window. The first cop banged his stick on the front of the bus, and the old porter turned to shout his complaints. The policeman raised his deadly club and screamed back. Krishna took the opportunity to swing the handle that closed the door of the bus. He snapped two syllables to the driver and we began to move, accelerating quickly down the dark driveway. There was a loud clang as a thrown rock struck the rear of the bus.

Then we were out of the airport and swinging onto an empty four-lane road. "VIP Highway," called Krishna from where he still stood by the door. "Traveled only by very important persons." A pale billboard flashed by to the right. The simple message—in Hindi, Bengali, and English—read WELCOME TO CALCUTTA.

We drove without headlights, but the interior lights of the

bus stayed on. Amrita's lovely eyes were set with circles of fatigue. Victoria—too exhausted to sleep, tired of crying—made mewling noises from her mother's arms. Krishna sat down sideways on the seat in front of us, hawk nose in profile, his angry countenance illuminated by the overhead bulbs and an occasional street light.

"I went to university in the States for almost three years," he said.

"Really?" I said. "That's very interesting." I felt like smashing the stupid son of a bitch's face in for creating such a mess.

"Yes, yes. I worked with blacks, Chicanos, red Indians. The oppressed people of your country."

The marshy fields of darkness that had bordered the highway gave way suddenly to a jumble of shacks that came right up to the shoulder of the road. Lanterns glowed through burlap walls. In the distance a bonfire showed sharp silhouettes moving jerkily in front of yellow flames. Seemingly without transition we were out of the country and winding through narrow, rain-filled streets that twisted past blocks of derelict high-rises, miles of tin-roofed slums, and endless vistas of decaying, blackened storefronts.

"My professors were fools. Conservative fools. They thought that literature was composed of dead words in books."

"Yes," I said. I had no idea of what Krishna was talking about.

The streets were flooded. Water stood two and three feet deep in places. Under tattered canvas, robed figures sat and slept and squatted and stared at us with eyes that showed only white in orbs of shadow. Each alley gave a glimpse of open rooms, starkly lit courtyards, shadows moving within shadows. A frail man pulling a heavy cart had to leap aside as our bus roared past, throwing a curtain of water across him and his load. He shook his fist, and his mouth shaped unheard obscenities.

The buildings seemed ancient beyond age, decayed remnants of some forgotten millennium—some pre-human age—for the shadows, angles, apertures, and emptinesses did not fit the architecture of man. Yet, on every second or third floor there were open-windowed glimpses of humanity inhabiting these druidic shambles: bare bulbs swinging, bobbing heads, peeled walls with plaster rotting off the white rib-bones of the building, garish illustrations of multi-armed deities clipped from magazines and taped crookedly to walls or windowpanes, the cries of children playing, running, fleeing through the knife-blackened alleys, the wail of infants half heard—and everywhere the random movement caught in the corner of one's vision, the sibilant rush of the bus's tires on wet clay and tarmac, and the sight of sheeted figures lying like corpses in the sidewalk shadows. A terrible feeling of *déjà vu* came over me.

"I quit in disgust when a fool of a professor would not accept my paper on Walt Whitman's debt to Zen Buddhism. An arrogant, parochial fool."

"Yes," I said. "Do you think we could turn off these inside lights?"

We were approaching the center of the city. Rotting residential slums gave way to larger, even more decayed-looking buildings. There were few street lights. Vague flickers of heat lightning were reflected in the deep pools of black water that filled the intersections. Every darkened storefront seemed to hold the silent, sheeted forms lying like unclaimed bundles of laundry or propped up to watch us pass. The yellow lights inside the bus made the three of us look like waxen corpses. I knew now how prisoners of war must feel while being paraded through the streets of the enemy's capital.

Ahead, a boy stood atop a crate in a black circle of water and swung what I took to be a dead cat by its tail. He threw it as the bus approached, and it was not until the furry corpse bounced hollowly off the windshield that I realized it had been a rat. The driver cursed and swerved toward the child. The boy leaped away with a flash of brown legs, and the crate he had been standing on splintered under our right wheel.

"You understand, of course, because you are a poet," said Krishna, and bared small, sharp teeth.

"What about the lights?" I asked. I could feel the rage rising in me. Amrita touched my arm with her left hand.

Krishna snapped something in Bengali. The driver shrugged and grunted an answer.

"The switch is broken," said Krishna.

We swung into an open square. What may have been a park cut a solid line of blackness through the maze of sagging buildings. Two streetcars sat abandoned in the center of a cluttered plaza while a dozen families huddled nearby under sagging canvas. It began to rain again. The sudden downpour beat at the metal of the bus like fists from the dark sky. Only the driver's side of the windshield had a wiper, and it moved sluggishly against the curtain of water that soon put a veil between the city and us.

"We must talk about Mr. M. Das," said Krishna.

I blinked. "I would like the lights *out*," I said slowly and distinctly. The irrational fury had been building in me since the airport. In a second I knew I would be choking this smug, insensitive cretin; choking him until his froglike eyes popped out of his stupid head. I felt the anger flow down into me like the heat from a strong drink. Amrita must have sensed my second of insanity, for her restraining hand closed on my arm like a vise.

"It is very important that I talk to you about Mr. M. Das," said Krishna. The heat in the bus was almost overpowering. Sweat stood on our faces like burn blisters. Our breath seemed to hang in the air like vapor while the world remained obliterated by the crashing downpour outside.

"I'll turn out the fucking lights," I said, and started to rise. Amrita would have held me back with both hands had it not been for Victoria.

Krishna's heavy brows went up in surprise as I towered over him. I freed my right arm just as Amrita said, "It doesn't matter, Bobby. We're here. Look, there's the hotel."

I paused and then stooped to look out the window. The downpour had stopped as suddenly as it had begun, and only a light drizzle continued to fall. My anger diminished with the ebbing sound of rain on the roof.

"We will perhaps speak later, Mr. Luczak," said Krishna. "It is most important. Tomorrow, perhaps."

"Yeah." I lifted Victoria in my arms and led the way off the bus.

The front of the Oberoi Grand Hotel was as dark as a granite cliff, but a little light escaped from the double doorway. A tattered awning ran to the curb. On either side, standing silently under rain-slicked umbrellas, were a dozen or so shadowy figures. Some were holding soggy placards. I could make out a hammer and sickle, and the English word UNFAIR on one. "Strikers," said Krishna as he snapped his fingers at a sleepy, red-vested porter. I shrugged. A picket line outside a pitch-black hotel at one-thirty A.M. in monsoon-drenched Calcutta did not surprise me. Sometime in the previous half-hour, my sense of reality had slipped its tether. A roaring filled my ears like the rasp of countless insect legs. *Jet lag*, I thought.

"Thank you for picking us up," said Amrita as Krishna hopped back aboard the bus.

He flashed his baby shark's grimace. "Yes, yes. I talk to you tomorrow. Good night. Good night."

The entrance to the hotel seemed to include several dark hallways that separated the lobby from the street like a protective labyrinth. The lobby itself was bright enough. The clerk was wide awake, smartly dressed, and pleased to see us. Yes, the reservations were right here for Mr. and Mrs. Luczak. Yes, they had received our Telex about the delay. The baggage porter was an old man, but he cooed at Victoria as we took the elevator to the sixth floor and I gave him ten rupees as he left us.

Our room was as cavernous and shadowy as everything else in the city, but it seemed relatively clean and there was a heavy bolt on the door.

"Oh, no!" It was Amrita's voice from the bathroom. I was there in three strides with my heart pounding.

"There are no towels," said Amrita. "Only washcloths." We both began to laugh then. One of us would stop, only to have the other start it up again.

It took us ten minutes to make a nest for Victoria on the empty bed, to strip off our sweat-sodden clothes, rinse up as well as possible, and crawl under the thin spread together. The air conditioner clunked and wheezed hollowly. Somewhere closeby, a toilet flushed explosively. The throbbing sound in my ears was the echo of jet engines.

"Sweet dreams, Victoria," said Amrita. The baby cooed softly in her sleep.

We were asleep in two minutes.

Chapter Four

"And on the great courtyard after the breaking of local barriers
Complete communication between men, affable loiterings begin."

—Purnendu Patri

"Everything always seems better in the morning light," said Amrita.

We were having breakfast in the Garden Café of the hotel. Victoria was gurgling happily from the highchair the obliging waiters had brought us. The café looked out on the gardens which filled the courtyard. Workers on scaffolds called merrily to one another.

I drank my tea, nibbled on the toasted muffin, and read the Calcutta English-language paper. The editorial called for a more modern transit system. Ads sold saris and motorcycles. A smiling Indian family held up bottles of Coca-Cola. Nearby on the page there was a close-up photo of a corpse—decomposing, face laid open like a burst rubber tire, glazed eyes protruding. The body had been discovered in an unclaimed steel trunk in Howrah Railway Station just yesterday—Thursday, July 14—and anyone who could furnish a clue as to the identity of the deceased should contact the Inspector of Police, Howrah, Govt Rly, and mention case No. 23 dt. 14.7.77 u/s 302/301 I.P.C. (S.R. 39/77).

I folded the paper and set it on the table.

"Mr. Luczak? Good morning!" I rose to shake hands with the middle-aged Indian gentleman who had approached us. He was short, light-skinned, almost bald, and wore thick, horn-rimmed glasses. His tropical worsted suit was impeccably tailored, and his handshake was gentle. "Mr. Luczak," he said, "I am Michael Leonard Chatterjee. Mrs. Luczak, a great pleasure to meet you." He bowed slightly and took Amrita's hand in his. "My sincere apologies for not meeting you at the airport last night. My driver mistakenly informed me that the Bombay flight had been delayed until this morning."

"No problem," I said.

"But unfortunate and inhospitable to have to enter a city without being properly welcomed. I do apologize. We are most pleased that you are here."

"Who is 'we'?" I asked.

"Please join us," said Amrita.

"Thank you. What a beautiful child! She has your eyes, Mrs. Luczak. 'We' are the Bengali Writers' Union, Mr. Luczak. We have been in repeated contact with Mr. Morrow and his fine publication, and we look forward to sharing with you the most recent work of Bengal's . . . no, of *India's* finest poet."

"So M. Das is still alive?"

Chatterjee smiled gently. "Oh, most assuredly, Mr. Luczak. We have received numerous correspondences from him in the past six months."

"But have you seen him?" I pressed. "Can you be sure it's M. Das? Why has he disappeared for eight years? When can I meet with him?"

"All in good time, Mr. Luczak," said Michael Leonard Chatterjee. "All in good time. I have arranged for an initial meeting for you with the executive council of our writers' union. Would two P.M. today be convenient for you? Or would you and Mrs. Luczak like a day to rest and sightsee?"

I glanced at Amrita. We had already decided that if I did not need a translator, she and Victoria would stay at the hotel and rest. "Today would be fine," I said.

"Marvelous, marvelous. I will send a car at one-thirty."

We watched as Michael Leonard Chatterjee left the café. Behind us, workmen on bamboo scaffolds shouted happily to hotel employees walking through the gardens. Victoria banged loudly on the tray of her highchair and joined in the merriment.

The billboard in the littered plaza across the street from the hotel was for the United Bank of India. It had no illustration, only black letters on a white background: *Calcutta—Cultural Capital of the Nation?—A Definition of Obscenity*? It seemed a strange way to advertise a bank.

The car was small, black Premiere with a driver in cap and khaki shorts. We set off down Chowringhee Road, and as we crawled through heavy traffic I had a chance to look at Calcutta in the daylight.

The scene was almost comical in its mad intensity. Pedestrians, flotillas of bicycles, oriental-looking rickshaws, automobiles, flatbed trucks adorned with swastikas, countless motorbikes, and creaking bullock carts all vied for our narrow lane of torn-up pavement. Cattle wandered freely, blocking traffic, poking their heads into shops, and wading through heaps of raw garbage which were stacked on curbs or piled in the center of the street. At one point the refuse lay knee-deep for three blocks, lining the street like a dike. Human beings also waded through it, competing with the cattle and crows for edible bits.

Farther on, schoolgirls in prim white blouses and blue skirts crossed the street in single file while a brown-belted policeman held up traffic for them. The next intersection was dominated by a small red temple that sat squarely in the center of the road. The sweet smell of incense and sewage came in through the open window of the car. Red banners hung from wires and decaying facades. And everywhere was the unceasing movement of brown-skinned humanity—an almost tidal flow of jostling, white- and tan-garbed population which seemed to make the very air heavy with its moist exhalations.

Calcutta in the light was impressive, perhaps a trifle intimidating, but it caused none of the strange fear and anger of the night before. I closed my eyes and tried to analyze the fury that had seized me on the bus, but the heat and noise prevented me from concentrating. Every bicycle bell in the universe seemed to be combining with car horns, shouts, and the rising susurration of the city itself to create a wall of noise that was almost physical in its impact.

The Writers' Union had its headquarters in a gray, hulking structure just off Dalhousie Square. Mr. Chatterjee met me at the base of the stairs and led the way to the third floor. The room was large and windowless. The fading remnants of a fresco looked down from the begrimed ceiling, and seven people looked up from a green-baized table.

Introductions were made. I was terrible at remembering people's names in the best of circumstances, and I felt a sense of vertigo as I tried to fix the lists of Bengali syllables I was hearing with the brown and cultured faces. The only woman there, tired face, gray hair, and heavy green sari, which she was constantly readjusting on her shoulder, seemed to be named Leela Meena Basu Belliappa.

There were several minutes of small talk made difficult by our dialects. I found that if I relaxed and let the singsong rush of Indian English flow over me, the meaning came soon enough. The choppy lilt of their speech was strangely soothing, almost hypnotizing. Suddenly a white-smocked retainer appeared from the shadows and distributed chipped cups heavy with sugar, clotted buffalo milk, and a little tea. I sat between the woman and the director of the executive council, a Mr. Gupta. He was a tall, middle-aged man with a thin face and a ferocious overbite. I found myself wishing that Amrita had come along. Her stolid presence would have been a buffer between me and these intense strangers.

"I believe that Mr. Luczak should hear our offer," said Gupta suddenly. The others nodded. As if on cue, the lights went off.

It was pitch-black in the windowless room. There were shouts from various places in the building, and candles were brought in. Mr. Chatterjee leaned across the table and assured me that this was a common occurrence. It seemed that there were daily blackouts as the inadequate electrical power was shunted from one part of the city to another.

Somehow the darkness and candlelight seemed to accentuate the heat. I felt somewhat light-headed and gripped the edge of the table.

"Mr. Luczak, you are aware that it is a unique privilege to receive the masterwork of a great Bengali poet such as M. Das." Mr. Gupta's voice was as reedy as an oboe. The heavy notes hung in the air. "Even we have not seen the complete version of this work. I hope that the readers of your magazine appreciate this honor."

"Yes," I said. There was a drop of sweat beading on the end of Mr. Gupta's nose. Our shadows were thrown fourteen feet high by the flickering candlelight. "Have you received more of the manuscript from Mr. Das?"

"Not as of yet," said Mr. Gupta. His dark eyes were moist and heavy-lidded. Wax from the candles dripped onto the baize. "This committee is to make the final decision as to the disposition of the English-language version of this epic work."

"I would like to meet with Mr. Das," I said. The people around the table exchanged glances.

"That will not be possible." It was the woman who spoke. Her voice was as high and shrill as a saw moving on metal. The irritable, nasal tones clashed with her dignified appearance.

"Why is that?"

"M. Das has not been available for many years," said Gupta smoothly. "For some time we all believed that he had died. We mourned the loss of a national treasure."

"And how do you know that he is alive now? Has anyone here seen him?"

There was another silence. The candles were already half-consumed and sputtering wildly, although no breeze stirred. I felt terribly hot and a little sick. It seemed for a mad second that the candles would burn out and we would continue talking in the humid darkness, bodiless spirits haunting a decaying building in the belly of a dead city.

"We have correspondence," said Michael Leonard Chatterjee. He removed half a dozen crackling envelopes from his briefcase. "They establish beyond a doubt that our friend is still alive and living in our midst." Chatterjee wet his fingers and flipped through the tightly folded pages of flimsy stationery. In the dim light the lines of Indian script looked like magical runes, ominous incantations.

Mr. Chatterjee read aloud several passages to prove his point. Relatives were inquired about, common friends mentioned. A discussion from twenty years earlier was recalled in detail. There was an inquiry to Mr. Gupta about a short poem of Das's that had been paid for years before but never published.

"All right," I said. "But it's important for my article that I see Mr. Das personally so that I can—"

"Please," said Mr. Chatterjee and held up his hand. His glasses reflected twin flames where eyes should have been. "This may explain why it is impossible." He folded a page, cleared his throat, and began reading.

". . . and so you see, my friend, things change but people do not. I remember the day in July of 1969. It was during the Festival of Shiva. The *Times* told us that men had left footprints on the moon. I was returning from my father's village: a place where men left footprints in the soil behind their laboring bullocks just as they have for five thousand years. In the villages our train passed by, the peasants labored to drag their heavy godcarts through the mud.

"All during that loud and crowded voyage back to our beloved city, I was struck by how empty and futile my life had been. My father had lived a long and useful life. Every man in his village, Brahman to Harijan, wished to attend his cremation. I had walked through fields which my father had flooded and tilled and recaptured from the vagaries of nature long before I was born. After his funeral, I left my brothers and went to visit in the shade of a great banyan which my father had planted as a youth. All around me were the evidences of my father's toils. The very land seemed to mourn his passing.

"And what, I asked myself, had I done? I would be fifty-four years old in a few weeks, and to what purpose had I spent my life? I had written some verse, amused my colleagues, and annoyed some critics. I had woven a web of illusion that I was carrying on the tradition of our great Tagore. Then I had enmeshed myself in my own web of deceit.

"By the time we reached Howrah Station, I had seen the shallowness of my life and art. For over thirty years I had lived and worked in our beloved city—the heart and bloodstone of Bengal—and never once had the essence of that city been recreated, nay, nor hinted at, in my feeble art. I had tried to define the soul of Bengal by describing its shallowest exterior, its foreign intruders, and its least honest face. It was as if I had tried to describe the soul of a beautiful and complex woman by listing the details of her borrowed garments.

"Gandhiji once said, 'A man cannot fully live unless he has died at least once.' By the time I had disembarked from my first-class coach at Howrah Station, I had acknowledged the imperative of that great truth. To live—in my soul, in my art—I would have to cast off the appurtenances of my old life.

"I gave my two suitcases to the first beggar who approached

me. His look of surprise is still a source of some pleasure to me. What he later did with my fine linen shirts, my Parisian ties, and the many books I had packed, I have no idea.

"I crossed the Howrah Bridge into the city knowing only one thing—I was dead to my old life, dead to my old home and habits, and necessarily dead to the people I loved. Only by entering Calcutta afresh, as I had some thirty-three years earlier as a hopeful, stammering student from a small village—only then could I see with the clear eyes I would need for my final work.

"And it is that work . . . my first true attempt to tell the story of the city which nurtures us . . . to which I have devoted my life. Since that day many years ago, my new life has led me to places I had never heard of in my beloved city—a city which I had foolishly thought to have known intimately.

"It has led me to seek my way among the lost, to own only what has been cast off by the dispossessed, to labor with the Scheduled Classes, to seek wisdom from the fools of Curzon Park, and to seek virtue from the whores of Sudder Street. In so doing I have had to acknowledge the presence of those dark gods who held this place in their palms before even the gods themselves were born. In finding *them* I have found myself.

"Please do not seek me. You would not find me if you searched. You would not know me if you found me.

"My friends, I leave it to you to carry out my instructions in relation to this new work. The poem is incomplete. Much more work must be done. But time grows short. I wish to have the existing fragments disseminated as widely as possible. Critical response means *nothing*. Credits and copyrights are unimportant. It *must* be published.

"Respond via usual channels.

—Das"

* * *

Chatterjee quit reading, and in the silence the distant carnival of street sounds became faintly audible. Mr. Gupta cleared his throat and asked a question about American copyrights. I explained as best I could—about both the *Harper's* offer and the more modest proposal from *Other Voices*. More discussion and questions followed. The candles burned low.

Finally Gupta turned to the others and said something in rapid-fire Bengali. I again wished that Amrita had come with me. It was Michael Leonard Chatterjee who said, "If you will wait outside in the hall for just a moment, Mr. Luczak, the Council will vote on the disposition of M. Das's manuscript."

I rose on pin-cushion legs and followed a servant with a candle out into the hallway. There was a chair on the landing and a small round table upon which the candle was placed. Some pale light came up the stairwell from frosted windows facing Dalhousie Square, but the dim glow only made the darkness in the corners of the landing and the branching corridors seem more absolute.

I had been sitting there for about ten minutes and was on the point of dozing when I noticed movement in the shadows. Something was moving stealthily just out of the circle of light. I lifted the candle and watched as a rat the size of a small terrier froze into immobility. Pausing at the edge of the landing, its long tail flicked wetly back and forth across the boards. Feral eyes gleamed at me from the borders of the light. It advanced half a step, and a chill of revulsion rippled through me. The thing's movement reminded me of nothing so much as a cat stalking its prey. I half rose and gripped the flimsy chair, ready to hurl it.

Suddenly a louder noise behind me caused me to jump. The shadow of the rat blended into the shadows of the hallway and there was a scrabbling as of many claws on woodwork. Mr. Chatterjee and Mr. Gupta emerged from the black council room. Flames reflected on Mr. Chatterjee's glasses. Mr. Gupta took a step forward into my pulsing circle of light. His smile was eager and his teeth were long and yellow.

"It is settled," he said. "You will receive the manuscript tomorrow. You will be contacted about arrangements."

Chapter Five

"No peace in Calcutta;
Blood calls at midnight . . .
—Sukanta Bhattacharjee

It was too easy. That was the thought that entered my mind as I was driven back to the hotel. I had held an image of being the trench-coated investigative journalist—Jesus, in that heat—carefully following up clues to piece together the mysterious disappearance and reappearance of the phantom Bengali poet. Now, on my first afternoon in the city, the puzzle had been assembled for me. Tomorrow, Saturday, I would have the manuscript and be free to take Amrita and the baby and fly home. What kind of article would that make? It was too easy.

My body insisted that it was early morning, but my wristwatch said it was five P.M. Workers were emerging from the age-stained office buildings near the hotel like white ants from gray stone carcasses. Families were brewing hot water for tea on the broken sidewalks while men with briefcases stepped over sleeping infants. A man in rags squatted to urinate in the gutter while another bathed in a puddle not six feet away. I brushed through the Communist pickets and entered the air-conditioned sanctuary of the hotel.

Krishna was waiting in the lobby. The hotel's assistant manager was watching him as though Krishna were a known terrorist. Little wonder. He looked even wilder than before. His black hair leaped out in electric exclamation marks, and the toad-like eyes were wider and whiter than ever under dark brows. He grinned widely when he saw me and came forward with hand extended. I was shaking it before I realized that the cordial greeting was Krishna's way of validating his presence to the assistant manager.

"Ah, Mr. Luczak! Very good to see you again! I have come to help you in your search for the poet, M. Das." He continued to pump my hand. He was wearing the same soiled shirt as the night before and smelled of musky cologne and sweat. I felt the sweat drying on my own body as the fierce air-conditioning raised goose bumps along my arms.

"Thank you, Mr. Krishna, but there is no need." I extricated my hand. "I've made all the necessary arrangements. I'll be completing my business here tomorrow."

Krishna froze in place. The smile faded, and the brows came even closer together over the great curve of nose. "Ahh, I see. You have been to the Writers' Union. Yes?"

"Yes."

"Ah, yes, yes. They would have had a very satisfactory story to tell you about our illustrious M. Das. You *were* satisfied by their story, Mr. Luczak?" Krishna almost whispered the last sentence, and his look was so blatantly conspiratorial that the assistant manager frowned across the entire length of lobby. God knows what he thought I was being offered.

I hesitated. I didn't know what the hell Krishna had to do with the whole thing, and I didn't really want to take time to find out. I mentally cursed Abe Bronstein for poking around in my arrangements and inadvertently putting me in touch with this creep. At the same time I was acutely aware of Amrita and Victoria waiting for me and of my own irritation at the direction this assignment was taking.

Interpreting my hesitation as uncertainty, Krishna leaned forward and grasped my forearm. "I have someone for you to meet, Mr. Luczak. Someone who can tell you the truth about M. Das."

"What do you mean, the truth? Who is this person?"

"He would rather I not say," whispered Krishna. His hands were moist. There were tiny veins of yellow in the whites of his eyes. "You will understand when you hear his story."

"When?" I snapped. Only the sense of incompleteness I had felt in the car kept me from telling Krishna to go to hell.

"Immediately!" said Krishna with a triumphant grin. "We can meet him at once!"

"Impossible." I abruptly pulled my arm out of Krishna's grasp. "I'm going upstairs. Take a shower. I promised my wife we would go out to dinner."

"Ah, yes, yes." Krishna nodded and sucked on his lower teeth. "Of course. I will make the arrangements for nine-thirty o'clock, then. That will be sufficiently good?"

I hesitated. "Does your friend wish to be paid for his information?"

"Oh, no, no!" Krishna raised both palms. "He would not

allow such a thing. It is only with the greatest difficulty that I have convinced him to speak to anyone about this."

"Nine-thirty?" I asked. The thought of going out into the Calcutta night filled me with a vague sickness.

"Yes. The coffee shop closes at eleven. We will meet him there."

Coffee shop. The words had an innocuous familiarity to them. If there were some angle I could use in the article. . . .

"All right," I said.

"I shall be waiting for you here, Mr. Luczak."

The woman holding my child was not Amrita. I stopped with my hand still on the doorknob. I might have stayed like that or even retreated into the hall in confusion if Amrita had not emerged from the bathroom at that moment.

"Oh, Bobby, this is Kamakhya Bharati. Kamakhya, this is my husband, Robert Luczak."

"It is a pleasure to meet you, Mr. Luczak." Her voice was wind through spring blossoms.

"Nice to meet you, Miss—ah—Bharati." I blinked stupidly and looked at Amrita. I had always thought that Amrita's features approached true beauty with her guileless eyes and the honest planes of her face, but next to this young woman I could see only the lines of approaching middle age in Amrita's flesh, the slight double chin, and the bump on the bridge of her nose. The afterimage of the young woman stayed in my retinas like a flashbulb's optical echo.

Her hair was jet-black and hung to her shoulders. Her face was a sharpened oval, perfect, punctuated with soft, slightly tremulous lips that seemed designed for laughter and great sensuality. Her eyes were startling—huge beyond all probability, accentuated by eye shadow and heavy lashes, pupils so dark and so penetrating that her gaze stabbed like dark beacons. There was something subtly oriental about those eyes while at the same time they projected a Western, almost subliminal sense of innocence and wordliness warring within.

Kamakhya Bharati was young—in her mid-twenties at most—and wore a sari of a silk so light that it seemed to float an inch above her flesh, buoyed up by some fragant pulse of feminity that seemed to emanate from her like a redolent breeze.

I had always associated the word *voluptuous* with a Rubens' weightiness, masses of alluring flesh, but this young woman's thin body, half-perceived through shifting layers of silk, struck me with a sense of voluptuousness so intense that it dried the saliva in my mouth and emptied my mind.

"Kamakhya is the niece of M. Das, Bobby. She came to inquire about your article, and we've spent the last hour talking."

"Oh?" I glanced at Amrita and looked back at the girl. I could think of nothing else to say.

"Yes, Mr. Luczak. I have heard rumors that my uncle has communicated to some of his old colleagues. I wished to know if you had seen my uncle . . . if he is all right. . . ." Her gaze dropped and her voice trailed off.

I sat on the edge of an armchair. "No," I said. "I mean, I haven't seen him but he's all right. I'd like to, though. See him. I'm doing an article—"

"Yes." Kamakhya Bharati smiled and set Victoria back in the center of the bed where her blanket and Pooh-bear lay. Elegant brown fingers brushed over the baby's cheek in an affectionate gesture. "I will not bother you further. I wished only to inquire about the health of my uncle."

"Of course!" I said. "Well, I'm sure we'd like to talk to you, Miss Bharati. I mean, if you knew your uncle well . . . it would help me out in my article. If you could stay a few minutes. . . ."

"I must go. My father will expect me to be home when he arrives." She turned and smiled at Amrita. "Perhaps I could talk when we see each other tomorrow, as we discussed?"

"Marvelous!" said Amrita. It was the first time I'd seen her so relaxed since London. She turned to me. "Kamakhya knows of a good sari dealer not far from here, near the Elite Cinema. I really would like to buy some material while we're here. That is, if you won't need me tomorrow, Bobby."

"Mmm, I'm not sure," I said. "Well, plan on your trip. I don't know when they'll arrange their appointment for me."

"I will call you in the morning then," said the girl. She smiled at Amrita, and I found myself jealous, wishing that I had been the recipient of that benediction. She rose and shook Amrita's hand while simultaneously adjusting her sari with the graceful move of her hand so universal with Indian women.

"Very good," said Amrita.

Kamakhya Bharati bowed slightly to me as she moved to the door. I returned the nod and then she was gone. A slight, tantalizing scent remained.

"Sweet Christ," I said.

"Relax, Robert," said Amrita. The proper British tones held a hint of amusement. "She's only twenty-two, but she's been engaged for eleven years. She's to be married this October."

"Damned waste," I said and dropped onto the bed next to

the baby. Victoria turned her head and waved her arms, ready to play. I swung her up in the air. She made noises of delight and kicked her feet. "Is she really Das's niece?"

"She used to help him with his manuscripts. Sharpen pencils. Go to the library for him. Or so she says."

"Yeah? She must have been ten years old." Victoria squealed as I swung her in an arc, spun her around, swung her back.

"Thirteen when he disappeared. Evidently her father had a falling-out with Das right before their father died."

"Their father? Oh, Das's—"

"Yes. At any rate, his name hasn't been mentioned in the household for years. I got the impression that she was too shy to approach Chatterjee or the Writers' Union."

"She approached us."

"That's different," said Amrita. "We're foreigners. We don't count. Are we still going to dinner?"

I lowered Victoria to my stomach. Her face was red with pleasure and she was pondering whether to cry. She dug her knees into my lap and began creeping up my chest. One pudgy hand tightened on the collar of my shirt in a death grip.

"Where shall we eat?" I asked. I explained about the nine-thirty meeting with Krishna's Mysterious Stranger. "It's a little late to go out on the town. Shall we call Room Service or go down to the Prince's Room? I hear they have Fatima the Exotic Dancer for a floor show."

"Victoria would undoubtedly create a fuss," said Amrita. "But I would imagine she would prefer Fatima to Room Service."

"Righto," I said.

"I'll be ready in a moment."

* * *

Fatima the Exotic Dancer was an overweight, middle-aged Indian woman whose dance could have been performed before a den of Exeter Cub Scouts without fear of scandal. Nonetheless, the crowd of overweight, middle-aged, predominantly male couples in the Prince's Room seemed appropriately titillated by her performance. Victoria was not. She began to cry, and the three of us left half way through Fatima's second round of gyrations.

Rather than return to the room, Amrita and I walked around the darkened hotel courtyard. It had been raining much of the evening, but now we could make out a few stars between the low, sulfurous clouds. Heavy curtains were drawn across most of the windows facing the courtyard, and only a few bands of light were visible. We took turns carrying the still-crying baby until the sobbing slowed and then stopped altogether. We paused by the pool and sat on a low bench near the dark café. Ripples of light from underwater spotlights danced across the heavy foliage and lowered bamboo curtains. I noticed a dark shape floating in the shallow end of the pool and realized that it was a drowned rat.

"Victoria's asleep," said Amrita. I glanced over to see the baby's hands clenched and her eyes closed in that intense, somehow satisfied-looking form of sleep that often followed intense crying spells.

I stretched my legs out and put my head back. I realized that I was very tired, probably still suffering from jet lag. I sat up and looked at Amrita. She was gently rocking the baby, her own gaze absent and meditative as it often was when she was working on a prolonged mathematical problem.

"How does it feel to be back?" I asked.

Amrita looked at me and blinked. "What, Bobby?"

"In India," I said. "How does it feel to be back?"

She patted the baby's ruff of hair and handed her to me. I settled Victoria in the hollow of my shoulder and watched as Amrita walked to the edge of the pool and smoothed down her tan skirt. The light from the pool illuminated her sharp cheekbones from below. *My wife is beautiful*, I thought for the thousandth time since our wedding.

"It feels a bit like *déjà vu*," she said very softly. "No, that's not quite the right word. It's actually more like reentering a recurring dream. The heat, the noise, the languages, the smell—everything is familiar and alien at the same time."

"I'm sorry if it upsets you," I said.

Amrita shook her head. "It doesn't upset me, Bobby. It *frightens* me, but it doesn't upset me. I find it very seductive."

"Seductive?" I stared at her. "What on earth have we seen that has been seductive?" It was not like Amrita to use a word loosely. Her precision with language often exceded mine.

She smiled. "Do you mean besides Kamakhya Bharati?" She slipped off her sandal and stirred the blue water with her foot. I could not see the drowned rat at the far end of the pool. "Seriously, Bobby, I find it all seductive in a strange way. It's as if I have been using only one part of my mind for all these years and now another part of me is being called to."

"Would you like to stay longer?" I asked. "After the assignment's over, I mean." I was confused.

"No," said Amrita, and there was no mistaking the finality in her voice."

I shook my head. "I'm sorry I left you alone all afternoon and agreed to this thing tonight," I said. "I guess it was a mistake for the three of us to come. I underestimated how difficult it would be for you with Victoria along." Somewhere from above came a sharp series of commands in what sounded like Arabic followed by a rush of nasal Bengali. A door slammed.

Amrita walked over to sit next to me again. She took Victoria and laid her across her legs. "It's all right, Bobby," she said. "I knew what it would be like. I guessed that you probably wouldn't need me as a translator until after you got the manuscript."

"I'm sorry," I said again.

Amrita looked back at the pool. "When I was seven years old," she said, "the summer before we moved to London, I saw a ghost."

I stared at her. I could not have been more surprised or incredulous if Amrita had told me that she had fallen in love with the old bellhop and was leaving me. Amrita was—or had been to that instant—the most unrelentingly rational person I had even known. Her interest and belief in the supernatural had until now seemed nonexistent. I had never even been able to interest her in the trashy Stephen King novels I would bring to the beach each summer.

"A ghost?" I said at last.

"We were on our way by train from our home in New Delhi to our uncle's in Bombay," she said. "It was always exciting when my sisters and I traveled with our mother to Bombay each June. But this year my sister Santha became ill. We got off the train west of Bhopal and stayed in a railway guest house for two days while a local doctor treated her."

"Was she all right?" I asked.

"Yes, it was just the measles," said Amrita. "But now I was the only one of the children who had not had them, so I slept outside our hotel room on a small balcony overlooking the forest. The only way to the balcony was through the room where my mother and sisters slept. The rains had not yet come that summer, and it was very hot."

"And you saw a ghost?"

Amrita smiled slightly. "I awoke in the middle of the night to the sound of crying. At first I thought it was my sister or mother, and then I realized that an old woman in a sari was sitting on the edge of my bed and sobbing. I remember feeling no fear, only wonder that my mother had allowed this person to go through their room to join me on the balcony.

"Her crying was very soft but somehow very terrible. I reached out my hand to console her, but before I touched her she stopped weeping and looked at me. I realized then that she was not really old, but that she had been aged by some terrible grief."

"And then what?" I prompted. "How did you know she was a ghost? Did she fade away or walk off on air or melt down to a pile of rags and grease, or what?"

Amrita shook her head. "The moon passed behind the clouds for a few seconds, and when there was light again the old woman was gone. I called out, and when my mother and sisters came out onto the balcony they assured me that no one had come through their room."

"Hmmm," I said. "Sounds sort of dull to me. You were seven years old and probably dreaming. Even if you were awake, how do you know it wasn't some chambermaid who'd come up a fire escape or something?"

Amrita lifted Victoria to her shoulder. "I agree it's not a very frightening ghost story," she said. "But it frightened me for years. You see, in that second before the moon was obscured, I looked right into the woman's face and I knew very well who she was." Amrita patted the baby's back and looked at me. "It was me."

"You?" I said.

"I decided then that I wanted to live in a country where I would see no ghosts."

"I hate to break it to you, kiddo," I said, "but Great Britain and New England are famous for having their share of ghosts."

"Perhaps," said Amrita and rose with Victoria secure in her arms. "But *I* can't see them."

At nine-thirty P.M. I was sitting in the lobby, nursing a growing headache from heat and fatigue, feeling queasy from too much bad wine at dinner, and going through various excuses to give to Krishna when he appeared. By nine-fifty I had decided to tell him that Amrita or the baby was sick. At ten P.M. I realized that I didn't have to tell him anything, and I had risen to go upstairs when suddenly he appeared, disheveled and distraught. His eyes looked red and puffy as though he had been crying. He came forward and shook my hand solemnly, as if the lobby were a funeral home and I the bereaved next of kin.

"What is it?" I asked.

"Very, very sad," he said, and the high voice broke. "Very terrible news."

"Your friend?" I asked. I felt a sense of relief in the sudden hunch that his mysterious source had broken his leg or been run over by a trolley or collapsed of a coronary.

"No, no, no. You must have heard. Mr. Nabokov has passed away. A great tragedy."

"Who?" Through the dialect I had heard only another rattling Bengali name.

"Nabokov! Nabokov! Vladimir Nabokov! *Pale Fire*. *Ada*. The greatest prose stylist in your native language. A very great loss for all of us. All men of letters."

"Oh," I said. I had never even got around to reading *Lolita*. By the time I remembered my resolve not to go with Krishna, we were outside in the humid dark and he was leading me to a rickshaw where a gaunt, wizened little rickshaw-coolie dozed in a red seat. I pulled back. Something in me rebelled at the thought of being pulled through filthy streets by this human scarecrow. "Let's take a cab," I said.

"No, no. This is reserved for us. It is a short ride. Our friend is waiting."

The seat was wet from the evening rains but not uncomfortable. The little man jumped down with a slap of his bare feet, grabbed the twin yokes, jumped into the air with a practiced agility, and came down straight-armed, balancing our weight expertly.

The rickshaw had no running lights, only a kerosene lantern that swung on a metal hook. It did not reassure me that the trucks and cars that swerved around us, horns blaring, also ran without lights. The trolleys were still running, and the sick, yellow pall of their interior bulbs showed sweaty faces crowded behind wire-mesh windows. Despite the late hour all of the public transit was loaded, buses swaying from the weight of people hanging from barred windows and outside grips, passing trains showing innumerable heads and torsos protruding from the black carriages.

There were few streetlights, but alleys and half-glimpsed courtyards glowed with that pale, decaying phosphorescence I had seen from the air. The darkness had not brought any relief from the heat. If anything, it was warmer now than it had been during the day. Heavy clouds could be seen just above the overhanging buildings, and their moist weight seemed to reflect the heat of the city streets back to us.

Anxiety rose in me again. It is hard even now for me to describe the nature of this tension. It had little to do with a sense of physical danger, although I felt absurdly exposed as we rattled over loose paving stones, heaps of garbage, and trolley tracks. I realized that I still had two hundred dollars' worth of travelers checks in my billfold. But that was not the real source of the nervousness that rose in my throat like bile.

Something about the Calcutta night worked directly upon the darkest regions of my mind. Brief clutches of an almost childlike fear tugged at my consciousness and were forced down again by the adult mind. The sounds of the night held no threat in and of themselves—distant shouts, sibilant scrapings, an occasional muffled snatch of conversation as we passed the sheeted figures—but they had the same gut-wrenching, attention-getting effect that the sound of someone breathing under your bed at night would generate.

"Kaliksetra," said Krishna. His voice was soft, barely audible over the panting of the rickshaw-coolie and the slap of bare feet on pavement.

"Excuse me?"

"Kaliksetra. It means 'the place of Kali.' Certainly you knew that this is where the name of our city has originated?"

"Ahh, no. That is, I may have. I must have forgotten."

Krishna turned toward me. I could not see his face clearly in the darkness, but I could feel the weight of his stare. "You must know this," he said flatly. "Kaliksetra became the village of Kalikata. Kalikata was the site of the great Kalighat, the most holy temple to Kali. It still stands. Less than two miles from your hotel. Certainly you must know this."

"Hmmm," I said. A trolley had turned the corner at high speed. Our rickshaw-coolie suddenly swerved across the tracks, avoiding the tram by less than a yard. Angry shouts followed us out onto a wider, emptier street. "Kali was a goddess, wasn't she?" I said. "One of Siva's consorts?" Despite my interest in Tagore, it had been many years since I had read any of the Vedas.

Krishna made an incredible sound. At first I thought it was an explosive burst of derision, but then I turned to look. He was stopping one nostril with his finger and loudly blowing mucus into his left hand. "Yes, yes," he said. "Kali is the sacred *sakti* of Siva." He inspected the contents of his hand, nodded as if satisfied, and flicked his fingers over the side of the rickshaw.

"Certainly you know her aspect?" he asked. From one of the shadowy, dilapidated buildings we had passed came the sound of several women screaming at each other.

"Her aspect? No, I don't believe so. She . . . the statues . . . they have four arms, don't they?" I looked around, and wondered if we were almost at our destination. There were fewer shops here. I found it hard to imagine a coffee shop among these ruins.

"Of course! Of course! She is a *goddess*; obviously she has four arms! You must see the great idol in the Kalighat. It is the *jagrata*, the "very awake" Kali. Very terrible. Beautifully terrible, Mr. Luczak. Her hands show the *abhaya* and *vara mudras*—the fear-removing and boon-granting *mudras*. But very terrible. Very tall. Very gaunt. Her mouth is open. Her tongue is long. She has the two . . . what is the word . . . the teeth of the vampire?"

"Fangs?" I gripped the wet seat cover and wondered what Krishna was going on about. We turned down a darker, narrower street.

"Ah, yes, yes. She alone of the gods has conquered time. She devours all beings, of course. *Purusam, asv́am, gām, avim, ajam*. She is unclad. Her beautiful feet tread on a corpse. In her hands she holds a pāsá . . . a noose, *khatvānga* . . . what is the word? . . . A stick, no, a *staff* with a skull, *khadga* . . . a sword, and a severed head."

"A severed head?"

"Certainly. You must know this."

"Listen, goddammit, Krishna, what is all this—"

"Ah, we are here, Mr. Luczak. Step down. Quickly, please. We are late. The coffee shop closes at eleven."

The street was little more than an alley filled with sewage and rainwater. There was no sign of any storefronts or shops, much less a café. The walls were unlit except for the dim reflection of lanterns glowing from one of the upper windows. The rickshaw-coolie had dropped the traces and was lighting a small pipe. I remained seated.

"Quickly please," said Krishna, and snapped his fingers at me in the way I had seen him deal with porters. He stopped over a sleeping man on the sidewalk and opened a door that I hadn't noticed. A single bulb illuminated a steep, narrow staircase. Faint undertones of conversation drifted down to us.

I jumped down and followed him into the light. Another door on the second-floor landing led to a wide hallway. "You saw the University down the street?" asked Krishna over his shoulder. I nodded, although I'd seen no building more imposing than a warehouse. "This, of course, is the University coffee shop. No, that is not right. *Coffee house*. Just like Greenwich Village. Yes."

Krishna turned left and led me into a truly cavernous room. The high ceiling, heavy columns, and windowless walls reminded me of a parking garage I used to know near the Chicago Loop. At least fifty or sixty tables were visible in the dim light, but only a few were occupied. Here and there a cluster of earnest-looking young men in loose white shirts sat at rough tables painted a dark green. Slow-moving fans hung from a twenty-foot-high ceiling; and although the moist air did not stir perceptibly, the light from the widely spaced bulbs was made to flicker slightly, imparting a dully stroboscopic, silent-film quality to the scene.

"A coffee house," I repeated stupidly.

"Come this way." Krishna led the way through tightly packed tables to the farthest corner. A young man of about twenty sat alone on a bench built into the wall. He rose as we approached.

"Mr. Luczak, this is Jayaprakesh Muktanandaji," Krishna said, and added something in Bengali to the youth. The deep shadows made it difficult for me to make out the young man's features clearly; but along with a moist, hesitant handshake, I registered a thin face, thick glasses, and a case of acne so severe that the pustules almost glowed.

We remained standing for a silent moment. The young man wiped his palms together and glanced furtively at the students at other tables. Some of them had turned to watch as we entered, but none continued to look our way.

We sat down just as an old man with stubble outlining a white beard brought coffee to the table. The cups were badly chipped and traced with fracture lines that radiated pale branches against the enamel. The coffee was strong and surprisingly good, except that someone had already added dollops of sugar and sour milk. Both Krishna and Muktanandaji looked at me as the old man stood quietly by the table, so I pawed through my billfold and set down a five-rupee note. The man turned and left without giving any change.

"Mr. Muktanandaji," I began, proud of remembering the name, "you have some information about the Calcutta poet M. Das?"

The boy bowed his head and said something to Krishna. Krishna replied abruptly and turned to me with his sharp-toothed smile. "Mr. Muktanandaji does not, I am sorry to say, speak such fluent English. Indeed, Mr. Luczak, he speaks no English. He has asked for me to interpret for him. If you are ready, Mr. Luczak, he will now tell you his story."

"I thought this was to be an interview," I said.

Krishna held up the palm of his right hand. "Yes, yes. You must understand, Mr. Luczak, Mr. Jayaprakesh Muktanandaji is speaking to you only as a personal favor to me, his onetime teacher. He is very reluctant. If you please to let him tell his story, I shall translate to the best of my abilities; and then, if you have questions, I shall put them to Mr. Muktanandaji."

Damn, I thought. That was twice in one day that I had made the mistake of not having Amrita with me. I considered canceling or rearranging the meeting, but discarded the idea. Better to get it over with. Tomorrow I would be receiving the Das manuscript, and with any luck we would be flying home in the evening.

"Very well," I said.

The young man cleared his throat and adjusted his thick

glasses. His voice was even higher pitched than Krishna's. Every few sentences he would pause and rub idly at his face or neck while Krishna translated. At first I found the delay irritating, but the musical flow of Bengali followed by the singsong rush of Krishna's dialect had a *mantra*-like, mesmerizing effect on me. It was similar to the heightened state of concentration and involvement one brings to a foreign movie simply because of the effort of reading the subtitles.

A few times I stopped them to ask a question; but this seemed to upset Muktanandaji, so after a few minutes I contented myself with sipping my cooling coffee and listening. Several times Krishna turned to say something in Bengali, and the boy would reply and I would curse myself for being a monolingual moron. I wondered if even Amrita could have followed the gist of the high-speed Bengali.

As the story began I found myself mentally rearranging Krishna's often tortured syntax or substituting the proper word for his sometimes comical replacement. Occasionally I jotted details in my notebook, but after a while even this became a distraction and I put my pen away. The overhead fans turned slowly, the light flickered like distant heat lightning on a summer's night, and I gave Jayaprakesh Muktanandaji my total attention as his story unfolded in Krishna's voice.

Chapter Six

A REQUEST
When I die
Do not throw the meat and bones away
But pile them up
And
Let them tell
By their smell
What life was worth
On this earth
What love was worth
In the end

—Kamela Das

"I am a poor person of Sudra caste. I am one of eleven sons of Jagdisvaran Bibhuti Muktanandaji who was with Gandhiji on his Walk to the Sea.

"My home is in the village of Anguda which is near

Durgalapur which is along the rail line connecting Calcutta and Jamshedpur. It is a poor village, and no one from the outside has taken any interest in it except for the time when a tiger ate two of the sons of Subhoranjan Venkateswarani and a man came from a newspaper in Bhubaneshwar to ask Subhoranjan Venkateswarani how he felt about this. I do not remember this well, as it occured during the war—which was some fifteen years before I was born.

"Our family has not always been poor. My grandfather, S. Mokeshi Muktanandaji, once loaned money to the village moneylender. By the time I was born, the eighth of eleven sons, we had long since borrowed back my grandfather's money and much more. To pay off some of the interest on his debts, my father was forced to sell the richest six acres of his land—those closest to the village. That left fifteen acres, spread over many miles, to be divided among the eleven us. One cannot raise cane for two bullocks on that small a share of land.

"The problem was made a small bit better when my older brother Marmadeshwar went off to do his patriotic duty in 1971 and was promptly killed by the Pakistanis. Still, the prospects for the rest of us were not good.

"Then my father had an idea. For eight years I had gone halftime to the Christian Agricultural Academy in Durgalpur. The school was sponsored by the very rich Mr. Debee of the Bengal Cattle Insemination Centre. It was a small school. We had few books and only two teachers, one of whom was slowly going mad from syphilis.

"Nonetheless, I was the only member of my father's family ever to have gone to school, and he decided that I would go off to university. He planned for me to become a doctor or—even better—a merchant, and bring much money to the family. This also solved the problem of my share of land. It was obvious to my father that a doctor or wealthy merchant would have no need for a small plot of poor farmland.

"I, myself, had mixed feelings about this idea. I had never been more than eight miles from Anguda. I had never ridden in a train or automobile. I could read very simple books and write basic sentences in Bengali, but I knew no English or Hindi and only enough Sanskrit to recite a few lines of the *Ramayana* and *Mahabharata*.

"In short, I was not sure that I was ready to become a doctor.

"My father borrowed more money—in my name, this time—from the village money-lender. My teacher, in his madness, wrote a recommendation for admission to Calcutta University and directed it to his old instructor there. Even Mr. Debee, who in his pre-Christian days had sworn to Gandhiji that he would humbly work for our villages and have his ashes spread on the main path of Anguda, wrote a note to the University requesting their kindness in admitting a poor, ignorant, low-caste peasant child to their honored halls of learning.

"Last year there was an opening. I paid most of my borrowed money as *baksheesh* to my teacher and to Mr. Debee's secretary, and then I left my home for the great city. How terrified I was!

"I will not describe my reactions to all of the wonders of Calcutta. Suffice it to say that every hour brought marvelous revelations. I was soon downcast, however. My meager funds barely paid the first semester's tuition and left not enough money for the expensive dormitories or student hostels near the University. I spent my first week in the city sleeping under the bushes in the Maidan, but the monsoon rains and two beatings by the police convinced me to seek a room.

"My four classes were somewhat of a disappointment. There were more than four hundred students in my Introduction to National History class. I could not afford the textbook and was rarely close enough to hear the lecturer, who mumbled and, in any case, spoke only in English, which I could not understand. I therefore spent my days hunting for lodging and wishing I were home in Anguda. Even by eating only one meal of rice and *chapatis* a day, I knew that I would be out of money within a few weeks. If I was lucky enough to find a room to rent, I would starve that much sooner.

"Then I answered an ad for a roommate in the *Student Forum* and everything changed. The room was six miles from the university on the seventh floor of a building which housed mostly refugees from Bangladesh and Burma. The student who wished to rent half of the room was a junior—a brilliant man several years older than I who was then studying pharmacy science but who wished to someday be a great author, or, failing that, a nuclear physicist. His name was Sanjay, and from the first time I saw him standing there amidst piles of his papers and unwashed clothing, I knew somehow that my life would never again be the same.

"He wanted two hundred rupees a month for my half of the room. My face must have shown my despair. At that time I had less than one hundred rupess to my name. I realized that I had made the two-hour walk for nothing. I asked if I could sit down. The soles of my feet were in great pain from the beating with *lathi* sticks I had received a few nights earlier. I later discovered that the policemen had broken the arches of my feet.

"Upon hearing this, Sanjay immediately took pity on me. He became furious when I told him of the beatings and the size of the bribes demanded by the University dormitory wardens. Sanjay's moods, as I was soon to learn, were like monsoon storms. One minute he could be calm, contemplative, as still as a statue, and the next he would fly off in a rage against some social injustice and put his fist through the rotting wallboards or kick some Burmese child down the back staircase.

"Sanjay was a member of both the Maoist Student Coalition and the Communist Party India. The fact that these two factions despised each other and frequently came to blows did not seem to bother him. He described his parents as "decadent capitalist parasites" who owned a small pharmaceutical company in Bombay and who sent him money each month. His parents at first had sent him out of the country to study, but when he returned to "renew contacts with the revolutionary struggle in my own country," he further offended them by choosing the brawling, plebeian Calcutta University in which to pursue his degree rather than a more prestigious college in Bombay or Delhi.

"After telling me these things about himself and listening to my own story, Sanjay promptly changed the rent request to five rupees a month and offered to loan me the money for the first two months. I confess that I wept with joy.

"During the following weeks, Sanjay showed me how to survive in Calcutta. In the morning, before sunrise, we rode to the center of the city with the Scheduled Class truck drivers who transported dead animals to the renderers. It was Sanjay who taught me that in a great city such as Calcutta, caste distinctions meant nothing and would soon disappear when the imminent revolution arrived. I agreed with Sanjay's points, but my upbringing still made it impossible for me to share a bus seat with a stranger or accept a piece of fried dough from a vendor without instinctively wondering what the caste of the man was. Nonetheless, Sanjay showed me how to ride the trains for free, where to be shaved by a street-corner barber who owed my friend favors, and how to squeeze into the cinema for free during the intermission of the nightly three-hour film.

"During this time I quit attending classes at the university, and my grades rose from four 'F's' to three 'B's' and and 'A.' Sanjay had educated me as to how to buy old papers and tests from upperclass students. To do this, I was forced to borrow another three hundred rupees from my roommate, but he did not mind.

"At first Sanjay took me to both the MMSC and CPI party meetings, but the endless potlitical orations and aimless internal bickerings served only to put me to sleep, and after a while he no longer insisted that I accompany him. Much more to my liking were the rare times when we went to the Lakshmi Hotel Nightclub to see the women dance in their underwear. Such a thing was almost unthinkable to a devout Hindu such as myself, but I confess I found it terribly exciting. Sanjay called it "bourgeois decadence" and explained that it was our duty to witness the sickening corruption which the revolution was destined to replace. In all, we went five times to witness the decadence, and each time Sanjay loaned me the princely sum of fifty rupees.

"We had been roommates for three months before Sanjay told me of his association with the *goondas* and Kapalikas. I had suspected that Sanjay was in some way involved with the *goondas*, but I knew nothing of the Kapalikas.

"Even I knew that for several years gangs of Asian *thugees* and Calcutta's own *goondas* had run entire sections of the city. They charged fees to the various refugees for entry and squatting rights; they controlled the flow of drugs to and through the city; and they murdered anyone who interfered with their traditional management of protection, smuggling, and crime in the city. Sanjay told me that even the pathetic slum-dwellers who paddled out from the *chawls* each evening to steal the blue and red navigation lights from the river for some purpose of their own paid a commission to the *goondas*. This commission was tripled after a *goondas*-chartered freighter—bound for Singapore with a cargo of opium and smugglers' gold—ran aground in the Hooghly because of missing channel lights. Sanjay said that it had taken most of the ship's profits to bribe the police and port authorities to pull it off the mud and let it proceed.

"At this time last year, of course, the country was going through the last stages of the Emergency. Newspapers were censored, the prisons bulged with political prisoners who had irritated Mrs. Gandhi, and it was rumored that young men in the South were being sterilized for riding trains without proper tickets. Calcutta, however, was in the middle of its own emergency. Refugees over the past decade had raised the population of the city beyond counting. Some guessed ten million. Some said fifteen. By the time I moved in with Sanjay, the city had gone through six governments in four months. Eventually, of course, the CPI assumed control out of sheer default, but even they have brought few solutions. The real masters of the city were not to be seen.

"Even today the Calcutta police will not enter major sections of the city. Last year they had tried daytime patrols in twos and threes, but after the *goondas* returned a few of these patrols in portions of seven and eight, the Commissioner refused to let his men go into those areas without the protection of soldiers. Our Indian Army announced that it had better things to do.

"Sanjay admitted that he had become associated with the Calcutta *goondas* through his pharmaceutical connections. But, he said, by the end of his first year at University, he had widened his role to include collection of protection money from many of his classmates and a runner's job as liaison between the *goondas* and the Beggarmasters' Union on the north side of the city. Neither of these tasks paid Sanjay very much, but they gave him considerable status. It was Sanjay who carried the order to the Union to temporarily reduce the number of child kidnappings when the *Times of India* began one of its seasonal and short-lived editorial outrages at the practice. Later, when the *Times* turned its moralizing eye to dowry murders, it was Sanjay who relayed permission to the Beggarmasters to replenish their depleted stock by increasing the kidnappings and mutilations.

"It was through the Beggarmasters that Sanjay received his chance to join the Kapalikas. The Kapalika Society was older than the Goonda Brotherhood, older even than the city.

"They worship Kali, of course. For many years they worshiped openly at the Kalighat Temple, but their custom of sacrificing a boy child each Friday of the month caused the British to ban the Society in 1831. They went underground and thrived. The nationalist struggle through the last century brought many to seek to join them. But their initiation price was high—as Sanjay and I were soon to learn.

"For months, Sanjay had tried to make contact with them. For months he had been put off. Then, in the autumn of last year, they offered him his chance. Sanjay and I were fast friends by then. We had taken the Brotherhood Oath together and I had done my small share by running a few messages to various people and once I made a collection run when Sanjay was ill.

"It surprised me when Sanjay offered to let me join the Kapalikas with him. It surprised and frightened me. My village had a temple to Durga, the Goddess Mother, so even so fierce an aspect and incarnation of her as Kali was familiar to me. Yet I hesitated. Durga was maternal and Kali was reputed to be wanton. Durga was modest in her representations while Kali was naked—not nude, but brazenly naked—wearing only the darkness as her cloak. The darkness and a necklace of human skulls. To worship Kali beyond her holiday was to follow the *Vamachara*—the perverse left-handed Tantra. I remember once as a child an older cousin was showing around a printed card showing a woman, a goddess, in obscene coitus with two men. My uncle found us looking at it, took the card, and struck my cousin in the face. The next day an old Brahmin was brought in to lecture us on the danger of such Tantric nonsense. He called it 'the error of the five M's'—*madya, mamsa, matsya, mudra, maithun*. These, of course, were the *Pancha Makaras* which the Kapalikas might well demand—alcohol, meat, fish, hand gestures, and coitus. To be truthful, coitus was much on my mind those days, but to first experience it as part of a worship service was a truly frightening thought.

"But I owed Sanjay much. Indeed, I began to realize that I might never be able to pay the debt I owed him. So I accompanied him on his first meeting with the Kapalikas.

"They met us in the evening in the empty marketplace near the Kalighat. I do not know what I expected—my image of Kapalikas grew out of the stories told to frighten unruly children—but the two men who waited there for us fit none of my imaginings and apprehensions. They were dressed like businessmen—one even carried a briefcase—and both were soft-spoken, refined in manner and dress, and courteous to both of us despite class and caste differences.

"The ceremonies in progress were most dignified. It was the day of the new moon in celebration of Durga, and the head of an ox was on the iron spike before Kali's idol. Blood still dripped into the marble basin beneath it.

"As someone who had worshiped Durga faithfully since infancy, I had no trouble joining in the Kali / Durga litany. The few changes were easily learned, although several times I mistakenly invoked Parvati / Durga rather than Kali / Durga. The two gentlemen smiled. Only one passage was so substantially different that I had to learn it anew:

> The world is pain,
> O terrible wife of Siva
> You are chewing the flesh;
> O terrible wife of Siva,
> Your tongue is drinking the blood,
> O dark Mother! O unclad Mother.
> O beloved of Siva
> The world is pain.

"Then large clay effigies were carried through the Kalighat in procession. Each was sprinkled with the blood of the sacrifice. Some were statues of Kali in her aspect of Chandi, The Terrible One; or as Chinnamasta, the 'she who is beheaded' of the ten *Mahavidyas* when Kali decapitated herself so as to drink of her own blood.

"We followed the procession outside and down to the banks of the Hooghly River, through which, of course, the waters of the Holy Ganges flow. There the idols were cast into the water in the sure faith that they would rise again. We chanted with the crowd:

Kali, Kali balo bhai
Kali bai aré gaté nai
O brethren take the name of Kali
There is no refuge except in her.

"I was moved to tears. The ceremony was so much more grand and beautiful than the simple village offerings in Anguda. The two gentlemen approved. So, evidently, did the Kalighat *jagrata,* for we were invited to a true meeting of the Kapalikas on the first day of next month's full moon."

Krishna paused in his translation. His voice was growing slightly hoarse. "Do you have any questions as of yet, Mr. Luczak?"

"No," I said. "Go on."

"Sanjay was very agitated all that month. I realized that he did not have the religious upbringing which I had been so fortunate to receive. Like all members of the Communist Party

India, Sanjay had to deal with political beliefs which were at war with his deeper heritage as a Hindu. You must understand that to us religion is no more an abstract 'belief' requiring an 'act of faith' than is the process of breathing. Indeed, it would be easier to will one's heart to stop beating than to will away one's perspective as a Hindu. To be a Hindu, especially in Bengal, is to accept all things as aspects of divinity and never to artificially separate the sacred from the profane. Sanjay shared this knowledge, but the thin layer of Western thought which had been grafted over his Indian soul refused to accept it.

"Once during that month, I asked him why he had bothered to seek membership with the Kapalikas if he could not truly worship the goddess. He grew angry at me then, and called me several names. He even threatened to raise my rent or call due his notes. Then, perhaps remembering our Brotherhood Oath and seeing the sorrow written on my face, he apologized.

" 'Power,' he said, 'Power is the reason I have sought this, Jayaprakesh. For some time I have know that the Kapalikas hold power far out of proportion to their numbers. The *goondas* fear nothing . . . nothing but the Kapalikas. The *thugees,* as stupid and violent as they are, will not oppose someone known to be a Kapalika. The common people hate the Kapalikas or pretend the society no longer exists, but it is a hatred born of envy. They fear the very name *Kapalika.*'

" 'Perhaps *respect* is the better word,' I said.

" 'No,' said Sanjay, 'the word is *fear.*'

"On the first night of the new moon following the feast of Durga, on the first night of the celebration of Kali, a man in black met us in the abandoned marketplace to take us to the meeting of the Kapalika Society. On the way we passed down the Street of the Clay Idols, and hundreds of aspects of Kali—straw bones piercing their unfinished clay flesh—watched us as we passed.

"The temple was in a large warehouse. The river flowed beneath part of it, just as it had at the Kalighat. We could hear its constant whispering throughout the ceremony which followed.

"It was a gentle twilight outside, but very dark once we were in the warehouse. The temple was a building within a building. Candles showed the way. A few snakes moved freely across the cool floor, but it was too dark for me to tell if they were cobras, vipers, or less worrisome serpents. I thought it a melodramatic touch.

"The idol of Kali was smaller than the one in the Kalighat—but also gaunter, darker, sharper of eye, and altogether more terrible. In the dim and trembling light, the mouth seemed now to open wider, now to close slightly into a cruel smile. The statue was freshly painted. Her breasts were tipped with red nipples, her groin was dark, and her tongue was bright crimson. The long teeth were very, very white in the gloom, and the narrow eyes watched as we moved closer.

"There were two other visible differences. First, the corpse upon which this idol danced was real. We could smell it as soon as we entered the temple proper. The stink mingled with the heavy scent of incense. The cadaver was that of a man—white of flesh, bones visible under the parchment flesh, its form molded into the attitudes of death with a sculptor's skill. One eye was open slightly.

"I was not totally surprised by the presence of a body. Tradition had it that Kapalikas wore necklaces of skulls, and raped and sacrificed a virgin before each ceremony. Only a few days earlier Sanjay had joked that I might well be the chosen virgin. But now, in the darkness of the warehouse temple, with the smell of corruption in our nostrils, I was glad enough that there was no sign of such a tradition being honored.

"The second difference in the statue was less noticeable and somehow more frightening. Kali continued to raise her four arms in fury; dangling from one hand the noose, from another the skullstaff, and from on high the sword. But her fourth hand was empty. Where there should have been the effigy of a severed head, there was only empty air. The idol's fingers grasped at nothing. I felt my heart begin to pound, and one glance at Sanjay told me that he too was holding back his terror. The smell of our sweat mixed with the holy odors of incense and dead flesh.

"The Kapalikas entered. They wore no robes or special garments. Most wore the simple white *dhoti* so common in rural areas. All were men. It was too dark to make out any Brahman castemarks, but I assumed there were several priests there. In all, they numbered about fifty. The black-garbed man who had led us to the warehouse blended back into the shadows which filled most of the temple, and I had no doubt that there were more unseen forms there.

"There were six other initiates besides Sanjay and myself. I recognized none of them. We made a trembling half-circle in front of the idol. The Kapalikas moved in behind us and began to sing. My useless tongue barely could form responses and they were always a second late. Sanjay gave up trying to join in the litany and held a thin smile through the entire worship service. Only the whiteness of his lips gave away his tension. Both of us kept returning our glances to the empty hand of Kali.

"The song was from my childhood. I associated its sentimental lyrics with sunlight on temple stone, the promise of holiday feasts, and the scent of scattered flower petals. Now, as I sang it in the night with the smell of carrion meat filling the moist air, the words took on a different meaning:

> O Mother mine,
> *Daughter of the Mountain*!
>
> The world is pain,
> Its load all bearing past;
> Never pine I, never thirst,
> For its kingdom vain.
>
> Rosy are her feet,
> A shelter free of fear;
> Death may whisper—*I am near;*
> She and I shall smiling meet.

"The service ended abruptly. There was no procession. One of the Kapalikas stepped onto the low dais below the idol. Now that my eyes had adjusted to the dark, I thought I recognized the man. He was an important figure in Calcutta. He would have to be important if I could know his face after only a few months in the city.

"The priest spoke softly. His voice was almost lost against the sound of the river. He spoke of the sacred society of the Kapalikas. *Many are called,* he intoned, *but few are chosen*. Our time of initiation, he said, would cover a period of three years. I gasped as he said this, but Sanjay merely nodded. I realized then that Sanjay had known more of what the initiation entailed than he had shared with me.

" 'You will be asked to do many things to prove your worth and faith in Kali,' the priest said gently. 'You may leave now, but once you have begun on the Path, you may not turn back.'

"There was a silence then. I looked at the other initiates. No one moved. I would have left then . . . I *would* have left . . . if Sanjay had not stayed where he was, unmoving, lips pulled tight in a bloodless smile. My own legs felt too heavy to move. My ribs ached from the thudding of my heart. I could hardly breathe. But I did not leave.

" 'Very well,' said the priest of Kali. 'You will be asked to fulfill two duties before we meet again tomorrow midnight. The first you may complete now.' So saying, the priest removed a small dagger from beneath the folds of his *dhoti*. I heard the slight intake of Sanjay's breath at the same instant as mine. All eight of us stood more erect, alert, alarmed. But the Kapalika only smiled and turned the blade across the soft flesh of his palm. The narrow line of blood swelled up slowly and looked black in the candlelight. The priest replaced the knife and then lifted what looked like several blades of grass from the clenched fist of the corpse under the idol's foot. One of these blades of grass he held up to the light. Then he turned his injured hand palm downward above it. The sound of the blood slowly dripping on the stone floor was clearly audible. One end of the three-inch stalk of grass was splashed with a few of these crimson tears. Immediately, another of the Kapalikas came out of the darkness, lifted all of the blades of grass, turned his back to us, and approached the idol.

"When he moved away, the slender stalks were only just visible, protruding from the clenched fist of the goddess Kali.

There was no way of telling which one of the identical stalks had been marked with the priest's blood.

" 'You may come forward,' said the priest. He pointed to Sanjay. 'Approach the goddess. Receive your gift from the *jagrata*.'

"To Sanjay's credit, he hesitated for only the smallest fraction of a second. He stepped forward. The goddess seemed to grow taller as Sanjay paused under the outstretched arm. Just as Sanjay reached upward there arose a hideous smell as if some bubble of decomposing gas had chosen that second to emanate from the trammeled corpse.

"Sanjay reached up, plucked a straw, and immediately covered it with his palms. It was not until he returned to our circle that he opened his cupped hands and looked at the blade of grass. It was unmarked.

"An overweight man at the far end of the line was pointed to next. His legs were shaking visibly as he approached the goddess. Instinctively, he hid the quickly grasped stalk, just as Sanjay had done; just as we all were to do. Then he held up the virgin blade of grass. Relief was written into every fold of his fat face.

"So it went with the third man, who could not stifle a soft gasp as he peered into his cupped hands and saw the clean stalk there. So it went with the fourth man who let out an involuntary sob as he reached for the fourth blade. The eyes of the goddess stared downward. The red tongue seemed inches longer than it had been when we arrived. The fourth stalk was clean.

"I was the fifth man chosen. I seemed to be watching myself from a great distance as I approached the goddess. It was impossible not to look into her face before reaching upward. The noose dangled. The empty eye sockets stared from the *khatvānga*. The sword was made of steel and looked razor-sharp. A gurgle seemed to rise from the twisted corpse as I stood there. It must have been only the river flowing directly under our feet.

"The goddess's cold stone fingers were reluctant to release the stalk of grass I had chosen. I thought that I felt her grip tighten as I tugged. The blade came free then, and without thinking I clapped my hands over it. Even I had not seen the surface of it in the poor light. I remember a great exhilaration coming over me as I returned to the circle. I felt a strange disappointment when I lifted my hand, turned the slender blade in my fingers, and found no mark. I threw back my head and stared directly into the goddess's eyes. Her smile seemed wider now, the long teeth whiter.

"The sixth man was younger than me, little more than a boy. However, he strode manfully to the *jagrata* and chose his blade of grass with no hint of hesitation. Upon returning to the circle, he held it up quickly, and immediately the red stain was visible to all of us. A final drop actually fell to the dark floor.

"We held our breath then, expecting . . . what? Nothing happened. The priest pointed, and the seventh man claimed his barren blade of grass. The last man lifted the last blade from the goddess's grip. We stood in the circle, silent, expectant, waiting for what seemed many moments, wondering what the boy was thinking, wondering what would come next. *Why doesn't he run?* Then the thought passed through my mind that although I was sure that the boy had somehow become the anointed of Kali, what if this meant that he was the only one *exempted* from some fate rather than chosen for it? *Many are called, few are chosen* the priest had said in what I had taken as a deliberate parody of the tiresome prattle of the Christian missionaries who wandered the plazas near the Maidan. But what if it meant that the boy was the only one to be smiled upon by this *jagrata* and approved for initiation into the Kapalikas? Disappointment mixed with relief in my confused swirl of thoughts and apprehensions.

"The priest returned to the dais. 'Your first duty is fulfilled,' he said quietly. 'Your second must be completed by the time you return tomorrow midnight. Go now to hear the command of Kali, bride of Siva.'

"Two men in black came forward and beckoned. We followed them to the far side of the warehouse temple to a wall that opened onto small alcoves covered by black curtains. The Kapalikas gestured like ushers at a wedding, assigning each of us a cubicle and then moving on a few paces to show the next man his place. Sanjay entered his black alcove and I unconsciously held back a second as the dark man before me beckoned.

"The cubicle was tiny and, as far as I could tell in the almost total darkness, empty of furniture or ornamentation on the three stone walls. The black-garbed man whispered 'Kneel' and closed the heavy curtain. The last bit of light was gone. I knelt.

"It was deathly quiet. Not even the sound of the river intruded on the hot silence. I decided to put the poundings of my heart to work and had counted twenty-seven pulse beats when a voice whispered directly in my ear.

"It was a woman's voice. Or rather, it was a soft, sexless voice. I jumped up then and threw out my hands but no one was there.

" 'You shall bring me an offering,' the voice had whispered.

"I got back down on my knees, trembling, waiting for another sound or for something to touch me. A second later the curtain was pushed aside and I rose and left the alcove.

"We had already formed the half-circle of initiates before the idol when I realized that only seven of us were there. *Good,* I thought. *He ran.* Then Sanjay touched my arm and nodded toward the goddess. The naked corpse she danced upon was younger, fresher. And headless.

"Her fourth hand was no longer empty. The burden she dangled by the hair swayed slightly. The expression on its young face was one of mild surprise. The dripping made a soft, starting-of-rainfall sound on the floor.

"I had heard no outcry.

" 'Kali, Kali, balo bhai,' we sang. 'Kali bai aré gaté nai.'

"The Kapalikas filed out. A man in black led us to a door in the darkness. In the anteroom we put on our sandals and left the building. Sanjay and I found our way through the maze of alleys to Strand Road. There we hailed a rickshaw and returned to our room. It was very late.

" 'What did she mean?' I asked when both of the lanterns were lit and we were in our *charpoys* and under the blankets. 'What kind of offering?'

" 'Idiot,' said Sanjay. He was trembling as fiercely as I was. His string bed shook. 'We have to bring her a body by tomorrow midnight. A human body. A dead body.' "

Chapter Seven

"Calcutta, Calcutta, you are a night obsessed field,
infinite cruelty,
Serpentine mixed current, on which I flow
to who knows where."

—Sunilkumar Nandi

Krishna stopped translating. His voice had grown more and more hoarse until the croak of it perfectly complemented his toad-like eyes. It was with an effort that I looked away from Muktanandaji. I realized that I had become so absorbed that I had forgotten Krishna's presence. Now I felt precisely the same irritation at him for stopping that one would feel toward a balky tape recorder or a television that malfunctioned at an inappropriate time.

"What's the matter?" I asked.

Krishna tilted his head, and I turned to look. The white-stubbled proprietor was approaching us. Incredibly, the huge room had emptied without my noticing it. Bulky chairs were upended on all of the other tables. The fans had ceased their slow turning. I glanced at my watch. It was 11:35.

The proprietor—if that is what he was—grumbled at Krishna and Muktanadaji. Krishna flicked his hand tiredly, and the man repeated something in a louder, more petulant voice.

"What's the matter?" I asked again.

"He must close," croaked Krishna. "He is paying for the electricity."

I glanced at the few dim bulbs still glowing and almost laughed aloud.

"We can finish this tomorrow," said Krishna. Muktanadaji had removed his glasses and was rubbing tiredly at his eyes.

"The hell with that," I said. I flipped through the few bills of Indian currency I'd brought with me and handed the old man a twenty-rupee note. He remained standing and mumbled something to himself. I gave him ten more rupees. He scratched at his whiskery cheeks and shuffled back toward his counter. I had parted with less than three dollars.

"Go on," I said.

"Sanjay was confident that we could find two corpses before midnight. This was, after all, Calcutta.

"In the morning, as we rode to the center of the city, we asked the Harijan dead-animal transporters if they ever carried human bodies in their trucks. No, they answered, the City Municipal Corporation hired other men—poor men but men of caste—to go out in the mornings and retrive the bodies which inevitably littered the sidewalks. And that was only in the business and downtown sections. Farther out, where the great *chawls* began, there was no arrangement. Bodies were left to the families or dogs.

"'Where are the bodies taken after they are collected downtown?' asked Sanjay. To the Sassoon Morgue, was the reply. By ten-thirty that morning, after eating a breakfast of fried dough along the Maidan, Sanjay and I were at the Sassoon Morgue.

"The morgue took up the first floor and two basement levels of a building in the old English section of the city. There were stone lions still guarding the front steps, but the door there was locked and boarded, obviously unused for many years. All business went through the back entrance where the trucks came and went.

"The morgue was crowded. Sheeted bodies lay on carts in the hallways and even outside the offices. There was a very strong smell. This surprised me.

"A man carrying a clipboard and wearing a yellow-stained white uniform came out of his office and smiled. 'Can I help you?'

"I had no idea what to say, but Sanjay began speaking immediately, convincingly. 'We are from Varanasi. We have come to Calcutta because two of our cousins, unfortunately dispossessed of their lands in West Bengal, recently came to the city to find other work. Alas, it seems they have taken ill and died on the streets before finding dutiful employment. The wife of our poor second cousin informed us of this by letter before she returned to her family in Tamil Nadu. The bitch made no attempt to retrieve the body of her husband or our other cousin, but now we have come, at great expense, to return them to Varanasi for proper cremation."

" 'Ahh.' the attendant grimaced. 'Those accursed Southern women. They have no sense of proper behavior. Animals.'

"I nodded agreement. It was so easy!

" 'Man or woman? Old, young, or infant?' asked the morgue man in a bored voice.

" 'Pardon?'

" 'The other cousin. I presume the wife who left was married to a man, but what was the sex of the other family member? And the age of each? Also, on what day would they have been collected? First, what sex?'

" 'A man,' said Sanjay.

" 'Female,' I replied at the same time.

"The attendant stopped in the act of leading us into another room. Sanjay gave me a look that could have removed skin.

" 'My apologies,' said Sanjay smoothly. 'Kamila, Jayaprakesh's poor cousin, is certainly female. I can think only of my own cousin, Samar. Jayaprakesh and I are related only through marriage, of course.'

" 'Ah,' said the attendant, but his eyes had narrowed as he looked from one to the other of us. 'You would not, by any chance, be students at the University?'

" 'No,' smiled Sanjay. 'I work at my father's rug shop in Varanasi. Jayaprakesh helps his uncle farm. I have some education. Jayaprakesh has none. Why do you ask?'

" 'No reason. No reason,' said the attendant. He glanced at me, and I worried that he could hear the loud thudding of my pulse. 'It is just that on occasion medical students from our university here . . . ah . . . lose loved ones on the street. This way, please." "The basement rooms were large, damp, cooled by throbbing air conditioners. Water had streaked the walls and floors. Bodies lay naked on gurneys and tables.

There was no order to their placement except for rough segregation by age and sex. The children's room we passed was quite crowded.

"Sanjay specified a date a week earlier as the time of our cousins' passing. It seemed that our cousin Samar had been in his forties.

"The first room we entered held about twenty men. All were in various stages of decomposition. It was not very cool in the room. Water dripped openly onto the corpses in a vain attempt to chill them. Both Sanjay and I lifted our shirts to our mouths and noses. Our eyes watered.

" 'Damned power outages,' grumbled the attendant. 'Every few hours these days. Well?' He walked over and pulled sheets off the few covered forms. He extended his hands as if offering a bullock for sale.

" 'No,' said Sanjay peering grimly into the first face. He went to another. 'No. No. Wait . . . no. It is hard to tell.'

" 'Mmmm.'

"Sanjay moved from table to table, cart to cart. The terrible faces stared back at him, eyes filmed over, jaws locked open, some with swollen tongues protruding. A few grinned obscenely as if courting our choice. 'No,'' said Sanjay. 'No.'

" 'These are all that came in during that week. Are you sure you have the dates right?' The morgue attendant did not try to hide the boredom and skepticism in his voice.

"Sanjay nodded, and I wondered what game he was playing. *Identify someone and let us be gone*! 'Wait,' he said. 'What about that one in the corner?'

"The cadaver lay alone on a steel table as if it had been tossed there absentmindedly. The knees and forearms were half raised, the fists clenched. The corpse was almost bald and had its face turned to the dank wall as if shamed by its own limp nakedness.

" 'Too old,' muttered the attendant, but my friend had taken five quick steps to the corner. He leaned over to look at the face. The raised white fist of the corpse brushed against Sanjay's lifted shirt and bare belly.

" 'Cousin Samar!' cried Sanjay with a half-sob. He clutched at the stiffened hand.

" 'No, no, no,' said the morgue man. He blew his nose into the tail of his stained tunic. 'He came in only yesterday. Too new.'

" 'Nonetheless, it is poor Cousin Samar,' said Sanjay in a choked voice. I saw real tears in his eyes.

"The morgue attendant shrugged and checked his clipboard. He had to look through several layers of forms. 'No identification. Brought in Tuesday morning. Found naked on Sudder Street . . . appropriate, yes? Estimated cause of death—broken neck resulting from fall or strangulation. Possibly robbed for his clothes. Estimated age, sixty-five.'

" 'Cousin Samar was forty-nine,' said Sanjay. He dabbed at his eyes and returned the shirt to his nose. Again the attendant shrugged.

" 'Jayaprakesh, why don't you look for Cousin Kamila?" said Sanjay. 'I will make arrangements for the transporting of Cousin Samar.'

" 'No, no,' said the morgue man.

" 'No?' Sanjay and I said together.

" 'No.' The man frowned down at his clipboard. 'You cannot transport this body until it is identified.'

" 'But I just identified him. It is Cousin Samar,' said Sanjay, still clutching the corpse's gnarled fist.

" 'No, no. I mean *officially* identified it. That must be done at the post office.'

" 'The post office?' I said.

" 'Yes, yes, yes. The city administration has its Office of Missing Persons and Unclaimed Bodies there. Third floor. After proof of identification is made, there is a two-hundred-rupee fee to the city. Two hundred rupees for each identified loved one, that is.'

" 'Ayeeh!' cried Sanjay. 'Two hundred rupees for what?'

" 'For the official identification and certification, of course. Then you must go to the Municipal Corporation offices on Waterloo Street. They are open to the public only on Saturdays.'

" 'That is three days away!' I cried.

" 'Why must we go there?' asked Sanjay.

" 'To pay the collection fee of five hundred rupees, of course. For their transporting service.' The attendant sighed. 'So, before releasing the body, I must have the identification certificate, the identification payment receipt, the collection payment receipt, and of course, a copy of your License to Transport Deceased Persons.'

" 'Ahhh,' said Sanjay. He released Cousin Samar's hand. 'And where do we get such a license?'

" 'From the Bureau of Licenses in the State Administrative Offices near Raj Bhavan.'

" 'Of course,' said Sanjay. 'And it costs—'

" 'Eight hundred rupees per deceased person you wish to transport. There is a group rate for more than five.'

" 'Is that all we need?' asked Sanjay, and his voice held the edge to it that I often had heard just before he struck out at walls or kicked the little Burmese children who cluttered our courtyard and stairways.

"'Yes, yes,' said the attendant. 'Except the death certificate. I can make that out.'

"'Aghhh,' breathed Sanjay. 'The cost?'

"'A mere fifty rupees,' smiled the attendant. 'Then there is the matter of the rent.'

"'Rent?' I repeated, speaking through my shirt.

"'Yes, yes, yes. We are very crowded, as you can see. There is a fifteen-rupee per day rental fee for space provided.' He consulted the clipboard. 'Your cousin Samar's rent comes to 105 rupees.'

"'But he's only been here one day!' I cried.

"'True, true. But I fear we must charge for the entire week because he received special facilities because of his . . . ah . . . advanced stage. Shall we look to your Cousin Kamila now?'

"'This will cost us almost two thousand rupees!' exploded Sanjay. 'For each body!'

"'Oh yes, yes,' said the morgue man with a smile. 'I trust that the rug business in Varanasi is healthy these days?'

"'Come along, Jayaprakesh,' said Sanjay as he turned to leave.

"'But what about Cousin Kamila?' I cried.

"'Come *along*!' Sanjay said and pulled me from the room.

"There was a white truck outside the morgue. Sanjay approached the driver. "The bodies,' he said. 'Where do they go?'

"'What?'

"'Where do the unclaimed bodies go when they're taken from here?'

"The driver sat up and frowned. 'To Naidu Infectious Diseases Hospital. Most of them. They dispose of them.'

"'Where is that?'

"'Way out on Upper Chitpur Road.'

"It took us an hour to get there by streetcar through heavy traffic. The old hospital was crowded with people hoping to recover or waiting to die. The long hallways, overflowing with beds, reminded me of the morgue. Birds came in through the bars on the windows and hopped among the tousled sheets, hoping to find stray crumbs. Lizards skittered across the cracked walls and I saw a rodent scurry under a bed as we passed.

"A mustached intern suddenly blocked our path. 'Who are you?'

"Sanjay, taken by surprise, gave our names. I could tell that his mind was working furiously to concoct an adequate story.

"'You're here about the bodies, aren't you?' demanded the intern.

"We both blinked.

"'You're reporters, aren't you?' asked the man.

"'Yes,' agreed Sanjay.

"'Damn. We knew this would get out,' growled the intern. 'Well, it's not our fault!'

"'Why not?' asked Sanjay. From his skirt pocket he removed the battered old notebook in which he kept records of the Beggarmasters' payments, our laundry bills, and our market lists. 'Would you care to make a statement?' He licked the end of a broken pencil.

"'Come this way,' snapped the intern. He led us through a ward of typhoid patients, into an adjoining kitchen, and outside past heaps of garbage. Behind the hospital there was an empty weeded field that covered several acres. In the distance were visible the burlap lean-tos and tin roofs of a growing *chawl*. A rusting bulldozer sat in the weeds and against it leaned an old man with baggy shorts and an ancient bolt-action rifle.

" 'Heeyah!' screamed the intern. The old man jumped and shouldered the rifle. 'There! There!' cried the intern and pointed out into the weeds. The old man fired and the sound of the shot echoed off the tall building behind us.

" 'Shit, shit, shit!' yelled the intern and bent quickly to rise with a large stone in his hand. Out in the weeds, a gray dog with prominent ribs had raised its head at the sound of the gunshot and now stared at us. The scrawny beast turned and loped off with its tail between its legs and something pink in its mouth. The intern threw his stone, and it dropped into the weeds halfway between him and the dog. The old man at the bulldozer was wrestling with the bolt of the rifle.

" 'Damn,' said the intern and led us out across the field. There were scars and mounds of dirt everywhere, as if the bulldozer had pawed at the earth here for years like a huge house cat. We stopped at the edge of a shallow pit where we had first seen the dog.

" 'Ay!' I said and backed away. The rotting human hand that rose out of the moist soil had brushed against my sandal and touched my bare foot. Other things were visible. Then I noticed the other pits, the other dogs in the distance.

" 'It was all right ten years ago,' said the intern, 'but now, with that industrial *basti* coming so close . . .' He broke off to throw another rock at another pack of dogs. The animals calmly trotted into the bushes. Behind us, the old man had succeeded in ejecting the spent cartridge and was levering another bullet in.

" 'Were these Muslims or Christians?' asked Sanjay. His pencil was poised.

" 'Hindus, most likely. Who knows?' the intern spat. 'The crematoria do not wish to have unpaying customers. But the damned dogs have been digging them up like this for months now. We were willing to pay until . . . Wait. You *have* heard about what happened today? That *is* why you're here, is it not?'

" 'Of course,' Sanjay said blandly. 'But perhaps you would like to tell us your side.'

"I was barely listening. I was too busy looking around, noticing the other bits and pieces rising from the churned soil like dead fish rising to the surface of a pond. From what I could see, there seemed little hope that Sanjay and I could find an intact offering here. Ravens circled overhead. The old man had sat down on the metal tractor tread and appeared to be dozing.

" 'There have been many complaints about today's business,' said the intern. 'But we had to do something. Make sure that you report that the *hospital* was prepared to pay for the cremations.'

" 'Yes,' said Sanjay and wrote something down.

"We began walking back to the hospital building. Families of patients were camped in makeshift tents and huts near the mountains of garbage. 'We had to do something,' said the intern. 'The power outages, you know. And with the dogs we couldn't just go on as we've done over the years. So we paid the Municipal Corporation to transport them, and this morning we loaded thirty-seven fresh from the cooler to be taken to

Ashutosh Crematorium Grounds. How were we to know that they would use an open truck and that it would be stuck in traffic for hours?'

" 'How indeed?' said Sanjay and scribbled something.

" 'And then, to make it worse, after the load was dumped on the cremation grounds, there was the festival crowd.'

" 'Yes!' I said. 'The *Kali Puja* begins today.'

" 'But how were *we* to know that the ceremony was to draw ten thousand people to *that* cremation park?' the intern asked sharply. I did not remind him that Kali was the goddess of all cremation grounds and places of deaths, including even battlefields and non-Hindu burial places.

" 'Do you know how *long* it takes for a full and proper cremation, even with the new electric pyres in the city?' asked the intern. 'Two hours,' he answered himself. 'Two hours *each*.'

" 'What happened to those bodies?' asked Sanjay as if the subject held little interest for him. It was already early afternoon. Ten hours until midnight.

" 'Ahh, the complaints!' wailed the intern. 'Several of the worshipers fainted. It was very hot this morning. But we *had* to leave most behind. The drivers refused to return here or to the Sassoon Morgue through afternoon traffic with a full load again.'

" 'Thank you,' said Sanjay and shook the man's hand. 'Our ..aders will be pleased to know the hospital's point of view. Oh, by the way, will your guard be here after dark?' Sanjay nodded toward the sleeping old man.

" 'Yes, yes,' snapped the sweating intern. 'For all the damned good it will do. Heeyah!' He shouted and bent to find a stone to throw at the slavering dog dragging something large into the bushes.

"We drove to the Ashutosh Crematorium Grounds at ten o'clock that night. Sanjay had arranged to borrow one of the small Premiere vans that the Beggarmasters used to take out and collect their crippled charges. The narrow compartment in the back was windowless and it smelled very bad.

"I had not known that Sanjay knew how to drive. After our reckless, honking, light blinking, lane-shifting ride through evening traffic, I was still not sure.

"The gates to the cremation park were locked, but we went in through the laundry grounds which adjoined it. The water had ceased running through the open pipes, the concrete stalls and slabs were empty of wash, and the workers of the launderer caste had left at nightfall. There was a stone wall separating the crematorium from the laundry grounds, but unlike so many walls in the city, it had no broken glass or razor blades set atop it and was easy to climb.

"Once over the wall, we hesitated for a minute. The stars were out, but the new moon had not yet risen. It was very dark. The tin-roofed cremation pavilions were gray silhouettes against the night sky. There was another shadow closer to the front gates: tall, domed, a huge wooden platform resting on giant wooden wheels.

" 'The godcart for the *Kali Puja*,' whispered Sanjay. I nodded. They had set tin shutters in place over the outer frame, but both of us knew the giant, angry, four-armed presence which waited within. Such a festival idol was rarely considered a *jagrata*, but who could know what power it gained at night, alone, in a place of death?

" 'This way,' whispered Sanjay and headed for the largest

pavilion, the one closest to the circular drive. We passed stacks of wood, fuel for the families with money, and stacks of dried cow-dung patties for the more common cremations. The roofless pavilion for the funeral band was an empty gray slab in the starlight. It seemed to me that it was a morgue slab, coldly awaiting the corpse of some huge god. I glanced nervously at the shuttered godcart.

" 'Here,' said Sanjay. They lay there in rough rows. If there had been a moon, the shadow of the godcart would have fallen across them. I took a step toward them and turned away. 'Ayah,' I said. 'I will have to burn my clothes tomorrow.' I could imagine the effect on the crowd, in the heat of the day.

" 'Pray there is a tomorrow,' hissed Sanjay and began stepping over the tumbled forms. A few had been covered by canvas tarpaulins or blankets. Most lay open to the sky. My eyes had adjusted to the faint starlight and I could make out pale glistenings and white glow of bones which had worked their way free of clinging flesh. Here and there a twisted limb rose above the indistinct heaps. I remembered the hand which had seemed to grasp my foot outside the hospital and I shuddered.

" 'Quickly!' Sanjay chose a body in the second row and began dragging it toward the back wall.

" 'Wait for me!' I whispered desperately, but he had already been swallowed by the shadows and I was alone with the dark obstacles underfoot. I moved to the middle of the third row and immediately regretted it. It was hard to put a foot down without it treading on something which yielded sickeningly to the touch. A slight breeze came up and a piece of tattered clothing fluttered a few feet from me.

"There was a sudden movement and noise in the row

nearest the looming godcart. I stood upright, hands clenching into feeble fists. It was a bird of some kind—huge, too heavy to fly, black pinions fluttering. It hopped over the corpses and disappeared into the darkness beneath the goddess's shelter. Rattling sounds echoed from under the loose tin shutters. I could imagine the great idol stirring, its four hands reaching for the containing wooden frame, its blind eyes opening whitely to view its domain.

"Something grasped my ankle in an encircling grip.

"I let out a yell then, jumped sideways, tripped, and went down among the tangle of cold limbs. My forearm ended up resting on the leg of a corpse whose face was buried in the grass. The grip on my ankle did not relax. If anything, it was tugging me backwards.

"I pushed myself to my knees and brushed wildly at my right leg. My shout had been so loud that I expected guards to come running from the front gate. I *hoped* someone would come running. But there were no guards. I yelled for Sanjay but there was no response. My ankle burned where something gripped it tightly.

"I forced myself to quit straining, to stand. The grip relaxed. I dropped to one knee and peered at the thing which held me.

"The body had been covered by a silky tarpaulin with many nylon lines attached. I had stepped into one of these loose coils of rope and pulled it tight with my next step. It took only a few seconds to untangle the cord.

"I smiled. Only a pale hand, grub-white in the starlight, protruded from the silken shroud. I nudged the hand back under the sheet with the toe of my sandal. *Perfect.* Let Sanjay wrestle with the flesh of the dead like a Scheduled Class renderer. Without actually touching the shape beneath the sheet, I rolled it deeper into the silky folds, used the dangling cords to bind it, lifted the soft mass to my shoulder, and was away, moving quickly past the dark pavilions. The noise in the godcart ceased as I moved away from it.

"Sanjay was waiting in the shadow of the wall. 'Hurry!' he hissed. It was after eleven. We were miles from the Kapalikas' temple. Together we hoisted the two bodies over the wall.

"The journey from the cremation grounds to the Kapalika temple was the stuff of nightmares—absurd nightmares. Our burdens rolled around in the back as Sanjay weaved in and out of traffic, forcing bullock carts off the road, causing pedestrains to leap into piles of garbage to escape being run down, and blinking his lights frantically to warn oncoming trucks that he would not surrender the right of way. Twice we had to bounce up on the sidewalks as he passed on the left. A wake of shouted obscenities marked our path through Calcutta that night.

"Finally, the inevitable occurred. Near the Maidan, Sanjay attempted to cross three lanes of oncoming traffic at an intersection. A metropolitan policeman jumped down from the giant tractor tire on which he was directing traffic and threw up his hand to halt us. For a mad second I was convinced that Sanjay was going to run him down. Then he slammed both feet on the brake and pulled back on the steering wheel as if he were trying to rein in a runaway bullock. Our van skidded broadside, almost tipped over, and came to a stop a foot from the policeman's outstretched palm. The engine stalled. One of the corpses in the back had tumbled forward until its bare foot protruded between the driver's seat and me. Luckily, the shroud was still tangled about both bodies. I hastily pulled the sheet over the foot just as the furious traffic policeman came around to Sanjay's side of the van. He leaned in the right window, and his face was almost rippling with outrage.

" 'What in fuck do you fucking well think you're fucking doing?' The officer's broad helmet bobbed as he shouted. I thanked all of the gods that he was not a Sikh. He was screaming at us in a West Bengali dialect. He punctuated his shouts with blows to Sanjay's door with his heavy *lathi* stick. A Sikh—and most metropolitan police tend to be Sikhs—would have been using the club on our heads. They are strange people, Sikhs.

"Before Sanjay could frame an answer or restart the engine, the policeman took a step back and threw his hand to his face. 'Pah!' he yelled. 'What the fuck do you have in there?'

"I sank in my seat. All was lost. The police would arrest us. We would get imprisoned for life in the terrible Hooghly Prison, but that would be only a few days because the Kapalikas would kill us.

"Sanjay, however, grinned broadly and leaned out the window. 'Ah, most honorable sir, surely you recognize this truck, sir?' He banged on the dented door with his palm.

"The policeman frowned fiercely but took another step back. 'Hmmrr,' he said through his hand.

" 'Yes, yes, yes,' cried Sanjay, still grinning stupidly. 'It is the very property of Gopalakrishna Nirendrenath G. S. Mahapatra, Chief Beggarmaster of the Chitpur and Upper Chittaranjan Union! And in the back are six of his most profitable and pitiable lepers. Very profitable beggars, honored sir!' Sanjay started the engine with his left hand and indicated the dark rear of the van with a sweep of his right hand. 'I am an hour late returning Master Mahapatra's property to their feeding-sleeping hall, respectful sir. He will have my head. But if you arrest us, honorable constable, I will have, at least, an excuse for my unworthy tardiness. Please, if you wish to arrest us I will open the back for you. The lepers, sir, however profitable, can no longer walk, so you will have to help me carry them out.' Sanjay fumbled at the outer door latch as if to get out.

"'No!' cried the officer. He shook the *lathi* club at Sanjay's fumbling hand. 'Begone! Immediately!' And so saying, he turned his back on us and walked quickly to the center of the intersection. There he began waving his arms and blowing his whistle at the screaming mass of tangled traffic which had blocked three streets in the short time he had been absent from his tire.

"Sanjay wrenched the truck into gear, drove around the snarled pack of vehicles by driving across the grass of Plaza Park, and turned against oncoming traffic onto Strand Road South.

"We parked as close as we could to the warehouse. The street was very dark, but there was a lantern in the back of the truck. Sanjay had to light it so we could untangle our offerings from the cords of my corpse's shroud. By my watch, a gift from Sanjay, it was ten minutes before twelve. My watch often ran slow.

"I could see by the sudden leap of light from the lantern that Sanjay had carried what had once been an old man from the cremation grounds. The corpse had no teeth, only a wisp of hair, and cataracts on both eyes. It was tangled in a spiderweb of ropes from my corpse's covering.

"'Damn!' muttered Sanjay. 'It's like a stinking parachute.

No, there's a fucking *net* tangled in with the tarp.' Sanjay finally had to use his teeth to bite through the cord.

" 'Quickly,' he said to me. 'Take that cloth off yours. They will not want it covered.'

" 'But I don't think . . ."

" '*Do* it, dammit,' snapped Sanjay in a full rage. His eyes seemed to leap out of his red face. The lantern spat and hissed. 'Shit, shit, shit!' he exploded. 'I should have used *you* as I first planned. It would have been so damned simple. Shit!' Sanjay angrily lifted his corpse under the arms and started dragging it free of the severed ropes.

"I stood there, transfixed, numb. Even when I slowly began untying the final knots and tugging away the last cords, I was not aware of what my hands were doing. *I tell you what, Jayaprakesh. You are a victim of social injustice. Your plight touches me. I will lower the rent from two hundred rupees a month to five rupees. If you need a loan for the first two or three months, I will be happy to advance it.*

"Tears ran down my cheeks and fell to the shroud. From far away I heard Sanjay's cry to hurry, but my hands moved slowly and methodically to untie the last of the tangled lines. I remembered my tears of gratitude when Sanjay took me in as a roommate, my surprise and gratitude at his including me in his Kapalika initiation.

"*I should have used* you *as I first planned.*

"I wiped brusquely at my eyes, angrily pulled the shroud away, and threw it into the far corner of the van.

" 'Ayeeeaa!' The scream was torn out of me. I leaped backwards and slammed into the wall of the van, almost pitching forward onto the *thing* revealed before me. The lantern tipped over and rolled along the metal floor. I screamed again.

" 'What?' Sanjay had run back to the van. Now he stopped and clutched at the door. 'Arhhh . . .'

"The thing I had carried like a bride from the cremation grounds may once have been human. No longer. No trace remained. The body was swollen twice the size of a man—more a giant, putrid starfish than a man. The face had no shape, only a white mass with wrinkled holes and swollen slits where the eyes, mouth, and nose might once have been. The thing was a sick simulacrum of a human form, crudely molded of suppurating fungus and dead, distorted meat.

"It was white—all white—the white of the bellies of dead carp washed up from the Hooghly. The skin had the texture of bleached, rotted rubber, like something peeled and shaped from the underside of a poisonous toadstool. The corpse was bloated taut; inflated from the awful internal pressure of expanding gases and organs swollen to the bursting point and beyond. Fractured splinters of ribs and bones were visible here and there in the puffy mass like sticks embedded in a rising dough.

" 'Ahh,' gasped Sanjay. 'A drowning victim.'

"As if to confirm Sanjay's statement, there came a whiff of foul river mud, and a sluglike thing appeared in one of the black eyeholes. Glistening feelers tasted the night air and then withdrew from the light. I sensed the movement of many other things in the swollen mass.

"I pressed back against the side of the van and slid my way to the rear door. I would have pushed past Sanjay and run into the welcoming night, but he blocked me, pushed me back into the narrow chamber with the thing.

" 'Pick it up,' Sanjay said.

"I stared at him. The fallen lantern threw wild shadows between us. I could only stare.

" 'Pick it up, Jayaprakesh. We have less than two minutes until the ceremony begins. Pick it up.'

"I would have jumped Sanjay then. I would have happily choked him until the last gasps of life rattled out of his lying throat. Then I saw the gun. It had appeared in his fist like the lotus flower suddenly popping into the palm of a clever traveling magician. It was a small pistol. It hardly looked large enough to be real. But it was. I had no doubt of that. And the black circle of the barrel was aimed right between my eyes.

" 'Pick it up.'

"Nothing on earth could have made me pick up the thing on the floor behind me. Nothing except the absolute certain knowledge that I would be dead in three seconds if I did not comply. *Dead*. Like the thing in the van. *Lying with it*. On it. *With it*.

"I knelt, set the lantern upright before it sputtered out or set fire to the shroud, and put my arms under the shape. It seemed to welcome my grasp. One arm moved against my side like the furtive touch of a timid lover. My fingers sank deep into the white. The flesh felt cool and rubbery, and I was sure that my fingers would break through at any second. Soft things shifted and stirred inside it as I backed out of the van and took a step. The thing sagged against me, and for a second I felt the terrible certainty that the corpse would deliquesce and flow down over me like moist river clay.

"I raised my face to the night sky and stumbled forward. Behind me, Sanjay shouldered his own cold burden and followed me into the Temple of the Kapalikas.

Chapter Eight

" 'Sa etān panca pasún apasýat—purusam, aśvam, gām, avim, ajam . . . Purusam prathaman alabhate, puruso hi prathamah paśunaṁm. . . .' "

"We sang the sacred words from the *Satapatha Brahmana*.

" 'And the order of sacrifice shall be this . . . first man, then horse, bull, ram, and goat . . . Man is foremost of the animals and most pleasing to the gods. . . .'

"We knelt in the darkness before the *jagrata* Kali. They had dressed us in plain white *dhotis*. Our feet were bare. Our foreheads were marked. We seven initiates knelt in a semicircle closest to the goddess. Then there was an arc of candles and the outer circle of Kapalikas. In front of us lay the bodies we had brought as offerings. On the belly of each corpse a Kapalika priest had placed a small white skull. The skulls were human, too small to be from adults. The empty sockets watched us with the same intensity as the goddess's hungry eyes.

"'The world is pain,
O terrible wife of Siva
You are chewing the flesh.'

"The head of our eighth initiate still hung from the hand of Kali, but now the young face was chalk-white and the lips had pulled back into a rictus grin. The corpse, however, was gone from its place at the base of the idol and the goddess's bangled foot was raised over empty air.

"'O terrible wife of Siva
Your tongue is drinking the blood,
O dark Mother! O unclad Mother.'

"I felt almost nothing as I knelt there. My mind continued to echo Sanjay's words. *I should have used* you. I was a provincial fool. Worse than that, I was a provincial fool who could never go home again to the provinces. Whatever else came from this night, I knew that the simple verities of life in Anguda were forever behind me.

"'O beloved of Siva
The world is pain.'

"The temple fell into silence. We closed our eyes in *dhyana*, the deepest contemplation possible only in the presence of a *jagrata*. Sounds intruded. The river whispered half-perceived syllables. Something slithered across the floor near my bare feet. I felt nothing. I thought nothing. When I opened my eyes, I saw that the crimson tongue of the idol had lolled farther from the gaping mouth. Nothing surprised me.

"Other Kapalikas came forward until each of us had a priest kneeling in front of us, facing us across the obscene altars we had supplied. My Brahman was a kindly-looking man. A banker, perhaps. Someone who was used to smiling at people for a living.

> "'O Kali, O Terrible One,
> O Chinnamasta, She Who Is Beheaded,
> O Chandi, Fiercest of Aspect,
> O Kamaski, Devourer of Souls,
> Hear our prayer, O Terrible Wife of Siva.'

"My priest lifted my right hand and turned it palm up as if he were about to read my fortune. His other hand went into the loose folds of his *dhoti*. When it emerged, I saw the quick gleam of sharp steel.

"The chief priest placed his forehead against the raised foot of the goddess. His voice was very soft. 'The goddess will be pleased to receive your flesh mixed with blood.'

"The other priests all moved in unison. The blades slid across our palms as if the Kapalikas were whittling bamboo. A fat sliver from the meaty portion of my palm sliced off neatly and slid across the blade. All of us gasped, but only the fat man cried out in pain.

"'Thou who art fond of sacrificial meat, O Great Goddess. Accept the blood of this man with his flesh.'

"The words were not new to me. I had heard them every October during the modest *Kali Puja* in our village. Every

Bengali child knows the litany. But never had I seen more than a symbolic sacrifice. Never had I seen a Brahman hold high a pink circle of my flesh and then bow to insert it in the gaping mouth of a corpse.

"Then the smiling, apologetic little man across from me took my injured hand and turned it palm downward. The Kapalikas in the darkness behind us began to recite the holiest of the *Gayatri mantri* in perfect unison while the dark drops fell slow and heavy to the white surface of the drowned thing at my knees.

"The *mantra* ended, and my banker-priest deftly retrieved a white cloth from his tunic and bound up my hand. I prayed to the goddess that it would soon be over. A sudden hollowness and sickness had risen in me. My arms began shaking and I feared that I might swoon. The fat man three places from me did faint, falling forward across the cold breast of the toothless old female corpse he had brought. His priest ignored him and returned to the darkness with others.

"*Please, goddess, let it end*, I prayed.

"But it did not end. Not yet.

"The first Brahman raised his forehead from the *jagrata's* foot and turned to us. He walked slowly along our semicircle as if inspecting the bodies we had brought as offerings. He paused for a lengthy moment in front of me. I could not raise my eyes to meet his. I was convinced that the drowned corpse would not be found worthy. Even now it gave off a stench of river mud and corruption like a foul breath rising from its gaping maw. But a second later the priest moved on in silence. He inspected Sanjay's offering and moved farther down the line.

"I risked a sideward glance in time to see the bare foot of

the priest roughly push the fat man's bulk off its cold pillow. Another Kapalika hurried forward and hastily set the child's skull back in place on the cadaver's sunken belly. The fat initiate lay unconscious next to his cold crone, two unlikely lovers torn from their embrace. Few of us doubted whose countenance the dark goddess would next raise up by the hair.

"I had no sooner begun to control my shaking than the priest was back in front of me again. This time he snapped his fingers and three Kapalikas came forward to join him. I sensed Sanjay's almost desperate desire to move farther away from me. I myself felt little. A great coldness had moved through me, cooling my throbbing hand, extinguishing my fear, and emptying my mind. I could have laughed aloud as the Kapalikas bent toward me. I chose not to.

"Tenderly, almost lovingly, they lifted the swollen excrescence that was the corpse and carried it to the slab at the foot of the idol. Then they motioned me forward to join them.

"The next few minutes run together in my memory like half-captured dreams. I remember kneeling with the Kapalikas before the shapeless dead thing. I believe we recited the *Purusha Sukta* of the tenth Mandala of the *Rig-Veda*. Others came forward from the shadows carrying pails of water to bathe the putrefying flesh of my offering. I recall that I found as very funny the idea of bathing someone who already had spent so much time in the holy river. I did not laugh.

"The chief priest brought out the stalk of grass, still marked with dried blood, which had decided our young inititate's fate the day before. The priest dipped the blade in a chalice of black lamp paste and painted half-circles above the holes in the corpse where once eyes had looked out on the world. I had seen holy effigies painted thus, and once again I fought back the urge to chuckle as I realized that it should have been the eyelids that were so marked. In our village ceremonies, such a ritual granted the clay form eyesight.

"Other men approached to place grass and flowers on the forehead. The tall and terrible Kali idol looked down as we recited the basic *mula-mantri* 108 times. Again the priest came forward, this time to touch each limb and place his thumb on the bloated white flesh where once a heart had beaten. Then, together we uttered a variant of the Vedic *mantra* which ended—'Om, may Vishnu endow you with genitals, Tvasta carve the form, Prajapati provide the semen, and Kali receive your seed.'

"The chorus of voices filled the darkness once again and rose in the chant of the holiest Veda, the *Gayatri mantra*. It was just then that a great sound and powerful wind rose to fill the temple. For a wild second I was sure that the river was rising to claim us all.

"The wind actually felt cold as it roared through the temple, blowing our hair, rippling the white fabric of our *dhotis*, and extinguishing most of the candles in the rows behind us. As clearly as I can recall, the temple never fell into *total* darkness. Some of the candles continued to burn as their flames danced to the eerie breeze. But if there *was* still light—any amount—I cannot account for what next occurred.

"I did not move. I continued to kneel less than four feet from the idol and its anointed offering. Nor did I perceive any other movement except for a few Kapalikas behind us striking several matches to relight some of the candles. It took only a few seconds to do this. Then the wind had passed, the sound abated, and the *jagrata* Kali was once again illuminated from below.

"*The corpse had changed.*

"The flesh was still grub-white, but now Kali's foot came down on a body which was visibly that of a man. It was as naked as it had been previously, flowers still strewn on its forehead, lampblack dabbed above the eyes, but a pale sex organ lay flaccid where only a rotting pustulence had been just seconds earlier. The face was not whole—the thing still had no lips, eyelids, or nose—but the ruined countenance was recognizably human. Eyes now filled the caves of the face. Open sores scoured the white flesh, but the splintered bones could no longer be seen.

"I closed my eyes and offered a wordless prayer—to which deity I do not recall. A gasp from Sanjay made me look again.

"The corpse breathed. Air whistled through the open mouth and the cadaverous chest rose once, twice, and then settled into a rasping, laboring rhythm. Suddenly, in one fluid movement, the body rose to a sitting position. Slowly, most reverently, it kissed the sole of Kali's foot with its lipless mouth. Then it swung its legs from the base of the idol and shakily stood. The face turned directly toward me and I could see slits of moist flesh where the nose had once been. It took a step forward.

"I could not look away as the tall form stiffly covered the three paces which separated us. It loomed above me, blocking out the goddess except for the gaunt face staring over its shoulder. It breathed with difficulty, as if the lungs were still filled with water. Indeed, when the thing's jaw lowered a bit as it walked, water gushed from the open mouth and streaked its heaving chest.

"Only when it stood a mere foot in front of me was I able to lower my eyes. The river stench of it flowed over me like a fog. The resurrected thing slowly brought forth its white palm until it touched my forehead. The flesh was cool, soft, slightly moist. Even after it lifted its hand and moved slowly to the next initiate, I could feel the imprint of its palm above my eyes, burning into my fevered skin like a cold flame.

"The Kapalikas began their final chant. My own lips moved without my volition to join in the prayer.

> " '*Kali, Kali, balo bhai*
> *Kali bai aré gaté nai.*
> O brethren take the name of Kali
> There is no refuge except in her.'

"The hymn ended. Two priests joined the first Brahman to help the newly reawakened one into the shadows at the rear of the temple. The other Kapalikas filed out another way. I looked around our inner circle and realized that the fat man was no longer with us. The six of us left stood in the dimness and stared at one another. Perhaps a minute thus passed before the chief priest returned. He was dressed the same, he looked the same, but he was *different*. There was a relaxed quality to his walk, an informality to his posture. It reminded me of an actor after a successful play, moving among the audience, removing one character to wear another.

"He smiled, approached us happily, and shook our hands, each in turn, saying to each, 'Namaste. You are now Kapalika. Await the next call of your beloved goddess.'

"When he said this to me, the touch of his hand on mine was less real than the imprint on my forehead which still tingled.

"A black-garbed man led us to the anteroom, where we

dressed in silence. The other four bade their farewells and left together, chattering like schoolchildren released from detention. Sanjay and I stood alone by the door.

"'We are Kapalika,' whispered Sanjay. He broke into a brilliant grin and held out his hand. I looked at him, looked at his open hand, and spat on the floor. Then I turned my back to him and left the temple without speaking.

"I have not seen him since. For months I have moved through the city, sleeping in hidden places, trusting no one. Always I have awaited and feared the 'call of my beloved goddess.' None came. At first I was relieved. Then I was more frightened than at first. Now I do not care. Recently I have openly returned to the University, to familiar streets, and to places I once frequented. Places like this.

"People seem to know that I have changed. If acquaintances see me they move away. People on the street glance at me and leave me room to pass. Perhaps I am Untouchable now. Perhaps I am Kapalika despite my panicked flight. I do not know. I have never returned to the temple or the Kalighat. Perhaps I am marked not as a Kapalika but as a prey of the Kapalika. I wait to find the answer.

"I would like to leave Calcutta forever but I have no money. I am only a poor person of Sudra caste from the village of Anguda, but also one who may never be able to go back to what he was.

"Only Mr. Krishna has continued to be my friend. It is he who called upon me to tell you my story. I am now finished with that story."

Krishna's voice barely croaked out the translation of the last sentence. I blinked and looked around. The proprietor's feet protruded from where he slept on the floor behind the counter. The room was quiet. There were no sounds from outside the building. My watch read 2:20.

I stood abruptly, accidentally knocking over the chair. My back ached and my spirit sagged from jet lag and fatigue. I stretched and kneaded the aching muscles near my spine.

Muktanandaji looked exhausted. He had removed his thick glasses and was rubbing tiredly at his eyes and the bridge of his nose. Krishna reached for the last of Muktanandaji's cold coffee, gulped it down, and tried repeatedly to clear his throat.

"Do you . . . hrrghhhh . . . do you have questions, Mr. Luczak?"

I stared down at the two of them. I didn't trust my own voice to work. Krishna noisily cleared his nostrils with his fingers, spat on the floor, and spoke again. "Do you have any questions, sir?"

I stared impassively for a few more seconds before replying. "Only one question," I said. Krishna's eyebrows went up politely.

"What the hell," I began, " . . . what the goddamned *hell* does that . . . that *story* . . . have to do with the poet M. Das?" My fist seemed to slam down on the table of its own accord. The coffee cups leaped.

It was Krishna's turn to stare. I seemed to remember such a stare from my kindergarten teacher when I was five and had soiled my pants one day during nap time. Krishna turned to Muktanandaji and spoke five words. The young man wearily returned the heavy glasses to his face and answered in even fewer syllables.

Krishna looked up at me. "Surely you must know that it was M. Das we spoke of."

"Which?" I said stupidly. "Who? What the shit do you mean? Do you mean to say that the priest was the great poet, M. Das? Are you serious?"

"No," said Krishna levelly. "Not the priest."

"Well, who—"

"The sacrifice," said Krishna slowly as if speaking to a dull child. "The offering. Mr. M. Das was the one Mr. Muktanandaji brought as sacrifice."

Chapter Nine

"Calcutta, you sell in the market
Cords for strangling the neck."
—Tushar Roy

That night I dreamed of corridors and caverns. Then the dream location shifted to the wholesale furniture warehouse on the near Southside of Chicago where I had worked during the summer of my sophomore year in college. The warehouse was closed but I continued to wander through an endless series of display rooms all crowded with furniture. The air smelled of Herculon fabric and cheap wood polish. I began to run, dodging through the tightly packed displays. I had suddenly remembered that Amrita and Victoria were still in the store somewhere and that if I didn't find them soon, we would all be locked in overnight. I didn't want them alone there, waiting for me, locked into the darkness. I ran, shouting their names, moving from room to room, shouting.

The phone rang. I reached for our travel alarm clock on the bedside table but the sound continued. It was 8:05 A.M. Just as I figured out that it was the telephone making the noise, Amrita came in from the bathroom and answered it. I dozed during her conversation. The sound of the shower running brought me up out of sleep again.

"Who was it?"

"Mr. Chatterjee," Amrita called over the running water. "You won't be able to pick up Das's manuscript until tomorrow. He apologized for the delay. Other than that, everything's all set."

"Mmmm. Damn. Another day."

"We're invited to tea at four."

"Hmmm? Where?"

"Mr. Michael Leonard Chatterjee's. He'll send his car. Do you want to go down to breakfast with your daughter and me?"

"Mmm." I pulled the extra pillow to my face and went back to sleep.

It seemed five minutes later that Amrita came through the door carrying Victoria. A waiter in white followed her with a tray. The travel clock read 10:28.

"Thank you," said Amrita. She set the baby on the carpet and tipped the waiter several rupees. Victoria clapped her hands and threw her head back to watch the man leave. Amrita picked up the tray, balanced it on one hand, and put a finger under her chin while executing a graceful curtsy in my direction. "Namastey and good morning, sahib. The management wishes you a wonderful and pleasant day although most of it is, alas, already gone. Yes, yes, yes."

I propped myself up in bed and she dusted off my lap with a

napkin and carefully set the tray in place. Then she curtsied again and held out her hand, palm up. I dropped a sprig of parsley in it.

"Keep the change," I said.

"Oh, thank you, thank you, most generous sahib," she sang while backing away in an obsequious series of bows. Victoria put three fingers in her mouth and watched us dubiously.

"I thought you were going sari hunting today," I said. Amrita pushed back the heavy curtains and I squinted in the gray glare. "Christ," I said, "is that really sunlight? In Calcutta?"

"Kamakhya and I have already been shopping. Very nice shop. Quite reasonable, actually."

"Didn't find anything?"

"Oh, yes. They'll deliver the material later. We each bought yards and yards. I probably spent your entire advance."

"Damn." I looked down and made a face.

"What's the matter, Bobby? Is your coffee cold?"

"No, it's fine. Very good, in fact. I just realized that I missed my chance to see Kamakhya again. Damn."

"You'll survive," Amrita said and placed Victoria on the bed to change her.

The coffee *was* good, and there was more in a small metal pot. I uncovered the plate to reveal two eggs, buttered toast, and . . . marvel of marvels . . . three strips of real bacon. "Fantastic," I said. "Thanks, kid."

"Oh, it was nothing," said Amrita. "Of course, the kitchen had been closed for hours, but I told them that it was for the famous poet in Room 612. The poet that stays out most of the night swapping war stories with the boys and then comes home chuckling to himself loudly enough to wake his wife and baby."

"Sorry."

"What was that conference about last night? You were mumbling to yourself in your sleep until I nudged you."

"Sorry, sorry, sorry."

She taped Victoria's new diaper in place, disposed of the old one, and came back to sit on the edge of the bed. "Honestly, Bobby, what revelations did Krishna's Mysterious Stranger come up with? Was he a real person?"

I offered her a wedge of toast. She shook her head no and then lifted it from my fingers and took a bite. "Do you really want to hear the story?" I asked.

Amrita nodded. I took a sip of coffee, decided not to give a blow-by-blow synopsis, and began talking in a light, slightly sarcastic tone of voice. Pausing occasionally to give my opinion of certain parts of the tale by shaking my head or making short remarks, I managed to retell Muktanandaji's three-hour monologue in less than ten minutes.

"My God," said Amrita when I was finished. She seemed distracted, even disturbed.

"Well, anyway, it was a hell of a way to end my first full day in beautiful downtown Calcutta," I said.

"Weren't you frightened, Bobby?"

"Good God, no. Why should I be, kiddo? The only thing that worried me was getting back to the hotel with my billfold still on my person."

"Yes, but . . ." Amrita stopped, went over to Victoria, returned a dropped pacifier to her hand, and came back to the bed. "If nothing else, I mean, you spent the evening with a madman, Robert. I wish . . . I wish I had been there to interpret."

"Me too," I said truthfully. "As far as I know, Muktananda-ji spent the entire time reciting the Gettysburg Address over and over in Bengali while Krishna made up the ghost story."

"Then you don't think the boy was telling the truth?"

"The truth?" I repeated. I frowned at her. "What do you mean? Corpses being brought back to life? Dead poets being resurrected from river mud? Hon, M. Das disappeared *eight years ago*. He'd be a pretty wasted zombie, don't you think?"

"No, I didn't mean that," said Amrita. She smiled, but it was a tired smile. I should never have brought her, I realized. I'd been so worried that I would need an interpreter, someone to help me out with the culture. *Dumb shit*. "I just thought maybe that the boy might have *thought* he was telling the truth," she said. "He could have tried to join the Kapalikas or whatever they're called. He might have seen *something* that he didn't understand."

"Yeah, that's possible," I said. "I don't know. The kid was a mess—red eyes, lousy skin, a mass of nervous mannerisms. He might have been on drugs, for all I know. I got the idea that Krishna was adding or changing a lot of things. It was like one of those comedy routines where the foreigner grunts and the interpreter chatters on for ten minutes. Know what I mean? Anyway, it could be that he tried to join this secret society and they played spooky games to impress him. But it's my guess that it was Krishna's idea of a scam."

Amrita took the tray and carried it to the dresser. She rearranged the cup and silverware in various patterns. She did not look at me. "Why is that? Did they ask for money?"

I pushed the sheet away and walked to the window. A

streetcar moved down the middle of the street, discharging and collecting passengers without stopping. The sky was still painted with low clouds, but there was enough sunlight to throw shadows on the cracked pavement. "No," I said. "Not in so many words. But Krishna ended the evening with a cute little epilogue—very *sotto voce*—explaining how his friend had to find a way to get out of the city, to get to Delhi or somewhere, possibly even South Africa. He left no doubt that a few hundred American dollars would be welcome."

"Did he *ask* for money?" Amrita's weighted British vowels were sharper than usual.

"No. Not in so many words—"

"How much did you give them?" She showed no sign of anger, only curiosity.

I padded over to my suitcase and began pulling out clean underwear and socks. Once again I realized that the greatest argument against marriage, the absolutely *irrefutable* argument against living with one person for years, was the destruction of the illusion of free will by the spouse's constant recognition of one's total predictability. "Twenty dollars," I said. "It was the smallest traveler's check I had. I left most of the Indian currency with you."

"Twenty dollars," mused Amrita. "At today's exchange rate, that would be about a hundred and eighty rupees. You made it out to Muktanandaji?"

"No, I left it blank."

"He might have a hard time getting all the way to South Africa on a hundred and eighty rupees," she said blandly.

"Goddammit, I don't care if the two of them go buy nose candy with it. Or use it to start a charity account—Save-

Muktanandaji-From-the-Wrath-of-the-Kapalikas-Fund. Tax-deductible. Give now."

Amrita said nothing.

"Look at it this way," I said. "We can't get a sitter, go into Exeter to see a bad movie, and go to McDonald's afterward for twenty bucks anymore. His story was a lot more enjoyable than some of the films we've driven to Boston to see. What was the name of that silly kiddie film we spent five dollars to see with Dan and Barb right before we left?"

"*Star Wars*," said Amrita. "Do you think you'll be able to use any of his story in the *Harper's* article?"

I belted my bathrobe. "The rendezvous and the coffee house, yes. I'll try to work in how surreal and absurd some of the characters were in my . . . what did Morrow call it? . . . my quest for M. Das. But I won't be able to use Muktanandaji's ravings. Not much, anyway. I'll mention it, but the whole Kapalika thing is just too weird. That sort of killer-goddess crap went out with the last of the movie serials. I'll check into the gang stuff—maybe the Kapalikas are sort of a Calcutta Mafia—but the rest of it's just too damn weird to put in a serious article about a fine poet. It's not just morbid, it's—"

"Perverted?"

"Naw, they wouldn't mind if I wrote about a little healthy perversion. The word I was thinking of was *trite*."

"God save us from clichés, is that it?"

"You got it, kiddo."

"All right, Bobby. What are we going to do next?"

"Hmmm, good question," I said. I was playing peek-a-boo with Victoria. Both of us were using part of the sheet as a hiding place. Each of us would giggle when I lifted it like a curtain from between us. Then Victoria would cover her eyes with her fingers and I would look around in bewilderment, trying to find her. She loved it.

"I think I'll take a shower," I said. "Then we're going to get you and the Little One here on this afternoon's flight to London. So far, there's been absolutely no need for you to translate anything but the porter's mumblings. I'm tired of paying for all those extra mouths to feed around here. There's no reason for you to stay an extra day even if I have to wait around for Chatterjee to get his act together. Today's Saturday. You could stay awhile in London, visit your parents overnight, and we could arrive in New York at about the same time . . . say, Tuesday evening."

"Sorry, Bobby. Impossible for several reasons."

"Nonsense," I said. "No such word as impossible." Victoria and I discovered each other and giggled. "Name the objections and I'll shoot them down."

"One, we have high tea at four o'clock with the Chatterjees—"

"I'll offer your regrets. Next?"

"Two, the material from the sari shop hasn't arrived yet."

"I'll bring it with me. Next?"

"Three, Victoria and I would miss you. Wouldn't we, Precious?" Victoria looked away from the game long enough to gape politely at her mother. Then she changed the rules by pulling the end of the sheet over her head.

"Sorry, three strikes," I said to Amrita. "You're out. I'll miss you guys, but maybe with you gone I'll be able to make time with your friend Kamakhya. I think there's a two P.M. flight to London today. If not, I'll stay at the airport with you until a later flight."

Amrita picked up some of the baby's toys and put them in a drawer. "There is a fourth problem," she said.

"What's that?"

"BOAC and Pan Am have canceled all flights out of Calcutta except BOAC's 6:45 A.M. layover from Thailand. Baggage-handling problems, the man said. I called last night when I was bored."

"Shit. You're kidding. *Damn.*" Victoria sensed the change in tone and dropped the sheet. Her face puckered toward tears. "There must be some way out of this stinking shithole of a—excuse me, Little One—this city."

"Oh, yes. All of the Air India in-country flights are going out. We could transfer to Pan Am in Delhi or to any of the overseas airlines there or in Bombay. But we've missed today's early New Delhi flight, and all of the others have horrendous layovers. I'd rather wait for you, Bobby. I don't want to travel in this country without you. I did enough of that as a child."

"Okay, hon," I said, and put my arm around her. "All right, then, let's try to make the Monday-morning BOAC flight. Christ, six-thirty in the morning. Well, at least it'll be a breakfast flight. Okay if I go ahead with my plan to shower?"

"Yes," said Amrita while picking up the baby. "I checked with the BOAC people and there's no problem with you showering."

That afternoon we went through the motions of sightseeing. I tucked Victoria into the backpack carrier, and we were out into the heat, noise, and confusion. The temperature and humidity both hovered near the 100 mark. We had a better than decent luncheon at a place called Shah-en-Shah's and then took a taxi up Chowringhee to the Indian Museum.

A small sign outside proclaimed ABSOLUTELY NO YOGIC EXERCISES PERMITTED IN GARDENS! The inside was very hot, the display cases were dusty, and the building was surprisingly empty except for a loud and obnoxious tour group of Germans. I was mildly interested in the anthropology displays on the first floor, but it was the exhibit of archaeological art that finally caught my eye.

"What is it?" asked Amrita as she saw me bending over a glass case.

The tiny black figurine was labeled *Representation of Durga Goddess in Kali Aspect: circa* 80 B.C. It fell short of being frightening. I saw no sign of a noose, skull, or severed head. One hand held what looked to be a wooden bough, another an inverted egg cup, a third what *might* have been a trident but looked more like an opened Swiss Army knife, and her last hand was extended palm up, offering a tiny yellow doughnut. As with all the statues of goddesses I'd seen in the museum, she was high-waisted, firm-breasted, and long of ear. Her face was scowling, her many teeth were sharp, but I could make out no vampirish canines or lolling tongue. She was wearing a headdress of flames. Much more fierce, to my eye, was a statue marked *Durga* that stood in a nearby case. This supposedly more benign incarnation of Parvati had ten arms, and each hand was filled with a weapon more fierce than the last.

"Your friend Kali doesn't seem too terrible," said Amrita. Even Victoria was leaning forward from the backpack carrier to look at the display case.

"This thing's two thousand years old," I said. "Maybe she's grown more hideous and bloodthirsty since then."

"Some women just don't age gracefully," agreed Amrita

and moved on to the next display. Victoria seemed to enjoy a large bronze idol of Ganesha, the playful, elephant-headed god of prosperity; and for the rest of our time in the museum we made a game out of finding as many representations of Ganesha as we could.

Amrita would have liked to visit the Victoria Memorial Hall to see artifacts of the Raj, but it was getting late and we contented ourselves with driving by in the taxi and pointing out to the baby the imposing white structure that we told her was named after her.

We entered the hotel in a torrential downpour, changed clothes quickly, and came back out to find Chatterjee's car waiting and the rain stopped.

I was wearing a tie for the first time in several days, and as the car pulled out into traffic I sat uncomfortably, tugging at the knot and wishing my collar were looser or my neck smaller. My short-sleeved white shirt had already soaked through the back and I was suddenly aware how scuffed and stained my faithful Wallabees looked. All in all, I felt wrinkled, tousled, and soaked in sweat. I glanced sideways at Amrita. She looked—as she always did—cool and contained. She was wearing the white cotton dress she had purchased in London and the lapis lazuli necklace I had given her before we were married. By all rights her hair should have been hanging down in limp strands, but it fell full and lustrous to her shoulders.

We drove for the better of an hour, a trip which reminded me that Calcutta was larger in area than New York City. Traffic was as insane and haphazard as ever, but Chatterjee's silent driver found the fastest route through the confusion. My concern about the traffic wasn't overly allayed by the large white signs in Bengali, Hindi, and English that sat in the center of several chaotic traffic circles we negotiated: DRIVE MORE CAREFULLY! THERE HAVE BEEN ☐ DEATHS ON THIS THOROUGHFARE THIS YEAR! The boxes were filled with the kind of nail-up number panels one used to see in old-time baseball parks. The highest number we saw on this trip was 28. I wondered idly whether that included that entire section of road or just those few square feet of pavement.

At times we sped down a highway bordered on each side by great *chawls*—those incredible slums of tin roofs, gunnysack walls, and mud-path streets—which extended for miles and were terminated only by gray monoliths of factories belching flame and unfiltered soot toward the monsoon clouds. I realized that sweeping philosophical convictions such as ecology and pollution control were luxuries for our advanced industrial nations. The air in Calcutta, already sweetened by raw sewage, burning cow dung, millions of tons of garbage, and the innumerable open fires eternally burning, was made almost unbreathable by the further effusion of raw auto emissions and industrial filth.

The factories themselves were huge artifacts of worn brick, rusted steel, rampant weeds, and broken windows—pictures from some grim future when the industrial age had gone the way of the dinosaur but left its rotting carcasses sprawled across the landscape. Yet, smoke rose from the most tumble-down ruin, and ragged human forms came and went from the black maws of the darkest buildings. I found it almost impossible to imagine myself living in one of those floorless hovels, working in one of those grim factories.

Amrita must have been sharing similar thoughts, for we rode in silence, each watching the panorama of human hopelessness pass by the car windows.

Then, in a space of a few minutes, we crossed a bridge over a wide expanse of railroad tracks, passed through a transitional neighborhood of tiny storefronts, and were suddenly in an old, established area of tree-lined streets and large homes guarded by walls and barred gates. The thin sunlight glinted off countless shards of broken glass set atop the flat walls. At one place there was a yard-wide swath cleared on top of a high wall, but the mud-colored masonry was smeared with dark streaks. Well-polished automobiles sat at the end of long driveways. The iron-spiked gates bore small signs warning *Beware of Dog* in at least three languages.

It took no great insight to realize that this once had been a British residential section, as separate from the pandemonium of the city and its natives as the English governing class could make it. Decay was evident even here—the frequently filthy walls, unshingled roofs, and crudely boarded windows—but it was a controlled decay, a rearguard action against the rampant entropy which seemed to govern Calcutta elsewhere; and the sense of dissolution was ameliorated somewhat by the bright flowers and other obvious attempts at gardening that one glimpsed through high entry gates.

We pulled up to one of these gates. The driver bustled out and unlocked a padlock with a key from a chain on his belt. The circular driveway was lined with tall, flowering bushes and drooping tree limbs.

We were greeted by Michael Leonard Chatterjee. "Ah, Mr. and Mrs. Luczak! Welcome!" His wife was also standing by the door next to a toddler whom I first took to be their son but then realized must be a grandson. Mrs. Chatterjee was in her early sixties, and I revised her husband's age upward. Chatterjee was one of those smooth-faced, perpetually balding gentlemen who reach fifty and seem to stay at that age until their late sixties.

We chatted on the front step for a moment. Victoria was duly complimented, and we praised their grandson. Then we were shown through the house quickly before being led through another door to a wide patio overlooking a side street.

I was interested in their home. It was the first chance I'd had to see how an upper-class Indian family lived. The first impression was one of juxtaposition: large, formal, high-ceilinged rooms with paint flaking from begrimed walls; a beautiful walnut sideboard covered with scratches on which was displayed a stuffed mongoose with dusty glass eyes and molting fur; an expensive, handmade carpet from Kashmir set atop chipped linoleum; a large, once modern kitchen now liberally cluttered with dusty bottles, old crates, crusted metal pans, and with a small, charcoal fireplace set squarely in the center of the floor. Smoke streaked a once white ceiling.

"It will be more comfortable outside," said Chatterjee, and held the door open for Amrita.

The flagstones were still wet from the last rainshower, but the cushioned chairs were dry and a table was set for tea. Chatterjee's grown daughter, a heavy young woman with lovely eyes, joined us long enough to chat with Amrita in Hindi for a few minutes and then to depart with her son. Chatterjee seemed bemused by Amrita's linguistic abilities and asked her something in French. Amrita answered fluently, and both of them laughed. He switched to what I later learned was Tamil, and Amrita responded. They began exchanging pleasantries in simple Russian. I sipped my tea and smiled at Mrs. Chatterjee. She smiled back and offered me a cucumber sandwich. We continued smiling at each other through a few more minutes of trilingual banter, and then Victoria began fussing. Amrita took the baby from my arms, and Chatterjee turned to me.

"Would you like more tea, Mr. Luczak?"

"No, thank you, this is fine."

"Perhaps something stronger?"

"Well . . ."

Chatterjee snapped his fingers and a servant quickly appeared. A few seconds later he reappeared with a tray laden with several decanters and glasses.

"Do you drink Scotch, Mr. Luczak?"

Is the Pope Catholic? I thought. "Yes." Amrita had warned me that most Indian Scotch was atrocious stuff, but one swallow told me that Chatterjee's decanter held only premium whiskey, almost certainly twelve years old, almost certainly imported. "Excellent."

"It's The Glenlivet," he said. "Unblended. I find it rather more authentic than the blended premiums."

For a few minutes we discussed poetry and poets. I tried to steer the conversation around to M. Das, but Chatterjee was reluctant to discuss the missing poet beyond mentioning that Gupta had arranged the details for tomorrow's transfer of the manuscript. We settled on discussing how hard it was for a serious writer in either of our countries to make a decent living. I got the impression that Chatterjee's money had come down through the family and that he had other interests, investments, and incomes.

Invariably, the talk steered to politics. Chatterjee was most eloquent about the relief the country was feeling after the ouster of Mrs. Gandhi in the previous election. The resurgence of democracy in India was of great interest to me and something I'd hoped to work into my Das article.

"She was a tyrant, Mr. Luczak. The so-called Emergency was merely a ruse to hide the ugly face of her tyranny."

"So you don't think she will ever reenter national politics?"

"Never! Never, Mr. Luczak."

"But I thought that she still has a strong political base and that the Congress Party is still a potential majority if the current coalition was to falter."

"No, no," said Chatterjee and waved his hand in dismissal. "You do not understand. Mrs. Gandhi and her son are *finished*. They will be in prison within a year. Mark my words. Her son is already under investigation for various scandals and atrocities; and when the truth comes out, he will be lucky to escape execution."

I nodded. "I've read that he alienated many people with his drastic population-control programs."

"He was a swine," Chatterjee said without emotion. "An arrogant, ignorant, dictatorial swine. His programs were little more than efforts at genocide. He preyed on the poor and the uneducated, although he was an essential illiterate himself. Even his mother was frightened of the monster. If he were to enter a crowd today, they would tear him apart with their bare hands. I would be pleased to take part. More tea, Mrs. Luczak?"

A car moved down the quiet side street beyond the iron fence. A rew raindrops pattered on the broad leaves of the banyan tree above us.

"Your impressions of Calcutta, Mr. Luczak?"

Chatterjee's sudden question caught me off guard. I took a drink of Scotch and let the warmth spread for a second before answering. "Calcutta is fascinating, Mr. Chatterjee. It's far too complex a city even to react to in two days. It's a shame we won't have more time to explore it."

"You are diplomatic, Mr. Luczak. What you mean to say is that you find Calcutta appalling. It has already offended your sensibilities, yes?"

"Appalling is not the correct word," I said. "It's true that the poverty affects me."

"Ah, yes, *poverty*," said Chatterjee and smiled as if the word had deeply ironic connotations. "Indeed, there is much poverty here. Much squalor by Western standards. That must offend the American mind, since America has repeatedly dedicated its great will to *eliminating* poverty. How did your ex-President Johnson put it . . . to declare *war* on poverty? One would think that his war in Vietnam would have satisfied him."

"The war on poverty was another war we lost," I said. "America continues to have its share of poverty." I set my empty glass down, and a servant appeared at my elbow to pour more Scotch.

"Yes, yes, but it is Calcutta we are discussing. One of our better poets has referred to Calcutta as that 'half-crushed cockroach of a city.' Another of our writers has compared our city to an aged and dying courtesan surrounded by oxygen tanks and rotting orange peels. Would you agree with that, Mr. Luczak?"

"I would agree that those are very strong metaphors, Mr. Chatterjee."

"Is your husband always so circumspect, Mrs. Luczak?" asked Chatterjee and smiled at us over his glass. "No, no, you should not be concerned that I will take offense. I am used to

Americans and their reaction to our city. They will react in either one of two ways: they will find Calcutta 'exotic' and concentrate only on their tourist pleasures; or they will be immediately horrified, recoil, and seek to forget what they have seen and not understood. Yes, yes, the American psyche is as predictable as the sterile and vulnerable American digestive system when it encounters India."

I looked at Mrs. Chatterjee, but she was bouncing Victoria on her lap and seemed not to hear her husband's pronouncements. At the same instant Amrita glanced at me, and I took it as a warning. I smiled to show that I was not going to get argumentative. "You may well be right," I said. "Although I wouldn't presume to say that I understood the 'American psyche' or the 'Indian psyche'—if there are such things. First impressions are necessarily shallow. I appreciate that. I've admired Indian culture for a long time, even before I met Amrita, and she's certainly shared some of the beauty of it with me. But I admit that Calcutta is a bit intimidating. There seems to be something unique . . . unique and disturbing about Calcutta's urban problems. Perhaps its only the scale. Friends have told me that Mexico City, for all of its beauty, shares the same problems."

Chatterjee nodded, smiled, and set down his glass. He steepled his fingers and looked at me the way a teacher looks at a student who may or may not be worth investing more time in. "You have not traveled extensively, Mr. Luczak?"

"Not really. I backpacked through Europe some years ago. Spent some time in Tangiers."

"But not in Asia?"

"No."

Chatterjee dropped his hands as if his point had been amply

demonstrated. But the lesson was not quite over. He snapped his fingers, fired a command, and a moment later the servant brought out a slim blue book. I could not make out the title.

"Please tell me if you find this a fair and reasonable description of Calcutta, Mr. Luczak," said Chatterjee and began to read aloud:

> ". . . a dense mass of houses so old
> they only seem to fall, through
> which narrow and tortuous lanes curve
> and wind. There is no privacy here
> and whoever ventures in this region
> find the streets—by courtesy so called
> —thronged with loiterers and sees,
> through half-glazed windows, rooms
> crowded to suffocation . . . the stagnant
> gutters . . . the filth choking up dark
> passages . . . the walls of bleached soot,
> and doors falling from their hinges . . .
> and children swarming everywhere,
> relieving themselves as they please."

He stopped, closed the book, and raised his eyebrows in polite interrogation.

I had made no great objection to continuing to act as a straight man if it amused our host. "It has its relevant parts," I said.

"Yes." Chatterjee smiled and held up the book. "This, Mr. Luczak, is a contemporary account of London written in the 1850's. One must take into account the fact that India is only now embarking on its own Industrial Revolution. The displacement and confusion which shocks you so—no, no, do not deny it—these are necessary by-products of such a revolution. You are lucky, Mr. Luczak, that your own culture has gone beyond that point."

I nodded, and resisted the impulse to tell him that the description he'd read would have been apt for the neighborhood on the Southside of Chicago where I'd grown up. I still felt it was worth one more effort to clarify my feelings.

"That's very true, Mr. Chatterjee. I appreciate what you say. I was thinking something similar on the ride here today and you've clarified the point very well. But I have to say that in our brief time here, I've sensed something . . . something *different* about Calcutta. I'm not sure what it is. A strange sense of . . . violence, I guess. A sense of violence seething just under the surface."

"Or insanity perhaps?" asked Chatterjee flatly.

I said nothing.

"Many would-be commentators on our city, Mr. Luczak, make note of this supposed sense of all-pervading violence here. Do you see that street? Yes, that one there?"

I followed his pointing finger. A bullock cart was moving down the otherwise empty side street. Except for the slowly moving cart and the multi-trunked banyan trees, the scene could have been in an old, well-worn section of any American city. "Yes," I said. "I see it."

"Some years ago," he said, "I sat here at breakfast and watched as a family was murdered there. No, murdered is not the correct word. They were butchered, Mr. Luczak, *butchered*. There. Right there. Where the cart is passing now."

"What happened?"

"It was during the Hindu-Muslim riots. There had been a

poor Muslim family that lived with a local doctor. We were used to their presence. The man was a carpenter and my father had used his services many times. Their children had played with my younger brother. Then, in 1947, they chose the tensest time of the riots to emigrate to East Pakistan.

"I saw them come up the street, five of them counting the youngest child, a babe in her mother's arms. They were in a horse-drawn wagon. I was eating breakfast when I heard the noise. A crowd of people had intercepted them. The Muslim argued. He made the mistake of using his braid whip on the leader of the mob. There was a great surge forward. I was sitting right where you are, Mr. Luczak. I could see very well. The people used clubs, paving stones, and their bare hands. They may well have used their teeth. When it was over, the Muslim carpenter and his family were stained bundles on the street. Even their horse was dead."

"Good God," I said. And then, into the silence, "Are you saying that you agree with those who say there's a streak of insanity in this city, Mr. Chatterjee?"

"Quite the contrary, Mr. Luczak. I mention this incident because the people in that mob were . . . and are . . . my neighbors: Mr. Golwalkar, the teacher; Mr. Sirsik, the baker; old Mr. Muhkerjee who works in the post office near your hotel. They were ordinary people, Mr. Luczak, who lived sane lives before that regrettable incident and who returned to sane lives afterward. I mention this because it shows the folly of anyone who singles out Calcutta as a bedlam of Bengali insanity. *Any* city can be said to have such 'violence seething just under the surface.' Have you seen the English-language newspaper today?"

"The paper? No."

Chatterjee unfolded the newspaper that had been lying near the sugar bowl. He handed it to me.

The lead story was datelined New York. The previous evening there had been a power failure, the worst since the 1965 total blackout. Almost as if on cue, looting erupted throughout the ghettos and poorer sections of the city. Thousands of people had taken part in seemingly mindless vandalism and theft. Mobs had gathered to cheer while entire families smashed store windows and ran off with television sets, clothing, and anything portable. Hundreds had been arrested, but the mayor's office and police spokesmen admitted that the police had been powerless in the face of the scope of the problem.

There were reprints of American editorials. Liberals saw it as a resurgence of social protest and decried the discrimination, poverty, and hunger that had provoked it. Conservative columnists acidly pointed out that hungry people don't steal stereo systems first and called for a crackdown in law enforcement. All of the reasoned editorials sounded hollow in light of the perverse randomness of the event. It was as if only a thin wall of electric lighting protected the great cities of the world from total barbarism.

I handed the paper to Amrita. "That's a hell of a thing, Mr. Chatterjee. Your point is well made. I certainly didn't want to sound self-righteous about Calcutta's problems."

Chatterjee smiled and steepled his fingers again. His glasses reflected gray glare and the dark shadow of my head. He nodded slightly. "As long as you understand that it is an *urban* problem, Mr. Luczak. A problem exacerbated by the degree of poverty here and by the nature of the immigrants who have flooded our city. Calcutta has been literally invaded by uneducated foreigners. Our problems are real but are not something unique to us."

I nodded silently.

"I don't agree," said Amrita.

Both Chatterjee and I turned in surprise. Amrita set the paper down with a quick flick of her wrist. "I don't agree at all, Mr. Chatterjee," she said. "I feel it *is* a cultural problem—one unique in many ways to India if not just to Calcutta."

"Oh?" said Chatterjee. He tapped his fingers together. Despite his smiling aplomb, it was obvious that he was surprised and irritated at being contradicted by a woman. "How do you mean, Mrs. Luczak?"

"Well, since it seems to be the time to illustrate hypotheses through the use of anecdotes," she said softly, "let me share two incidents that I observed yesterday."

"By all means." Chatterjee's smile held the tense undertones of a grimace.

"Yesterday I was having breakfast in the garden café of the Oberoi," she began. "Victoria and I were alone at our table, but there were many others in the restaurant. Several Air India pilots were at the next table. A few feet from us, an Untouchable woman was cutting the grass with hand clippers—"

"Please," said Chatterjee, and the grimace was visible now on the smooth features. "We prefer to say Scheduled Class person."

Amrita smiled. "Yes, I'm aware of that," she said. "Scheduled Class or Harijan, 'Beloved of God.' I grew up with the conventions. But they are mere euphemisms, as I'm sure you are well aware, Mr. Chatterjee. She was 'Scheduled

Class' because she was born out of caste and will die there. Her children will almost certainly spend their lives performing the same menial jobs as she. She is Untouchable."

Chatterjee's smile was frozen but he did not interrupt again.

"At any rate, she was squatting, cutting grass a blade at a time, moving across the yard in what would be, for me at least, a very painful duck walk. No one took notice of her. She was as invisible as the weeds she was trimming.

"During the night, an electric line had fallen from the portico. It dropped across the courtyard lawn, but no one had thought to repair it or to shut off the current. Waiters ducked it on their way to the pool area. The Untouchable woman encountered it in her clipping and went to move it out of her way. It was not insulated.

"When she touched it, she was knocked backwards violently; but she could not let go of the wire. The pain must have been very great, but she let out only one terrible cry. She was literally writhing on the ground, being electrocuted before our eyes.

"I say 'our,' Mr. Chatterjee. The waiters stood by with their arms folded and watched. Workmen on a platform near the woman looked down without expression. One of the pilots near me made a small joke and turned back to his coffee.

"I'm not a quick-thinking person, Mr. Chatterjee. All of my life I've tended to let other people carry out even the simplest actions for me. I used to beg my sister to purchase train tickets for us. Even today, when Bobby and I order a pizza to be delivered, I insist on his placing the telephone call. But when half a minute had elapsed and it became obvious that the men in the courtyard—and there were at least a dozen—were not going to prevent this poor woman from being electrocuted, I acted. It did not take much thought or courage. There was a broom near the door. I used the wooden handle to move the wire from her hand."

I stared at my wife. Amrita had mentioned none of this to me. Chatterjee was nodding in a distracted way, but I found my voice first. "Was she badly hurt?"

"Evidently not," said Amrita. "There was talk of sending her to hospital, but fifteen minutes later she was cutting the grass once again."

"Yes, yes," said Chatterjee. "That is quite interesting but should not be taken out of context—"

"The second incident occurred only an hour or so after that," Amrita continued smoothly. "A friend and I were shopping for saris near the Elite Cinema. Traffic was backed up for blocks. An aged cow was standing in the middle of the street. People shouted and honked but no one tried to move it. Suddenly the cow began urinating, pouring a powerful stream into the street. There was a girl on the sidewalk near us—a very pretty girl, about fifteen years old, wearing a crisp white blouse and red kerchief. This girl immediately ran into the street, thrust her palm into the stream of urine, and splashed some on her forehead."

Leaves rustled in the silence. Chatterjee glanced at his wife and looked back at Amrita. His fingertips were tapping silently against each other. "That is the second incident?" he asked.

"Yes."

"Surely, Mrs. Luczak, even though you have been out of your country—India—since your childhood, you must remember the respect we bestow upon cows as symbols of our religion?"

"Yes."

"And you must know that not all people in India have the Westerner's . . . ah . . . horror at the idea of class differences."

"Yes."

"And did you know that urine . . . especially human urine . . . is thought by many here to have strong spiritual and medicinal properties? Did you know that our current Prime Minister, Mr. Moraji Desai, drinks several ounces of his own urine each morning?"

"Yes, I know that."

"Then, in all honesty, Mrs. Luczak, I do not see what your 'incidents' reveal except perhaps culture shock and a revulsion at your former culture's traditions."

Amrita shook her head. "Not just culture shock, Mr. Chatterjee. As a mathematician I tend to view different cultures rather abstractly, as adjoining sets with certain common elements. Or, if you will, as a series of human experiments as to how to live, think, and behave toward one another. Perhaps because of my own background, because I moved around so much as a child, I've felt a sense of some objectivity toward different cultures I've visited and lived in."

"Yes?"

"And, Mr. Chatterjee, I find some elements in India's set of cultural mind-sets that few other cultures have—or, if they did possess them, have not chosen to retain. I find in my own country here an ingrained racism that is probably beyond current comparison. I find here that the nonviolent philosophy which I was raised in—and feel most comfortable with—continues to be shattered by deliberate and callous acts of savagery by its proponents. And the fact that your prime minister drinks several glasses of his own urine each day, Mr.

Chatterjee, does not commend the practice to me. Nor to most of the world. My father often reminded me that when the Mahatma went from village to village, the first thing he would preach would not be human brotherhood or anti-British stratagems or nonviolence, but the basics—the absolute basics—of human hygiene.

"No, Mr. Chatterjee, speaking as an Indian person, I do not agree that all of Calcutta's difficulties are simply a microcosm of urban problems everywhere."

Chatterjee stared at her over his fingers. Mrs. Chatterjee stirred uneasily. Victoria looked up at her mother but did not make a noise. I'm not sure what would have been said next if the first large raindrops had not chosen that second to begin falling around us like moist cannon fire.

"I think we would be more comfortable inside," said Mrs. Chatterjee as the full force of the storm broke around us.

The presence of Chatterjee's driver inhibited us during the ride back to the hotel, but we did communicate through elaborate codes known only to married couples.

"You should have worked for the United Nations," I said.

"I *did* work for the U.N.," said Amrita. "You forget that I worked there one summer as an interpreter. Two years before we met."

"Hmmm, start any wars?"

"No. I left that to the professional diplomats."

"You didn't tell me that you saw a woman almost electrocuted during breakfast."

"You didn't ask."

There are some times when even a husband knows when to shut up. We watched the passing slums through shifting curtains of rain. Some of the people there made no effort to get out of the downpour but squatted dully in the mud, heads bowed under the onslaught.

"Notice the children?" asked Amrita quietly. I hadn't, but I did now. Girls of seven and eight stood with even younger children on their hips. I now realized that this was one of the most persistent images from the past couple of days—children holding children. As the rain came down they stood under awnings, overpasses, and dripping canvases. Their ragged clothes were brightly dyed, but even the brilliant reds and royal blues did not hide the dirt and wear. The girls wore gold bracelets on their emaciated wrists and ankles. Their future dowries.

"There are a lot of children," I said.

"And almost none," said Amrita so softly that it was almost a whisper. It took me only a few seconds to realize that she was correct. For most of the youngsters we saw, their childhood was already past them. They faced a future of rearing younger siblings, heavy labor, early marriage, and rearing their own offspring. Many of the younger children we could see running naked through the mud would not survive the next few years. Those that did reach our age would greet the new century in a nation of a billion people facing famine and social chaos.

"Bobby," Amrita said, "I know that American elementary schools don't teach mathematics very seriously, but you did have Euclidean plane geometry in your secondary school, didn't you?"

"Yeah, even American high schools teach that, kiddo."

"Then you know that there are non-Euclidean geometries?"

"I've heard nasty rumors to that effect."

"I'm serious, Bobby. I'm trying to understand something here."

"Go ahead."

"Well, I began thinking about it after I mentioned alternate sets and experiments to Chatterjee."

"Uh-huh."

"If Indian culture was an *experiment*, then my Western prejudices tell me that it's a failure. At least in terms of its ability to adapt and protect its people."

"No argument there."

"But if it's just another *set*, then my metaphor suggests a much worse possibility."

"What is that?"

"If we think in terms of set theory, then I'm convinced that my two culture sets are eternally incompatible. And *I* am the product of these two cultures. The common element in two sets without common elements, as it were."

"East is East and West is West and never the twain shall meet?"

"You see my problem, don't you, Bobby?"

"Perhaps a good marriage counselor could—"

"Shut up, please. The metaphor made me think of a more frightening analogy. What if the differences we're reacting to in Calcutta are the result of the culture's not being another *set* but a different *geometry*?"

"What's the difference?"

"I thought you knew Euclid."

"We were introduced but never got on a first-name basis."

Amrita sighed and looked out at the industrial nightmare through which we traveled. It occurred to me that this was Fitzgerald's industrial wasteland imagery from *Gatsby* taken to the tenth power. It also occurred to me that my own private literary references were beginning to be contaminated by Amrita's mathematical metaphors.

I watched as a man squatted by the roadside to defecate. He lifted his shirt over his head and prepared a small bronze bowl of water for the fingers of his left hand.

"Sets and number theories overlap," said Amrita. I suddenly realized by the tension in her voice that she was very serious. "Geometries don't. Different geometries are based on different theorems, postulate different axioms, and give rise to different realities."

"Different realities?" I repeated. "How can you have different realities?"

"Perhaps you cannot," said Amrita. "Perhaps only one is 'real.' Perhaps only one geometry is true. But the question is, What happens to me—to all of us—if we've chosen the wrong one?"

The police were waiting for us when we returned to the hotel.

"A gentleman has been waiting to see you, sir," said the assistant manager as he handed me our room key. I turned to the lobby expecting to find Krishna, but the man who rose from the plum-colored sofa was tall, turbaned, and bearded—obviously a Sikh.

"Mr. Luck-zak?"

"Loo-*zack*. Yes."

"I am inspector Singh of the Calcutta Metropolitan Police." He showed me a badge and a faded identity photo behind yellowed plastic.

"Inspector?" I did not offer to shake hands.

"Mr. Luczak, I would like to speak to you concerning a case which our department is investigating."

Krishna's got me into some sort of trouble. "And what is that, Inspector?"

"The disappearance of M. Das."

"Ah," I said and gave the room key to Amrita. I had no intention of inviting this policeman up to our room. "Do you need to speak to my wife, Inspector? It's time for our little one to eat."

"No. It will take only a minute, Mr. Luczak. I am sorry to interrupt your afternoon."

Amrita carried Victoria to the elevator and I looked around. The assistant manager and several porters were watching curiously. "What do you say we go into the License Room, Inspector?" This was the Indian hotel euphemism for a bar.

"Very good."

It was darker in the bar, but as I ordered a gin and tonic and the Inspector asked for just tonic, I was able to take time to appraise the tall Sikh.

Inspector Singh carried himself with the unselfconscious authority of a man who was used to being obeyed. His voice held the echo of years in England, not the Oxbridge drawl but the clipped precision of Sandhurst or one of the other academies. He wore a well-tailored tan suit that fell just short of being a uniform. The turban was wine-red.

His appearance confirmed what little I knew about Sikhs. A minority religious group, they made up possibly the most aggressive and productive segment of Indian society. As a people they tended to understand machinery, and although the majority of Sikhs inhabited the Punjab, they could be found driving taxis and operating heavy equipment throughout the country. Amrita's father had said that ninety percent of his bulldozer operators had been Sikhs. It was also the Sikhs who made up the upper echelons of the military and police forces. From what Amrita had told me, only the Sikhs had capitalized on the Green Revolution and modern agricultural technology to make a go of their extensive cooperative farms in the north of India.

It also had been the Sikhs who were responsible for many of the massacres of Muslim civilians during the partition riots.

"Cheers," said Inspector Singh and sipped at his tonic water. A steel bracelet rattled against his heavy wristwatch. The bracelet was a constant symbol of his faith, as was the beard and a small ceremonial dagger he would be carrying. A security guard at the Bombay airport on Thursday had asked a Sikh ahead of us in line, "Are you carrying any weapons other than your sabre?" The rest of us had submitted to body searches, but the Sikh had been passed through after his negative grunt.

"How can I help you, Inspector?"

"You can share any information you have about the whereabouts of the poet M. Das."

"Das has been missing for a long time, Inspector. I'm surprised you're still interested."

"M. Das's file is still open, sir. The 1969 investigation concluded that he was most probably the victim of foul play. Does your country have a statute of limitations on murder?"

"No, I don't think so," I said. "But in the States we have to produce a body for it to be a murder."

"Exactly. That is why we would appreciate any information you could share with us. M. Das left many influential friends, Mr. Luczak. Many of these people are in even more respected positions now, eight years after the poet's disappearance. We would all be relieved to conclude this investigation."

"All right," I said, and proceeded to tell him of my involvement with *Harper's* and the arrangement with the Bengali Writers' Union. I debated telling him about Krishna and Muktanandaji, and then decided that such a fantastic story would only cause complications with the police.

"So you have no confirmation that M. Das is alive other than the poem which you may or may not receive through the Writers' Union?" asked Singh.

"That and the letter Michael Leonard Chatterjee read at the meeting with the executive council," I said. Singh nodded as if he was well aware of the correspondence.

He asked, "And you plan to pick up the manuscript tomorrow?"

"Yes."

"Where will this take place?"

"I don't know. They haven't told me yet."

"At what time?"

"Again, they haven't told me."

"Will you meet with Das at this time?"

"No. At least, I don't think so. No, I'm sure I won't."

"Why is that?"

"Well, all of my requests to meet with the great man and actually confirm his existence have met with a stone wall."

"A stone wall?"

"Negative response. A flat refusal."

"Ah. And you have no further plans to meet with him later?"

"No. I'd hoped to. My article certainly needed an interview. But to tell you the truth, Inspector, I'll be just as happy to get the damned manuscript, take my wife and child with me out of Calcutta tomorrow morning, and leave it to the literary experts as to whether M. Das wrote the poem."

Singh nodded as if this was a reasonable enough attitude. Then he jotted a few things in a small spiral notebook and finished his tonic. "Thank you, Mr. Luczak. You have been most helpful. Again, I apologize for taking up your Saturday evening."

"Quite all right."

"Oh," he said, "there is one thing."

"Yes?"

"Tomorrow, when you go to pick up the alleged Das manuscript, would you have any objections to police officers from the Metropolitan Force discreetly following you? It might help us in our investigation."

"A tail?" I said. I sipped at the last of my drink. If I objected, I might cause trouble for myself, and the cops would almost certainly still follow us. Besides, having the police nearby might allay some of the anxiety I was feeling about the rendezvous.

"Your associates need not know," added Singh.

I nodded. Personally, I didn't give a damn if Chatterjee, Gupta, and the whole Union became implicated. "All right," I said. "That would be fine. If it would help in your investigation. I have no idea myself whether Das is really alive. I'd be happy to help."

"Ah, excellent." Inspector Singh rose and we shook hands at last. "Have a good trip, Mr. Luczak. I wish you luck with your writing."

"Thank you, Inspector."

* * *

The rain continued falling for the rest of the evening. Any lingering thought Amrita and I had of spending Saturday night out on the town was squelched by the sight of mud, monsoon, and squatting misery we would glimpse when we opened the curtains. The tropical twilight was a brief transition between the gray, rainy day and the black, rainy night. A few lanterns glowed from under canvas across the flooded plaza.

Victoria was tired and fussy, so we put her down in her nest early. Then we called down to Room Service and waited an hour for dinner to arrive. When it did show up, it consisted mostly of a lesson to me never to order cold roast-beef sandwiches in a Hindu country. I begged some of Amrita's excellent Chinese dinner.

At nine P.M., while Amrita was showering before bed, there was a knock at the door. It was a boy with the fabric from the sari shop. The youngster was dripping wet, but the material was safely wrapped in a large plastic bag. I tipped him ten rupees, but he insisted on exchanging the bill I gave him for two five-rupee notes. The ten-rupee bill was torn slightly, and Indian currency evidently became non-negotiable when damaged. That exchange put me in a less than pleasant mood, and when Amrita emerged in her silk robe she took one look in the bag and announced that it was the wrong fabric. The shop had switched her bolts of material with Kamakhya's. We then spent twenty minutes going through the phone book trying to find the proper Bharati, but the name was as common as Jones would be in a New York directory and Amrita thought that Kamakhya's family probably didn't have a phone anyway.

"To hell with it," I said.

"Easy for you to say. You didn't spend over an hour picking out the material."

"Kamakhya will probably bring your stuff by."

"Well, it will have to be tomorrow if we're leaving early Monday morning."

We turned in early. Victoria awoke once, sobbing slightly in some baby's dream that made her arms and legs paddle in frustration, but I carried her around the room for a while until she drifted off to sleep, drooling contentedly on my shoulder. During the next couple of hours the room seemed alternately too hot and then chilly. The walls rattled from various mechanical noises. It sounded as if the place were honeycombed with dumbwaiters, each being pulled laboriously by chains and pulleys. An Arab group two doors away shouted and laughed, never thinking to move the party into their suite and close the door.

At around 11:30 I rose from the damp sheets and went to the window. The rain still pelted the dark street. No traffic moved.

I opened my suitcase. I had brought only two books along: a hardback copy of my own recent publication, and a Penguin paperback I'd picked up in a London bookstore of M. Das's poetry. I sat down in a chair near the door and snapped on a reading lamp.

I confess that I opened my own book first. The pages fell open to the title poem, *Winter Spirits*. I tried to read through it, but the once sharp imagery of the old woman moving through her Vermont farmhouse and communing with the friendly ghosts in the place while the snow piled in the fields did not go well with the hot Calcutta night and the sound of the heartless monsoon rattling the panes. I picked up the other book.

Das's poetry immediately captivated me. Of the short works at the beginning of the book, I most enjoyed "Family Picnic," with its humorous but never condescending insight into the need to patiently suffer the eccentricities of one's relatives. Only the passing reference to ". . . the blue, shark-sharpened waters of the Bay of Bengal/ Unclouded by sail or smoke of distant steamer" and a quick description of a ". . . Mahabalipuram temple/ sandstone worn with sea age and prayer/ a smooth-cornered plaything now/ for children's climbing knees and Uncle Nani's/ snapshots" placed the locale in Eastern India.

I came to his "The Song of Mother Teresa" with new eyes. Less visible to me now were the academic echoes of Tagore's influence in the hopeful theme and more apparent were the blunt references such as ". . . street death/ curb death/ the hopeless abandonments she moved among/ a warm infant's plaint for succor/ against the cold breast of a milkless city." I wondered then if Das's epic tale of the young nun who heard her calling while traveling to another mission, who came to Calcutta to help the suffering multitudes if only by providing them a place to die in peace, would ever be recognized as the classic of compassion I felt it was.

I turned the book over to look at the photo of M. Das. It reassured me. The high forehead and sad, liquid eyes reminded me of photographs of Jawaharlal Nehru. Das's face had the same patrician elegance and dignity. Only the mouth, those slightly too-full lips upturned at the corners, suggested the sensuality and slight self-centeredness so necessary in a poet. I fancied that I could see where Kamakhya Bharati had received her sensuous good looks.

When I clicked off the light and crawled in next to Amrita, I felt better about the coming day. Outside, the rain continued to tear and batter at the huddled city.

Chapter Ten

Calcutta, Lord of Nerves,
Why do you want to destroy me entirely?
I do have a horse and eternal foreign-stay
I go to my own city.

—Pranabendu Das Gupta

It was a strange mixture of people that set off for the manuscript rendezvous on Sunday morning. Gupta had called at 8:45. We had been up for two hours. During breakfast in the Garden Café, Amrita had announced her decision to go along on this trip and I couldn't sway her from it. Actually, I was relieved at the idea.

Gupta began the phone conversation in the inimitable style of all Indian telephonic communications.

"Hello," I said.

"Hello, hello, hello." The connection sounded as if we

were using two tin cans and several miles of string. Static rasped and snickered.

"Mr. Gupta?"

"Hello, hello."

"How are you, Mr. Gupta?"

"Very fine. Hello, Mr. Luczak? Hello?"

"Yes."

"Hello. The arrangements have been . . . hello? Mr. Luczak? Hello?"

"Yes. I'm here."

"Hello! The arrangements have been made. You will come alone when we meet you at your hotel at ten-thirty o'clock this morning."

"Sorry, Mr. Gupta. My wife's coming. We decided that—"

"What? What? Hello?"

"I say, my wife and child are coming along. Where are we going?"

"No, no, no. It is arranged. You are to come alone."

"Yes, yes, yes," I said. "Either my family goes along today or I don't go at all. To tell you the truth, Mr. Gupta, I'm a little tired of this James Bond bullshit. I came twelve thousand miles to pick up a piece of literary work, not to sneak around Calcutta alone. Where is the meeting to take place?"

"No, no. It would be better if you were to go alone, Mr. Luczak."

"Why is that? If it's dangerous, I want to know—"

"No! Of course it is not dangerous."

"Where's the meeting to take place, Mr. Gupta? I really don't have time for this nonsense. If I go home empty-handed, I'll write some sort of article, but you'll probably be hearing from my magazine's lawyers." It was an empty threat, but it caused a silence broken only by the hiss, crackle, and hollow clunks normal to the line.

"Hello? Hello, Mr. Luczak?"

"Yes."

"Very well. Your wife will, of course, be very welcome. We are to meet M. Das's representative at Tagore's home—"

"*Tagore's* home?"

"Yes, yes. It is a museum, you know."

"Marvelous!" I said. "I had hoped to see Tagore's house. That's excellent."

"Mr. Chatterjee and I will be at your hotel at ten-thirty o'clock then. Hello, Mr. Luczak?"

"Yes?"

"Good-bye, Mr. Luczak."

Gupta and Chatterjee did not show up until after eleven, but Krishna was in the lobby when we went down. He was wearing the same soiled shirt and rumpled trousers. He acted overjoyed to see us, bowing to Amrita, tousling Victoria's thin hair, and shaking my hand twice. He had come, he said, to inform me that our "mutual friend, Mr. Muktanadaji" had used my most gracious gift to return to his village of Anguda.

"I thought that he said he couldn't go home again."

"Ahh," said Krishna and shrugged.

"Well, I guess both he and Thomas Wolfe were wrong," I said. Krishna stared a second and then exploded with a laugh so loud that Victoria began to cry.

"You have received the Das poem?" he asked when both his laughter and Victoria's crying had subsided.

Amrita answered. "No, we're going to get it right now."

"Ahh," smiled Krishna, and I could see the gleam in his eyes.

On an impulse I asked, "Would you like to accompany us? Perhaps you'd like to see what kind of manuscript a water-logged corpse can produce."

"Bobby!" said Amrita. Krishna only nodded, but his smile was more sharklike than ever.

Gupta and Chatterjee were less than thrilled at the size of our party. I didn't have the heart to tell them that an unknown number of Calcutta's Finest were also going along.

"Mr. Gupta," I said, "this is my wife, Amrita." Pleasantries were exchanged in Hindi. "Gentlemen, this is our . . . guide, Mr. M. T. Krishna. He will also accompany us."

The two gentlemen nodded tersely, but Krishna beamed. "We have already met! Mr. Chatterjee, you do not remember me?"

Michael Leonard Chatterjee frowned and adjusted his glasses.

"Ah, you do not. Nor you, Mr. Gupta? Ah, well, it was some years ago, upon my return from Mr. Luczak's fair country. I petitioned for membership in the Writer's Union."

"Oh, yes," said Chatterjee, although it was obvious that he remembered none of it.

"Yes, yes." Krishna smiled. "I was told that my prose 'lacked maturity, style, and restraint.' Needless to say, I was not granted admission to the Writers' Union."

Everyone squirmed in embarrassment except for Krishna. And me. I was beginning to enjoy this. Already, I was glad that I'd invited Krishna along.

It was a crowded little Premiere that drove east from the hotel. Gupta, Chatterjee, and Chatterjee's liveried driver were crammed into the front seat. As far as I could tell, the driver had one arm out the window, the other hand was frequently adjusting his cap, and he was driving with his knees. The effect was no different than usual.

In the back, I sat squeezed between Krishna and Amrita holding Victoria on her lap. We were all perspiring freely, but Krishna seemed to have started earlier than the rest of us.

It was absurdly hot. Upon leaving the air-conditioned hotel, Amrita's camera lens and Chatterjee's glasses had steamed up. It was at least 110 degrees, and my cotton shirt immediately became plastered to my back. In the littered plaza across from the hotel, forty or fifty men squatted with their bony knees higher than their chins, trowels, mortar boards, and plumb bobs on the pavement in front of them. It seemed to be some sort of work lineup. I asked Krishna why they were there, and he shrugged and said, "It is Sunday morning." Everyone else seemed satisfied with this Delphic utterance, so I said nothing.

Moving down Chowringhee, we made a right turn in front of Raj Bhavan—the old Government House—and drove south on Dharamtala Street. The air coming in the open windows did not cool us but rasped at our skins like hot sandpaper. Krishna's matted hair whipped around like a nest of snakes. At every stop sign or traffic policeman, the driver would turn off the engine and we would sit in sweaty silence until the car moved again.

We drove east onto Upper Circular Road and then swung onto Raja Dinendra Street, a winding road which paralleled a canal. The stagnant water reeked of sewage. Naked children splashed in the brown shallows.

"Look there," ordered Chatterjee, pointing to our right. A

large temple was painted in Technicolor glory. "The Jain Temple. Very interesting."

"The Jain priests will take no life," said Amrita. "When they leave the temple, they have servants sweep the walk so that they won't inadvertently step on an insect."

"They wear surgical masks," said Chatterjee, "so that they will not accidentally swallow any living thing."

"They do not bathe," added Krishna, "out of respect for the bacteria which live on their bodies."

I nodded, and silently speculated on whether Krishna himself honored this particular Jain code. Between the usual Calcutta street smells,the reek of raw sewage, and Krishna, I was beginning to feel a little overwhelmed.

"Their religion forbids them to eat anything which *is* living or *was* living," Krishna said happily.

"Wait a minute," I said. "That rules out everything. What do they live on?"

"Ahh." Krishna smiled. "Good question!"

We drove on.

Rabindranath Tagore's home was in Chitpur. We parked on a narrow sides street, walked through a gate into an even narrower courtyard, and removed our shoes in a small anteroom before entering the two-story building.

"Out of reverence to Tagore, this home is treated like a temple," Gupta said solemnly.

Krishna kicked off his sandals. "Every public monument in our country becomes a temple sooner or later," he laughed. "In Varanasi, the government built a structure housing a large relief map of India to educate the ignorant peasants about our national geography. Now it is a holy temple. I have seen people worship there. It even has its own feast day. A relief map!"

"Quiet," said Chatterjee. He led us up a dark stairway. Tagore's suite of rooms was empty of furniture, but the walls were lined with photographs and display cases showing off everything from original manuscripts that must have been worth a fortune to cans of the Master's favorite snuff.

"We seem to be alone," said Amrita.

"Oh, yes," agreed Gupta. The writer looked even more like a rodent when he smiled. "The museum is usually closed on Sundays. We are privileged to be here only by special arrangement."

"Great," I said to no one in particular. Suddenly, from speakers on the wall, there came recordings of Tagore's voice, high and squeaky, reading excerpts of his poetry and singing some of his ballads. "Marvelous."

"M. Das's representative should be here shortly," said Chatterjee.

"No hurry," I said. There were large canvases of Tagore's oil paintings. His style reminded me of N. C. Wyeth's—an illustrator's version of impressionism.

"He won the Nobel Prize," said Chatterjee.

"Yes."

"He composed our national anthem," said Gupta.

"That's right. I'd forgotten," I said.

"He wrote many great plays," said Gupta.

"He founded a great university," said Chatterjee.

"He died right there," said Krishna.

We all stopped and followed Krishna's pointing finger. The corner was empty except for small balls of dust. "It was 1941," Krishna said. "The old man was dying, running down like an unwound clock. A few of his disciples gathered here. Then more. And more. Soon all of these rooms were filled with people. Some had never met the poet. Days passed. The old man lingered. Finally a party began. Someone went to the American military headquarters . . . there were already soldiers in the city . . . and returned with a projector and reels of film. They watched Laurel and Hardy, and Mickey Mouse cartoons. The old man lay in his coma, all but forgotten in the corner. From time to time he would swim up out of his death sleep like a fish to the surface. Imagine his confusion! He stared past the backs of his friends and the heads of strangers to see the flickering images on the wall."

"Over here is the pen that Tagore used to write his famous plays," Chatterjee said loudly, trying to draw us away from Krishna.

"He wrote a poem about it." continued Krishna. "About dying during Laurel and Hardy. In those last days he dated his poems, knowing that each one could be his last. Then, in the brief periods between coma, he wrote down the hour as well. Gone was his sentimental optimism. Gone was the gentle *bonhomie* that marked so much of his popular work. For you see, between poems, he now was facing the dark face of Death. He was a frightened old man. But the poems . . . ahh, Mr. Luczak . . . those final poems are beautiful. And painful. Like his dying. Tagore looked at the cinema images on the wall and wondered—'Are we all illusions? Brief shadows thrown on a white wall for the shallow amusement of bored gods? *Is this all*?' And then he died. Right there. In the corner."

"Come this way," snapped Gupta. "There is much more to see."

There was indeed. Photographs of Tagore's friends and contemporaries included autographed images of Einstein, G. B. Shaw, and a very young Will Durant.

"The Master was a strong influence on Mr. W. B. Yeats," said Chatterjee. "Did you know that the 'rough beast' in 'The Second Coming'—the lion body with the head of a man—was drawn from Tagore's description to Yeats of the fifth incarnation of Vishnu?"

"No," I said. "I don't think I knew that."

"Yes," said Krishna. He ran his hand over the top of a dusty display case and smiled at Chatterjee. "And when Tagore sent Yeats a bound edition of his Bengali poetry, do you know what happened?" Krishna ignored the frowns from Gupta and Chatterjee. He dropped into a crouch and wielded an invisible weapon with both hands. "Why, Yeats charged across his London sitting room, grabbed a large samurai sword which had been a gift, and smote Tagore's book thus . . . Ayehh!!"

"Really?" asked Amrita.

"Yes, really, Mrs. Luczak. And Yeats then cried out, 'Tagore be damned! He sings of peace and love when blood is the answer!' "

The tape recordings of Tagore's music stopped abruptly. We all turned as a poorly dressed boy of about eight stepped into the room. The boy carried a small canvas bag, but it was too small and too irregular to hold a manuscript. He looked from face to face until he came to me.

"You are Mr. Luczak?" The words sounded memorized, as if the boy did not speak English.

"Yes."

"Follow me. I take you to M. Das."

* * *

A rickshaw waited in the courtyard. There was room beside the boy for Amrita, Victoria, and me. Gupta and Chatterjee hurried to their car to follow. Krishna seemed to lose interest, and stood by the door.

"You're not coming?" I shouted.

"Not now," said Krishna. "I will see you later."

"We're leaving in the morning," called Amrita.

Krishna shrugged. The boy said something to the rickshaw *wallah*, and we moved out onto the street. Chatterjee's Premiere pulled out behind us. Half a block back, a small gray sedan also pulled away from the curb. Behind it, a bullock cart lumbered along with half a dozen ragged people in it. I amused myself by imagining that the bullock cart driver was the Metropolitan Policeman assigned to following us. The boy yelled a sentence in Bengali and the rickshaw-coolie shouted back and broke into a faster trot.

"What'd he say?" I asked Amrita. "Where are we going?"

"The boy said, 'Hurry up,'" said Amrita with a smile. "The rickshaw man said that the Americans are heavy pigs."

"Hmmm."

We crossed Howrah Bridge in a mass of brawling traffic that made all previous traffic jams I'd seen pale in comparison. There was as much pedestrain movement as wheeled traffic and it jammed the two levels of the bridge to capacity. The intricate puzzle of gray girders and steel mesh stretched more than a quarter of a mile across the muddy expanse of the Hooghly River. It was a child's Erector Set version of a bridge, and I took Amrita's Minolta to snap a picture of it.

"Why did you do that?"

"I promised your father."

The boy waved both hands at me and repeated something that sounded urgent and angry.

"What's he saying?"

Amrita frowned. "I'm not sure through the dialect, but it's something about photos of the bridge being against the law."

"Tell him it's okay."

She spoke in Hindi, and the boy scowled and responded in Bengali.

"He says it's not okay," said Amrita. "He says that we Americans should let our satellites do our spying."

"Jesus."

The rickshaw pulled up in front of an interminable brick building that was the Howrah Railway Station. There was no sign of Chatterjee's Premiere or of the gray sedan in the snarl of traffic coming off the bridge. "Now what?" I said.

The boy turned to me and handed over the canvas bag. I was surprised by its weight. I tugged the drawstring loose and looked inside.

"Good heavens," said Amrita. "They're coins."

"Not just coins," I said, holding one up. "Kennedy half-dollars. There must be fifty or sixty of them here."

The boy pointed to the entrance of the building and spoke quickly. "He says you are to go inside and give these away," said Amrita.

"Give them away? To whom?"

"He says someone will ask you for them."

The boy nodded as if satisfied, reached into the bag, grabbed four of the coins, and was out of the rickshaw, into the crowd.

Victoria reached for the coins. I tugged the drawstring tight and stared at Amrita. "Well," I said, "I guess it's up to us."

"After you, sir."

When I was a child, the Merchandise Mart in Chicago was the biggest building I could possibly imagine. Then in the late 60's I had the opportunity to see the interior of the Vehicle Assembly Building at the Kennedy Space Center. The friend who was showing me around told me that clouds formed indoors on some days.

Howrah Railway Station was more impressive.

It was a structure built to a giant's scale. There were a dozen tracks immediately visible; five locomotives at rest, several pouring steam; several score of vendors selling unnamed things from carts that sent up eye-scalding plumes of smoke, thousands of sweating, jostling people; more thousands squatting, sleeping, cooking—*living* there; and a cacophony of sound so deafening that one couldn't hear himself shout, much less think. That was Howrah Railway Station.

"Mother of Mercy," I said. A few feet from my head, an aircraft propeller protruded from a girder and slowly stirred the heavy air. Dozens of similar fans added their racket to the ocean of noise.

"What?" shouted Amrita. Victoria cringed against her mother's breast.

"Nothing!" We began walking aimlessly, shoving through a crowd moving nowhere. Amrita tugged at my sleeve, and I leaned over so she could speak in my ear. "Shouldn't we wait for Mr. Chatterjee and Mr. Gupta?"

I shook my head. "Let them get their own Kennedy half-dollars."

"What?"

"Never mind."

A short woman came up to us. On her back was a thing that might have been her husband. The man's spine was twisted cruelly, one shoulder grew out of the middle of his humped back, and his legs were boneless tentacles that disappeared inside the folds of the woman's sari. A black arm more bone than flesh unfolded our way and his palm opened. "Baba, Baba."

I hesitated a second and then reached into the bag and handed him a coin. His wife's eyes opened wide, and both her hands thrust at us. "Baba!"

"Should I give him the whole thing?" I shouted at Amrita, but before she could reply there were a dozen hands being thrust into my face.

"Baba! Baba!"

I tried to back away, but more imploring palms struck at my back. Quickly I began dispensing coins. The hands would grasp the silver, disappear into the fray, and then thrust back for more. I caught a glimpse of Amrita and Victoria ten feet away and was glad there was some distance between us.

The crowd grew magically. One second there were ten or fifteen people shouting and holding their hands out, and a few seconds later the mob had grown to thirty, then fifty. I felt as if it were Halloween and I was dispensing candy to a crowd of trick-or-treaters, but this harmless illusion disappeared when a dark hand rotted from leprosy came out of the crowd and scabrous fingers batted at my face.

"Hey!" I shouted, but it was a weak sound against the noise of the mob. There must have been a hundred people pushing toward the packed center of a circle which held me as its locus. The pressure was frightening. A groping hand accidentally ripped my shirt open and left parallel tracks across my chest.

An elbow struck me in the side of the head and I would have gone down then if the press of bodies had not kept me upright.

"Baba! Baba! Baba!" The entire mob was moving toward the edge of the platform. It was a six-or seven-foot drop to the metal rails. The woman with the cripple on her back screamed as the man was torn loose and fell into the surging pack. A man near me began screaming and repeatedly striking another in the face with the side of his hand.

"The shit with this," I said and threw the bag of coins into the air. The canvas pouch turned over once in a lazy arc and spewed coins across the mob and a shouting rice vendor. The screaming rose in pitch and the frenzied mass lunged away from the edge of the platform, but not before I heard something or someone heavy fall to the rails. A woman screamed inches from my face and saliva spattered over me. Then a heavy blow caught me in the back and I pitched forward, grabbed at a sari, then went down on my knees.

The mob pressed around me, and for a second I panicked, covering my heads with my hands. Stained trouser legs and sharp knees in rags struck at my face. Someone tripped over me, and for a second the full weight of the mob was on my back, forcing my face to the floor, crushing me. I distantly heard Amrita's shouts above the animal roar of the crowd. I opened my mouth to scream, but at that instant a filthy bare foot struck me in the face. Someone stepped on the back of my leg and a searing pain shot up my calf muscle.

One second I was lost in the darkness of tumbling forms and in the next I could see the glow from broken skylights high above and Amrita was bending over me, holding Victoria in her left arm while she used her right arm to shove aside the last of the jostling beggars. Then the mob was past and Amrita was helping me to a sitting position on the filthy platform. It was as if a tidal wave had appeared from nowhere, spent its violence, and was now flowing back into the random sea of people and pools of huddled families. Nearby an old man crouched over a large pot of boiling water that had remained miraculously unspilled in the confusion.

"I'm sorry, I'm sorry," I kept repeating to Amrita when I could get my breath. Now that the danger was past, Amrita began sobbing and laughing as she hugged me and helped me to my feet. We checked Victoria for bruises or scratches, and the baby chose that instant to begin wailing so loudly that both of us had to reassure her with hugs and kisses. "I'm sorry," I said again. "That was so stupid."

"Look," said Amrita. There, next to my feet, lay a plain brown briefcase. I picked it up, and we pushed our way outside past packs of rickshaw coolies clamoring for our business. We found a relatively open space near the street and leaned against a brick pillar while the flow of people broke around us. I checked Victoria again. She was fine, blinking in the stronger light and obviously debating whether to resume her wailing.

Amrita grasped my forearm. "Let's see what's in the briefcase and get out of here," she said.

"I'll open it later."

"Open it *now*, Bobby," she said. "We'll feel pretty foolish if you went through all that to come away with some businessman's lunch."

I nodded and snapped open the latches. It was not someone's lunch. The manuscript lay in a heap of several hundred pages. Some were typewritten, some were scrawled in longhand, and at least half a dozen different sizes and colors of paper had been used. I glanced at enough pages to confirm that it was poetry and that the manuscript was in English. "Okay," I said, "Let's get out of here."

I closed the briefcase and we had turned to choose a taxi when the Premiere screeched to a halt and Mr. Chatterjee and Mr. Gupta jumped out, shouting excitedly.

"Greetings," I said wearily. "What kept you?"

Chapter Eleven

"I think with my body and soul about the women of Calcutta . . ."
—Ananda Bagchi

The apparition in the mirror was a mess. His hair was in disarray, his shirt was torn, his white cotton slacks were filthy, and there were fingernail tracks across his chest. I grimaced at myself and tossed the ruined shirt on the floor. I grimaced again as Amrita applied a cotton swab soaked with peroxide to my cuts.

"You didn't make Mr. Chatterjee or Mr. Gupta very happy," she said.

"It's not my fault that there wasn't a Bengali version of the manuscript."

"They would have liked to have had more time to study the English version, Bobby."

"Yeah. Well, they can catch excerpts in *Harper's* or wait for the spring edition of *Other Voices*. That is, if Morrow's experts decide it *is* a Das manuscript. I have my doubts."

"And you're not going to read it today?"

"Nope. I'll look at it tomorrow during the flight and study it when we get home."

Amrita nodded and finished swabbing the cuts on my chest. "Let's have Dr. Heinz look at these when we get home."

"All right." We went into the other room and sat on the bed. The electricity was out, the air conditioning had failed, and the room was a steam bath. Opening the windows only served to let in the noise and stench from the street below. Victoria sat on her quilt on the floor. She wore nothing but diapers and rubber pants and was wrestling with a big ball with bells in it. The ball was on top and appeared to be winning the match.

I had surprised even myself by not reading the manuscript immediately. I had never been known for either stifling my curiosity or deferring gratification of any sort. But I was tired and depressed and had a strong and completely illogical aversion to even looking at the manuscript until the three of us were safely out of the country.

Where had the police been? I had not seen the gray sedan again and now had my doubts as to whether it had ever actually followed us. Well, nothing else had appeared to work efficiently in Calcutta. Why should the police force be an exception?

"So, what do we do today?" asked Amrita.

I flopped back on the bed and picked up a tourist guide. "Well, we can see impressive Fort William, or view the imposing Nakhoda Mosque—which, by the way, was modeled on Akbar's tomb, whoever Akbar was—or go back across the river to see the botanical gardens."

"It's *so hot,*" said Amrita. She had changed into shorts and a T-shirt that read A WOMAN'S PLACE IS IN THE HOUSE—AND THE SENATE. I wondered what Chatterjee would think if he saw her dressed that way.

"We could go to the Victoria Memorial."

"I bet they don't even have *fans* there," she said. "Where would it be cool?"

"A bar?"

"It's Sunday."

"Yeah. I've been meaning to ask. Why is it that every place closes down in a Hindu country on—"

"The park!" said Amrita. "We could go for a walk on the Maidan near the racecourse we saw from the taxi. There should be a breeze."

I sighed. "Let's try it. It's bound to be cooler than this place."

It was no cooler there. Small groups of beggars, a painful reminder of the morning's folly, flocked to us everywhere. Even the frequent and violent bouts of rainfall did not discourage them. I had long since emptied my pockets of change, but their insistent clamoring only grew louder. We paid two rupees to duck into a zoological garden in the park. There were only a few animals caged there, miserably swatting their tails back and forth to keep away clouds of insects, tongues hanging out from the heat. The zoo smell mixed with the heavy sewer sweetness of the river tributary that flowed past the park. We pointed out a tired tiger and some sullen monkeys to Victoria, but the baby wanted only to nestle against my damp shirt and sleep. When the rains struck again we found shelter in a small pavilion which we shared with a six- or seven-year-old boy who was watching over an infant lying on the cracked stone. Occasionally the boy would wave a hand to shoo the flies which hovered above the baby's face. Amrita tried talking to the youngster, but he continued to squat silently and stare at her with his large brown eyes. She pressed several rupees and a ballpoint pen into his hand and we left.

The electricity was on at the hotel, but the laboring air conditioner had not cooled the room appreciably. Amrita showered first and I had just pulled off my soaked shirt when there was a heavy knock at the door.

"Ah. Mr. Luczak! Namastey."

"Namastey, Mr. Krishna." I remained standing in the doorway, blocking it.

"You had a successful conclusion to your transaction?"

"Yes, thank you."

The heavy eyebrows went up. "But you have not read Mr. Das's poem?"

"No, not yet." I braced myself for a request to borrow the manuscript.

"Yes, yes. I do not want to bother you. I wish to give you this in anticipation of your meeting with Mr. M. Das." Krishna handed over a wrinkled paper sack.

"I have no plans to meet with—"

"Yes, yes." Krishna shrugged from the waist up. "But who is to know? Good-bye, Mr. Luczak." I shook Krishna's extended hand. Before I could look in the sack he was gone, whistling down the corridor toward the elevators.

"Who was that?" called Amrita from the bathroom. I sat on the bed.

"Krishna," I said and opened the sack. There was something wrapped in a loose bundle of rags.

"What did he want?"

I stared at the thing in my hands. It ws an automatic pistol: metal, chromed, tiny. It was as small and light as cap pistols I'd played with as a boy. But the muzzle opening looked real enough, and when I figured out how to slide the small clip out, the jacketed cartridges were all too real. Tiny lettering above the handgrip read GUISSEPPE .25 CALIBRE. "Goddamn it to shit," I said softly.

"I said, What did he want?" called Amrita.

"Nothing!" I yelled and looked around. Four steps took me to the closet. "Just to say good-bye."

"What did you say just now?"

"Nothing." I stuffed the pistol and clip in the bag separately, wrapped them tightly in rags, and tossed the bag as far back as I could on the wide shelf above the hangars.

"You mumbled something," said Amrita as she emerged from the bathroom.

"Just trying to get you to hurry up," I said and pulled a green knit shirt and tan slacks from the closet and closed the door.

We made arrangements for a cab to take us to the airport at 4:45 A.M. and then we turned in early. I lay there for hours, watching the silhouettes of furniture slowly materialize as my eyes adjusted to the darkness.

It would have been an understatement to say that I felt dissatisfied with myself. I lay there in the moist Calcutta night and realized that my actions during the entire time I'd been in the city had been either pointless or hesitant or both. Half the time I had behaved like a brainless tourist, and the other half I had let the locals treat me like one. What the hell was I going to write about? How had I let a city frighten me for no real reason? Fear . . . nameless, asinine *fear* . . . had controlled my reactions more than any attempt at logic.

Krishna. That insane son of a bitch. *What is the gun for?* I tried to convince myself that the present of the gun was another one of Krishna's senseless, melodramatic gestures, but what if it was part of some elaborate scam? What if he contracted the police and told them that the American was carrying an illegal firearm? I sat up in bed, my skin clammy. No. How the hell could that benefit Krishna? *Are handguns illegal in Calcutta?* For all I knew, Calcutta was the home office of the N.R.A.

Sometime before midnight I arose and turned on the tiny table lamp. Amrita stirred but did not wake. Victoria was asleep with her rump raised under the light blanket. The catches on the briefcase made a soft click in the silence.

The pages were yellowed, tattered, and strewn about the inside of the briefcase, but they were also numbered with bold strokes of a fountain pen and it took me only minutes to set them in order. There were over five hundred pages, and it made for a heavy stack of poetry. I smiled ruefully as I thought of any American magazine editor being confronted with five hundred pages of verse.

There was no cover page, no title, no cover letter, and no author's name on the pages. If I hadn't know that the massive work was purported to have been written by M. Das, there would have been no way to guess from the manuscript.

The first page looked like a poor carbon copy. I leaned closer to the light and began reading.

And the demon Mahishasura
Came forth from its vile pit,
Summoning its vast army to it,
And Devi, Bhavani, Katyayani;
Parvati in her many robes,
Bid Siva farewell and rode forth
To do final battle with her foes.

Several more stanzas of this rough verse painted a grisly picture of the demon Mahishasura, a powerful, malevolent thing which threatened even the gods. Then, on page 3, the meter and "voice" changed drastically. I translated a scrawled marginal notation as *Kālidāsa: Kumarāmbhava* 400 *A.D. new trans*.

A fearful flock of evil birds
ready for the joy of eating the army of demons
flew over the host of the gods,
and clouded the sun.

Suddenly monstrous serpents, as black as powdered soot,
scattering poison from their upraised heads,
frightful in form,
appeared in the path of Parvati.

The sun put on a ghastly robe
of great and terrible snakes, curling together,
as if to mark his joy
at the death of god or demon.

I yawned. "A fearful flock of evil birds." God help me when I give this to Chet Morrow. Nothing could help me if I brought this as my "new Das epic" to Abe Bronstein. I skimmed through several pages of similar turgid verse. The only reason I didn't put it down then was a vague curiosity as to how Parvati was going to beat the apparently invincible Demon Mahishasura. Stanza after stanza described the opening of the battle between the gods and demons. It was vintage Homer via Rod McKuen.

> Lighting heaven from end to end
> with flames crashing all around,
> with an awful crash, rending the heart with terror,
> a thunderbolt fell from a cloudless sky.
>
> The host of the foe was jostled together.
> The great elephants stumbled, the horses fell,
> and all the footmen clung together in fear,
> as the earth trembled and the ocean rose
> to shake the mountains.
>
> And, before the host of the foes of the gods,
> dogs lifted their muzzles to gaze on the sun,
> then howling together with cries that rent the eardrums,
> wretchedly slunk away.

I could identify with that. Still, I continued reading. Things looked bad for the goddess Parvati. Even with the assistance of the great god Siva, she could not best the mighty Mahishasura. Parvati was reborn as the warrioress Durga, ten hands brandishing weapons of battle. Millennia passed as the struggle progressed, but Mahishasura could not be conquered.

And before the very disc of the sun
jackals brayed harshly together,
as though eager fiercely to lap the blood
of the mightiest of the gods, fallen in battle.

The gods retreated from the field to review their options. Mere mortals petitioned them not to abandon the earth to the less than tender mercies of Mahishasura. A grim decision was made. The will of all the gods was bent to dark purpose. From Durga's forehead leaped a goddess more demon than divine. She was power incarnate, violence personified, unfettered even by the bonds of time which held other gods and mere men in check. She strode the heavens wrapped in darkness deeper than night, casting fear into the hearts of even the deities who had brought her forth.

She was called to battle. She accepted the call. But before opposing Mahishasura and the rampaging legions of demons, she demanded her sacrifice. And it was a terrible one. From every town and village on the young earth, men and women, children and elders, virgins and depraved were brought before the hungry goddess. Das's marginal note, only just decipherable, read: *Bhavabhūti Mālatīmādhava*.

Now wake the terrors of the place, beset
With crowding and malignant fiends; the flames
From funeral pyres scarce lend their sullen light
Clogged with fleshy prey to dissipate
The fearful gloom that hems them in. Pale ghosts
Spirit with foul goblins, and their dissonant mirth
In shrill resplendent shrieks is echoed round.

All hail the Age of Kali.
The Age of Kali has begun.
All hail the Age of Kali.
The Song of Kali now is sung.

That would have been enough for one night, but the next line kept me in my chair. I blinked and read on.

To: Central Construction Office
From: I. A. Topf and Sons, Erfurt
Subject: Crematoria 2 and 3
We acknowledge receipt of your order
For five triple furnaces
Including two electric elevators
For raising the corpses
And one emergency elevator.
A practical installation for stoking coal
Was also ordered
And one for transporting ashes.
We guarantee the effectiveness
Of the furnaces and ovens mentioned,
As well as their durability,
The use of the best material
And our faultless workmanship.

Awaiting you further word,
We will be at your service,
I. A. Topf and Sons,
Erfurt

And then, without transition, the style reverted to the fifth-century *sambhava*.

The sky poured down torrents of red-hot ashes, With
which were mixed blood and human bones,
Till the flaming ends of heaven were filled with smoke
And bore the dull hue of the neck of an ass.

Hail, hail! Camundā-Kali, Mighty Goddess, hail!
We glórify thy sport, when in the dance
That fills the court of Siva with delight,
Thy foot descending spurns the earthly globe.
The darkness which hides and robes thee, to thy steps
Swings to and fro: the whirling talons rend
The crescent on thy brow; from the torn orb
The trickling nectar falls, and every skull
That gems thy necklace laughs with horrid life;
The Age of Kali has begun; thy Song can now be sung.

All this was mere prelude as the poem unfolded like some dark flower. Das's strong poetic voice would appear occasionally, only to fade and be replaced by a classic Veda or a piece of news raised from archives or the banal tones of journalism. But the song was the same.

For ages beyond time, the gods conspired to contain this black power they had created. It was circumscribed, propitiated, and hidden in the pantheon, but its essential nature could not be denied. It alone—*she* alone—grew in strength as other divinities faded from mortal memory, for she alone embodied the dark underside of an essentially benign universe—a universe whose reality had been forged through the millennia by the consciousness of gods and men alike.

But *she* was not the product of consciousness. She was the focus and residue of all the atavistic urges and actions which ten thousand years of conscious strivings had hoped to put behind.

The poem unfolded through countless small stories, anecdotes, and folk tales. All had the indefinable taste of truth to them. Each story reflected a rip in the sense-deafening fabric of reality, a rip through which the Song of Kali could be faintly heard. People, places, and points in time became conduits, holes through which powerful energies poured.

In this century the Song of Kali had become a chorus. The smoke of sacrifice rose to the clouded dwelling place of Kali, *and the goddess awoke to hear her song.*

Page after page. Sometimes entire lines were gibberish, as if typed out by someone using fists on the keys. Other times, whole pages of scribbled English were indecipherable. Fragments of Sanskrit and Bengali interrupted clear passages and crawled up the margins. But random images remained.

> —A whore on Sudder Street murdered her lover and greedily devoured his body in the name of love.
> *The Age of Kali has begun.*
> —Screams are torn from the dead bellies of the slaughtered millions of our modern age; a chorus of outrage from the mass graves which fertilize our century.
> *The Song of Kali now is sung.*
> —The silhouettes of children playing etched permanently on a shattered wall when the bomb flash instantaneously scorched the concrete black.
> *The Age of Kali has begun.*
> —The father waited patiently for the last of his four daughters to come home from school. Gently he placed the revolver to her temple, fired twice, and placed her

warm body next to those of her mother and sisters. The police find him crooning a soft lullaby to the silent forms. *The Song of Kali now is sung.*

I quit with only another hundred pages left to read. My eyes had been shutting of their own accord, and twice I'd awakened to find my chin on my chest. I clumsily stuffed the manuscript in the briefcase and checked my watch on the dresser.

It was 3:45 A.M.. In a few minutes the alarm would go off and we would have to get ready for the ride to the airport. The flight home, counting the London layover, would be a 28-hour marathon.

I groaned with exhaustion and crawled into bed next to Amrita. For the first time, the room seemed pleasantly cool. I pulled up the sheet and closed my eyes for just a few minutes. A few minutes to doze before the alarm went off and we had to get dressed.

Just a few minutes.

I awake elsewhere. Someone has carried me here. It is dark but I have no trouble knowing where I am.

It is the Kali Temple.

The goddess stands before me. Her foot is raised over empty air. All four of her hands are empty. I cannot see her face because I am lying on the floor to one side of the idol.

I am not afraid.

I realize that I am naked. It does not matter. There is a rush mat under me and it is cool against my skin. A few candles illuminate the statue. The air smells of musk and incense. Somewhere men's high voices chant softly. Or perhaps it is only the sound of the moving water. It is not important.

The idol moves.

Kali turns her head and looks at me.

I feel only wonderment. I marvel at her beauty. Her face is oval, perfect, flushed. Her lips are full and moist. She smiles at me.

I stand. My bare feet feel the parallel weave of the mat. A breeze sends a shiver up my bare abdomen and belly.

Kali stirs herself. Fingers move. Her arms bend and balance her. Her foot comes down on the pedestal and she stands lightly on both legs. Her luminous eyes never leave mine.

I close my eyelids, but vision persists. I see the soft light on her flesh. Her breasts are high, full, heavy with promise. The broad nipples rise from the soft circles of their areolae. Her waist is high and impossibly narrow, widening to full hips made to cradle a man's thrusting pelvis. Her lower belly is a soft, protruding crescent, throwing shadow into the pubic darkness below. The dancer's thighs do not touch, but curve sensuously inward at their juncture. Her feet are tiny and high-arched. Bracelets circle her ankles. They jingle as she moves. Her legs part and I can see the folds in the triangle of shadow; the soft, inward-curving cleft.

My penis stirs, hardens, and rises stiffly into the night air. My scrotum pulls tighter as I feel the *power* flow through me and center there.

Kali lightly steps down from her pedestal. Her necklace clicks softly, the bracelets on her ankles jingle faintly, and her bare soles make soft, fleshy sounds on the stone floor.

She is five paces from me. Her arms move in silhouette, sensuous reeds weaving to an unfelt breeze. Her whole body sways to the pulsing music-beat of the lapping river and her left knee rises, rises, until it touches the elbow or her cocked arm. A woman scent rises from her perfumed flesh and enfolds me.

I want to go to her, but I cannot move. My pounding heart fills my chest with the drumbeat of the chanting. My hips begin to move of their own accord, thrusting involuntarily. All of my consciousness is centered at the base of my throbbing penis.

Kali swings her left leg around and down.

She steps toward me. Her anklets tinkle.

Unnāla-nabhi-pamke-ruha sings the river, and I understand it perfectly.

Her four arms sway in a silent dance. Fingers curl, touch fingertips, move gracefully through the sweet air toward me. Her breasts bob together heavily.

Victory to the face of the Daughter of the Mountain.

She takes another step forward. Her fingers sway, caress my cheek, glance lightly against my shoulder. Her head is thrown back, eyes half closed with passion. I see the perfection of her features, the flushed cheeks and trembling mouth.

Kamakhya?

Iva yenāvabhāti Sambhur'api

Jayati purusāyitāyās'tadānanam 'Ṣaila-kanyāyāh

Kali's next step brings her arms around me. Her long hair flows down over her shoulders like rivulets on a soft hillside. Her glowing skin is lightly perfumed, and sweat glistens in the tender valley between her breasts. Two hands hold my upper arms while a third softly caresses my cheek. Her other hand moves upward to gently cup my testicles. Her tapered fingers move up the length of my stiff penis, curve lightly around the glans.

I am Sambhu-Siva appearing as Visnu

The lotus and its stalk rise from my navel

I cannot stifle a moan. My erection touches the cusp of her belly. She looks down, and then her beautiful eyes turn up wantonly at me through heavy lashes. The wiry softness of her *mons veneris* moves against me, withdraws, comes again.

Finally I can move. My arms immediately go around her while she encloses me. Soft breasts flatten against me. Hands slide up and down my back. Her right leg rises, crooks itself around my hip, fingers guide, and she mounts me. Her ankles clasp beneath my thrusting buttocks.

Kali, Kali, balo, bhai

The chanting fills the world with the rhythm of our movement. Her warmth scalds me. She opens her mouth wetly against my neck, slides to find my tongue. I grip her, lift her. Breasts move across my chest on a cushion of sweat. My feet are arching, my calves straining in the effort to strike more deeply inside Kali.

The universe focuses on a circle of flame growing in me, rising in me, exploding through me.

I am Siva
Kali, Kali balo bhai
Kali bai aré gaté nai
I am a God

"Sweet Jesus!" I sat up in bed. The sheets were soaked with my sweat and my pajama bottoms wet from the growing stain of an ejaculation.

"Oh, Christ." I cradled my aching head in my hands and rocked. Amrita was gone. Heavy sunlight poured through the curtains. The travel clock said 10:48.

"Goddammit to goddam hell." I went into the bathroom,

flung the pajamas into a bag of dirty laundry, and scrubbed myself under a pounding shower. My hands and legs were still shaking when I emerged fifteen minutes later. My head hurt so fiercely that small dots danced in the periphery of my vision.

I dressed quickly and took four aspirin. Dark stubble stood out against my pale cheeks, but I decided not to shave. I came out of the bathroom just as Amrita returned with Victoria.

"Where the fuck were you?" I snapped.

She froze, her smile of greeting slowly fading. Victoria stared at me as at a stranger.

"Well?"

Amrita's back straightened. Her voice was level. "I went back to the sari shop to get Kamakhya's address. I tried to phone but the lines have been dead. As long as we're staying another day, I wanted to exchange the material. Didn't you see my note?"

"We're supposed to be almost to London by now. What the hell happened?" My voice was harsh, but the anger was already beginning to flow away.

"What do you mean, Bobby? Just what do you mean?"

"I mean what happened to the damn alarm, the cab we'd arranged, the BOAC flight? *That's* what I mean."

Amrita moved briskly to set the baby down. She crossed to the window, jerked the curtains back, and folded her arms. "The 'damn alarm' went off at four. *I* got up. *You* refused to wake up, even after I shook you. Finally, when I did get you to sit up, *you* said, 'Let's wait another day.' And all this was because *you* sat up all night reading."

"I said that?" I shook my head and sat down on the edge of the bed. The world's worst hangover still throbbed and threatened to make me throw up. *Hangover from what?* "I said that?"

"*You* said that." Amrita's voice was cold. In our years of marriage, I'd cursed at her very few times.

"Damn. I'm sorry. I wasn't awake. That damned manuscript."

"You said you were going to wait to read it on the plane."

"Yeah."

Amrita uncrossed her arms and went over to the mirror to replace a strand of hair that had come loose. The color was coming back to her lips. "That's all right, Bobby. I don't mind staying another day."

An urgency rose in my throat. My voice sounded strange to me. "Goddamn it, *I* mind. You and Victoria aren't staying another day. What time are the Air India flights to Delhi?"

"Nine-thirty and one o'clock. Why?"

"You're taking the one o'clock flight and catching the evening Pan Am flight out of Delhi."

"Bobby, that will mean . . . What do you mean 'you'? Why aren't you going? You have the manuscript."

"You two are going. Today. I have to finish something relating to this stinking article. One more day will do it."

"Oh, Bobby, I *hate* to travel alone with Victoria—"

"I know, kiddo, but it can't be helped. Let's get your stuff repacked."

"It's still packed."

"Good. Get Victoria ready and the bags together. I'll go downstairs and arrange for a taxi and a porter." I kissed her on the cheek. Normally there would have been an argument at any attempt by me to be dictatorial, but Amrita heard something in my voice.

"All right," she said. "But you'd better hurry. You can't reserve tickets over the phone in India, you know. You just have to show up early and stand in line."

"Yeah. I'll be right back."

"Mr. Gupta?" The phone in the lobby was working.

"Hello. Yes. Hello?"

"Mr. Gupta, this is Robert Luczak."

"Yes, Mr. Luczak. Hello?"

"Listen, Mr. Gupta, I want you to arrange a meeting with M. Das. A private meeting. Just him and me."

"What? What? This is not possible. Hello?"

"It had better be possible, Mr. Gupta. Make whatever contacts you have to and tell Das that I want to meet with him *today.*"

"No, Mr. Luczak. You do not understand. M. Das had not permitted anyone to—"

"Yes, I've heard all of that. But he'll meet with me, I'm sure. I urge you to expedite this, Mr. Gupta."

"I am very sorry, but—"

"Listen, sir, I'll explain the situation. My wife and baby are leaving Calcutta in a few minutes. I'm flying out tomorrow. If I have to leave without seeing Das, I'm still going to have to write an article for *Harper's*. Would you like to hear what that article is going to say?"

"Mr. Luczak, you must understand that it is impossible for us to arrange for you to meet M. Das. Hello?"

"My article will say that for some reason known only to themselves, the members of the Bengali Writers' Union have attempted to perpetrate the biggest literary fraud since the Clifford Irving hoax. For some reason known only to themselves, this group has accepted money in exchange for a manuscript they claim is the work of a man who has been dead for eight years. And what is more—"

"Completely untrue, Mr. Luczak! Untrue and actionable. We will press charges. You have no proof of these allegations."

"And what's more, this group has despoiled a great poet's name by producing a pornographic paean to a local demon goddess. Authoritative sources in Calcutta suggest that the Writers' Union may have done this because of contacts they have with a group called the Kapalikas—an outlawed cult involved in the city's crime world and reputed to offer human sacrifices to their demented goddess. How do you like it so far, Mr. Gupta? Hello, Mr. Gupta? Hello?"

"Yes, Mr. Luczak."

"What do you think, Mr. Gupta? Shall I go with that or shall I interview M. Das?"

"It will be arranged. Please call back in three hours."

"Oh . . . and Mr. Gupta?"

"Yes."

"I've already mailed one copy of my . . . ah . . . first article to my editor in New York with instructions not to open it unless I'm delayed in my return home. I hope that it won't be necessary to do that version. I'd much rather do the Das story."

"It will not be necessary, Mr. Luczak."

All cabs to and from Dum-Dum Airport were driven by veterans of the '71 Indo-Pakistani War. Our driver had scar tissue covering his right cheek and a broad, black patch over his eye that made me speculate idly about monocular vision and depth perception as we weaved in and out of heavy traffic on VIP Highway.

It was raining again. Everything was the color of mud—the clouds, the road, the burlap-tin hovels piled on one another, and the distant factories. Only the red and white stripes painted around the occasional banyan tree near the roadside added color to the scene. Near the edge of town there were new apartment buildings going up. I could tell they were new by the bamboo scaffolding girdling them and the bulldozers parked nearby in the mud, but the structures looked as decayed and age-streaked as the oldest ruins in the center of the city. Beyond the bulldozers were clusters of lean-tos occupied by huddled forms. Were these the families of construction crews or new residents waiting to occupy the buildings? Most likely the shacks were just the nucleus of a new *chawl;* the growing edge of 250 square miles of unrelieved slum.

To our left was the white sign I'd glimpsed at night. This side read—

CALCUTTA WISHES YOU
GOOD-BYE
GOOD HEALTH.

A woman with pans and a large bronze jug stacked atop her head squatted in the mud beneath the sign.

The airport was crowded, but not as insanely so as the night we arrived. The Delhi flight was already filled but there had just been a cancellation. Yes, the Pan Am flight would leave New Delhi at 7 P.M. It should be possible to get tickets.

We checked the luggage through and wandered through the terminal. There were no empty chairs, and it took awhile to find a quiet corner where we could change Victoria's diaper. Then we went into a small coffee shop to have a soft drink.

We said little to each other. Amrita seemed lost in her own thoughts and my head still ached abominably. Occasionally I would remember fragments of my dream, and the muscles in my gut would clench in tension and embarrassment.

"If worse came to worst," I said, "and you missed this evening's Pan Am connection, you could stay overnight with your aunt in New Delhi."

"Yes."

"Or stay at a good hotel near the airport."

"Yes, I could do that."

A Belgian tour group squeezed into the coffee shop. One of them, an incredibly ugly woman wearing open mesh trousers, was carrying a large plaster statue of the elephant-headed god Ganesha. They were all laughing uproariously.

"Call Dan and Barb when you get to Boston," I said.

"All right."

"I should be there the day after you. Hey, are you going to call your parents from Heathrow?"

"Bobby, I really wouldn't mind staying another day. You might need help . . . with the translating. It's about the manuscript, isn't it?"

I shook my head. "Too late, kiddo. Your luggage is already loaded. You could do without any clothes, I suppose, but we'd be doomed without the extra disposable diapers."

Amrita did not smile.

"Seriously," I said and took her hand, "I've just got to do some follow-up work with Gupta and those clowns. Hell, I just don't have enough stuff to put into an article yet. One day should do it."

Amrita nodded and tapped my ring. "All right, but be

careful. Don't drink any unbottled water. And if Kamakhya comes by to exchange my material, make sure she gives you *just* the material . . ."

I grinned. "Yeah."

"Bobby, why didn't you let the maid in?"

"What?"

"To clean the room. Right before we left you told her to wait until tomorrow."

"The Das manuscript," I said quickly. "I don't want anyone nosing around."

Amrita nodded. I drank the last of my warm Fanta, watched a small ghekko scurry across the wall, and tried not to think about the .25-caliber automatic on the shelf of the hotel room closet.

The plane was ready to board and I had kissed both of them farewell when Amrita remembered something. "Oh, in case Kamakhya doesn't come to the hotel, would you drop by her home to get the material?" She began rummaging through her purse.

"Is it that important?"

"No, but I'd appreciate it if it works out."

"Why didn't you just exchange her material at the shop?"

"It was all cut to length. And I was certain we would see her again. Darn, I was sure I had the slip here. Never mind. I remember the address." Amrita took out a book of matches she'd picked up at the Prince's Room and jotted the address inside the cover. "Only if you have time," she said.

"All right." I would not have time. We kissed again. Victoria twisted between us, confused by the crowd and noises. I cupped the baby's head in my hand, feeling the infinite softness of her hair. "You two have a good trip. I'll see you in a couple of days."

There were no enclosed boarding ramps at Dum-Dum Airport. The passengers crossed a wet expanse of tarmac and climbed a stairway into the waiting Air India jet. Amrita turned and waved Victoria's pudgy arm before disappearing into the French-made Airbus. Normally I would have waited for the plane to take off.

I checked my watch and walked quickly back through the terminal to a stand of telephones. Gupta answered on the fifth ring.

"It is arranged, Mr. Luczak. Here is the address . . ." I fumbled for my notebook but came up with the matchbook Amrita had given me. I jotted the street number next to Kamakhya's address.

"Oh . . . and Mr. Luczak . . ."

"Yes?"

"This time you *will* come alone."

The rain had stopped when I stepped out of the taxi. Vapor rose from the streets and drifted between the old buildings. I had no idea where I was. The address Gupta had given me was a street corner in the old section of the city, but I had seen no familiar landmarks on the way there.

The streets and sidewalks were filling up with people after the rainstorm. Bicycles glided by with bells jangling. The steamy air was thickened further by the fumes from motorcycles. An old bullock, its back a mass of scabs and open sores, lay down heavily in the center of the busy street. Traffic swerved around it.

I stood and waited. The sidewalk there was actually a a four-foot-wide strip of pockmarked mud between the gutter and the walls of old buildings. There were three-foot gaps between the buildings, and after being assaulted by a terrible smell, I walked over and peered into one of the narrow apertures.

Garbage and organic wastes rose eight to twelve feet high down the length of the long alley. It was obvious that the residents had thrown their refuse out the upper windows for many years. Dark shapes moved through the stinking heaps. I quickly moved away from the opening and stood by the stream of rainwater and sewage that marked the separation of street and sidewalk.

I watched every face in the moving crowd. As in any large city, the pedestrians had set their faces in masks of hurried irritability. Many of the men wore stiff polyester shirts and bell-bottomed polyester slacks. I marveled that—in a nation which produced some of the world's best and least expensive cotton clothing—the sign of middle-class prestige was the more expensive, unbreathable polyester. Occasionally a sweaty face under oiled black hair would glance my way, but no one stopped except some children, naked except for filthy khaki shorts, who danced around me for several minutes calling "Baba! Baba!" and giggling. I handed out no coins, and after several minutes they ran off splashing through the gutter.

"You are Luczak?"

I jumped. The two men had come up behind me while I was watching the traffic go by. One of them was dressed in the usual polyester, but the other wore the stained khaki of the service classes. Neither looked especially bright or pleasant. The tall, thin one in a print shirt had a wedge-shaped face with sharp cheekbones and a narrow mouth. The man in khaki was shorter, heavier, and dumber-looking than his friend. There was a sleepy, disdainful look about his eyes that reminded me of all the bullies I'd ever known.

"I'm Luczak."

"Come."

They moved off through the crowd so quickly that I had to jog to catch up. I asked several questions, but their silence and the uproar of the street convinced me to keep quiet and follow them.

We walked for the better part of an hour. I had been lost to start with, but I was soon terminally disoriented. Because of the omnipresent clouds, I couldn't even use the sun for dead reckoning. We went down crowded side streets no wider than an alley and actual alleys crowded with people and debris. Several times the two led the way through short tunnels into courtyards of residential buildings. Children ran, squealed, and squatted everywhere. Women pulled their saris half over their faces and watched with dark, suspicious eyes. Other tunnels led to other courtyards. Old men hung over rusted iron railings and looked down with glazed expressions. Babies screamed. Cooking fires burned on concrete landings and smoke hung in the foggy air.

Another short tunnel brought us out into alley which was several blocks long and more crowded than most American main streets. This led to an area where buildings had been razed, but tents and impromptu shelters sat between mounds of rubble. One large pit, perhaps a basement in some previous time, had been flooded by monsoon rains and the filthy drainage. Scores of men and boys splashed and shouted in the water while others leaped from second-floor windows in buildings surrounding the brown pool. Nearby, two naked boys laughingly poked sticks at what appeared to be a drowned and bloated rat.

Then we were out of the residential buildings completely and into a *chawl* of loosely piled rock walls, gunnysack apartments and multi-leveled condominiums constructed of old billboards, sheets of tin, and bleached scrapwood. An empty lot held twenty or thirty men squatting to defecate. Farther on, young girls sat on a rocky terrace behind their younger siblings, carefully pulling lice from matted hair. An occasional scrawny dog slunk away as we passed, but none seemed to possess any territorial instincts here. Human eyes watched from the deep shadows of the hovel doorways. Every once in a while a child would run out, palm extended, but a shout from an unseen adult would quickly call him back.

Suddenly, incense filled the air and stung the eyes. We passed a ramshackle green building which from the sounds of bells and atonal singing rising from an inner courtyard gave the impression of being a temple. Outside the green temple, an old woman and her granddaughter scooped heaps of cow dung from a large basket and kneaded them into hamburger-sized fuel patties for the evening fire. The temple wall was coated for thirty feet with rows of round and drying chunks of finger-patterned dung. Across the mud path of a street, several men were working on a bamboo frame of a hut no larger than a big backpacking tent. The men stopped their good-natured shouting and watched silently as we passed. If I had retained any doubt that my two guides were Kapalikas, it was dispelled by the wake of silence we left in our passing.

"Is it much farther?" It was beginning to rain again, and I'd left our umbrella back at the hotel. My white slacks were muddy half-way to my knees. My tan Wallabees would never be the same again. I stopped. "I said, Is it much farther?"

The heavy man in khaki turned and shook his head. He stabbed a finger at a wall of gray industrial buildings visible just beyond the sea of shacks. We had to climb a muddy hillside for the last hundred yards and I went down on my knees twice. The top of the hill was guarded by a high mesh fence with overhanging barbed wire. I looked through and saw rusted oil barrels and empty railroad sidings between the buildings.

"Now what?" I turned to admire the view of the *chawl*. The tin roofs were held down by countless rocks, black on gray. Here and there open flames were visible in dark doorways. Far off in the direction from which we had come, tenements stretched out of sight into the heavy drizzle. Smoke rose from a hundred sources and blended into the gray-brown sky.

"Come." The thin, hatched-faced man had peeled back a section of fence.

I hesitated. My heart was pounding from more than the climb up the hill. I was filled with that exhilarating, stomach-clenching lightness that one feels approaching the end of a high diving board.

I nodded and stepped through the fence.

The factory area was *silent*. I realized how I had grown used to the constant sounds of conversation, of movement . . . of *people* in this crowded city. Now, as we moved from one dim alley to the next, the silence grew as thick as the moist air. I could not believe that this factory complex was still active. Small brick buildings were almost overgrown with weeds and vines. Far up a wall, a window that had once held a hundred glass squares could now show only ten or twelve intact. The rest were jagged black holes through which small birds occasionally flitted. Everywhere were the empty oil drums—once a bright red, yellow, blue, but now scabrous with rust.

We turned into an even narrower alley, a *cul-de-sac*. I stopped abruptly. My hand went to the lower right pocket of my safari shirt and to the heavy, palm-sized rock I had picked up on the hillside. Incredibly, I felt no fear now that I was here, only a strong curiosity as to what the two men would do next. I glanced over my shoulder to make sure my back was clear, mentally traced a retreat through the maze of alleys, and turned back to the two Kapalikas. *Watch the heavy one*, a part of me warned.

"There." The one in khaki pointed up a narrow outside wooden stairway. The door at the top was a little higher than a normal second floor would be. Ivy matted the brick wall. There were no windows.

I did not move. My hand closed around the stone. The two men waited a long moment, glanced at each other, and turned on their heels to walk back the way we had come. I stepped to the side with my back against a wall and let them go. I could tell that they did not expect me to follow. Their footsteps on gravel were audible for a short while, and then there was only the sound of my own heavy breathing.

I glanced up at the steep stairway. The high walls and narrow strip of sky made me a little dizzy. Suddenly a flock of pigeons exploded from some dark cavity under the rooftop and wheeled away, wings flapping like rifle shots, circling into the heavy sky. It seemed very dark for 3:30 in the afternoon.

I walked back to the junction of alleys and looked both directions. Nothing was visible for at least a hundred paces. The rock in my hand felt cool and properly heavy, a caveman's utensil. Red clay still clung to its smooth surface. I raised the stone to my cheek and looked again at the door thirty feet up the overgrown wall. There was a pane of glass in the door but it had been painted over long ago.

I closed my eyes a second and let my breathing slow. Then I dropped the stone into my shirt pocket and climbed the rotting staircase to meet whatever waited there.

Chapter Twelve

". . . You bitch Calcutta
You piss yellow leprosy, like jaundiced urine,
Like a great artistic fresco . . ."

—Tushar Roy

The room was very small and very dark. A tiny oil lamp, open flame sputtering above a pool of rancid *ghee*, sat in the center of a square wooden table but the little light it produced was swallowed by the tattered black curtains which hung on every side. The chamber was less a room than a black-shrouded crypt. Two chairs waited at the table. On the splintered table's surface lay a book, its title not quite legible in the sick light. I did not have to read the cover to know what book it was. It was *Winter Spirits*, the collection of my poetry.

The door had opened on a corridor so narrow and so black that I almost had smiled, remembering the fun house at old Riverview Park. My shoulders brushed the flaking plaster on either side. The air was thick with the smell of wood rot and mold, bringing memories of times as a child when I'd crawled under our latticed front porch to play in the moist soil and darkness there. I would not have entered the narrow hall had not the faint glow of the oil lamp been visible.

The black gauze curtain hanging just inside the room struck my face as I entered. It swept aside easily enough, crumbling at my touch like a spider's abandoned web.

If the copy of my book was meant to intrigue me, it did. If it was meant to put me at my ease, it failed.

I remained standing four feet from the table. The rock was in my hand again, but it seemed a pitiful thing, a child's response. I again remembered the fun house at Riverview Park, and this time grinned despite myself. If anything leaped out of the curtained darkness at me, it would damn well get a face full of granite.

"Hey!" The black curtains absorbed my shout as effectively as they did the light. The open flame danced at the movement of air. "Hey! Ollie Oxen in Free! Game's over! Come on in!" Part of me was close to giggling at the absurdity of the situation. Part of me wanted to scream.

"All right, let's get this show on the road," I said and stepped forward, pulled the chair out, and sat at the table. I laid the rock on my book like a clumsy paperweight. Then I folded my hands and sat as still and upright as a schoolchild on the first day of school. Several moments passed. No sound intruded. It was so hot that sweat dripped from my chin and made small circles in the dust on the table. I waited.

Then the flame bent to an unfelt movement of air.

Someone was coming through the black curtains.

A tall form brushed back the netting, paused while still in shadow, and then shuffled hesitantly into the light.

I saw the eyes first—the moist, intelligent eyes tempered by time and too great a knowledge of human suffering. There was no doubt. They were the eyes of a poet. I was looking at M. Das. He stepped closer, and I gripped the edge of the table in a convulsive movement.

I was looking at a thing from the grave.

The figure wore gray rags that might have been the remnants of a shroud. Teeth gleamed in an involuntary rictus grin—the lips were rotted away except for tattered polyps of pulpy flesh. The nose was almost gone, seemingly nibbled away to a moist, pulsating membrane of raw tissue that did not conceal the twin openings to the skull. The once impressive forehead had been spared the ravages of the lower faces, but irregular scaly patches cut through the scalp and left tufts of white hair standing out at odd angles. The left ear was a shapeless mass.

M. Das pulled out the other chair to sit, and I noticed that two fingers of his right hand were missing at the middle joint. A rag was wrapped around what was left of the hand, but it did not conceal patches of corruption at the wrist which left muscle and tendons clearly visible.

He sat down heavily. The massive head bobbed as if the narrow neck could not support it, and the rags over the bowl of a chest rose and fell rapidly. The room was filled with the sound of our ragged breathing.

"Leprosy." I whispered the word but it seemed as if I'd shouted it. The small flame flickered wildly and threatened to extinguish itself. Liquid brown eyes stared across the oil lamp at me and I could see now that parts of the eyelids themselves had been eaten away. "My God," I whispered. "Oh, dear God. Das, what have they done to you? Leprosy."

"Yesss . . ."

I cannot adequately explain the quality of that voice. The ruined lips made some sounds impossible, and others were accomplished only with a sibilant lisp as the tongue batted against exposed teeth. I do not know how he managed to speak at all. Adding to the insanity of the moment was the still-audible Oxford accent and elegant syntax in the labored, hissing phrases. Spittle moistened the bare teeth and flew in the lamplight, but the words were intelligible. I could not move and I could not look away.

"Yesss," said the poet M. Das, "leprosy. But it is called Hansen's Disease these days, Mr. Luczak." *Dēsss dayss, Missser Lussak.*

"Of course, I'm sorry." I nodded, blinked, but still could not look away. I realized that I was still clinging tightly to the edge of the table. The splintery wood connected me to reality somehow. "My God," I repeated dully, "how did this happen? How can I help?"

"I have read your book, Mr. Luczak," hissed M. Das. "You are a sentimental poet."

"How did you get a copy?" *Idiot. Get a grip on yourself.* "I mean, why do you think the verse is sentimental?"

Das blinked slowly. The ruined eyelids came down like frayed window shades and never completely covered the whites of his eyes. With the intelligent gaze hidden, the apparition before me was a thousand times more horrible. I resisted the impulse to run, and held my breath until he was looking at me again.

Das's voice managed to sound wistful. "Does it really snow that much in Vermont, Mr. Luczak?"

"What? Oh, you mean . . . yes. Yes. Not always, but some winters. Especially in the mountains. They mark the roadsides and mailboxes with batons and little orange pennants." I was babbling, but it was either that or stuff my knuckles in my mouth to stifle other sounds.

"Ahhh," sighed Das, and the sound was air escaping from a dying sea creature. "I would have liked to have seen that. Yesss."

"I read your poem, Mr. Das."

"Yesss?"

"The Kali poem, I mean. Of course, you know that. You sent it to me."

"Yess."

"Why?"

"Why what, Mr. Luczak?"

"Why are you sending it out of the country for publication? Why did you give it to me?"

"It *must* be published." For the first time Das's odd voice conveyed emotion. "You did not like it?"

"No, I did not like it," I said. "I did not like it at all. But there were parts that are very . . . memorable. Terrible and memorable."

"Yesss."

"Why did you write it?"

M. Das closed his eyes again. The awful head bowed forward, and for a second I thought that he had gone to sleep. The lesions on his scalp glowed a gray-green in the lamplight. "It must be published," he whispered hoarsely. "You will help me?"

I hesitated. I was not sure if the last thing he had said was a question. "All right," I said at last. "Tell me why you wrote it. What you're doing here."

Das returned his gaze to me, and in the electric contact of it he somehow communicated that we were not alone. I glanced to the side but there was only blackness. Sweat dripped from my cheeks in the terrible heat. "How did you . . ." I hesitated. "How did you come to be like this?"

"A leper."

"Yes."

"I had been one for many years, Mr. Luczak. I ignored the signs. The scaly patches on my hands. The pain followed by numbness. Even as I signed autographs on tours and led seminars at the University, the feeling fled my hands and cheeks. I knew the truth long before the open sores appeared, long before the week I went east to my father's funeral."

"But they have drugs now!" I cried. "Surely you must have known . . . medicines! It can be cured now."

"No, Mr. Luczak, it cannot be cured. Even those who believe in such medicines claim only that the symptoms can be controlled, sometimes arrested. But I was a follower of Gandhi's health philosophy. When the rash and pain came I fasted, I followed diets, I administered enemas and purified my body as well as my mind. For years I did this. It did not help. I knew it would not."

I took a deep breath and wiped my palms on my trousers. "Well, if you knew that—"

"Listen, please," whispered the poet. "We do not have much time. I will tell you a story. It was the summer of 1969—a different century to me now, a different world. My father had been cremated in the small village of my birth. The bleeding sores had been visible for many weeks. I told my brothers it was an allergy. I sought solitude. I did not know what to do.

"The long ride back to Calcutta gave me time to think. Have you ever seen a leprosarium in our country, Mr. Luczak?"

"No."

"You do not wish to. Yesss, I could have gone abroad. I had the money. Doctors in such enlightened nations as yours rarely see advanced cases of Hansen's Disease, Mr. Luczak. Leprosy does not truly exist in most modern nations, you see. It is a disease of filth and muck and unhygienic conditions forgotten by the West since the Middle Ages. But it is not forgotten in India. No, not in my beloved India. Did you know, Mr. Luczak, that there are half a million lepers in Bengal alone?"

"No," I said.

"No. Nor did I. But so I have been told. Most die of other causes before the disease progresses, you see. But where was I in our story? Ah, yes. I had arrived in Howrah Station in the evening. By then I had decided upon my course of action. I had considered going abroad for medical help. I had considered enduring the years of pain as the disease followed its slow encroachment. I had considered submitting myself to the humiliation and isolation such treatment would demand. I considered it, Mr. Luczak, but I rejected it. And once I had made my decision, I felt very calm. I was very much at peace with myself and the universe that evening as I watched the lights of Howrah Station through the window of my first-class coach.

"Do you believe in God, Mr. Luczak? I did not. Nor do I now . . . believe in any god of light, that is. There are other . . . but where was I? Yes. I left the coach in a peaceful state of mind. My decision allowed me to avoid not only the pain of being an invalid, but also the pain of parting. Or so I thought.

"I gave away my luggage to a surprised beggar there in the railway station. Ah, yes, you must forgive me my method of transferring the manuscript to you yesterday, Mr. Luczak. Irony is one of the few pleasures left to me. I only wish that I could have seen it. Where were we? Yes, I left the station and walked to the marvelous structure we call the Howrah Bridge. Have you seen it? Yes, of course you have. How silly of me. I have always considered it a delightful piece of abstract sculpture, Mr. Luczak, quite unappreciated as the work of art it truly is. The bridge that night was relatively empty—only a few hundred people were crossing it.

"I stopped in the center. I did not hesitate for long, because I did not wish to have time to think. I must confess that I composed a short sonnet, a farewell verse you might say. I too was once a sentimental poet.

"I jumped. From the center span. It was well over a hundred feet to the dark water of the Hooghly. The fall seemed to go on forever. If I had known the interminable wait between execution and culmination of such a suicide, I would have planned differently, I assure you.

"Water struck from such a height has precisely the consistency of concrete, Mr. Luczak. When I hit, the impact was like a flower blossoming in my skull. Something in my back and neck snapped. Loudly. Like a thick branch breaking.

"My body sank then. I say 'my body' because I died then, Mr. Luczak. There is no doubt of that. But a strange phenomenon occurred. One's spirit does not depart immediately after death, but, rather, watches the disposition of events much as a disinterested spectator might. How else can I describe the sensation of seeing one's twisted body sink to the mud at the bottom of the Hooghly? Of seeing fish preying on the eyes and soft parts of one's self? Of seeing all this *and of feeling no concern, no horror, only the mildest of interest*? Such is the experience, Mr. Luczak. Such is the dreaded act of dying . . . as banal as all of the other necessary acts which make up our pitiful existence.

"I do not know how long my body lay there, becoming one with the river mud, before the tides or perhaps the wake of a ship brought my discarded form to shore. Children found me. They poked at me and they laughed when their sticks penetrated my flesh. Then the Kapalikas came. They carried me—tenderly, although such distinctions meant nothing to me then—to one of their many temples.

"I awoke within the embrace of Kali. She is the only deity who defies both death and time. She resurrected me then, Mr. Luczak, but only for her own purposes. Only for her own purposes. As you can see, the Dark Mother did not see fit to remove the scourge of my affliction when she restored the breath to my body."

"What were those purposes, Mr. Das?" I asked.

The poet's lipless grimace was a cruel imitation of a smile. "Why, it must be obvious to what end my poor powers have been spent," said Das. "I am the poet of the goddess Kali. Unworthy as I am, I serve her as poet, priest, and avatar."

During this entire conversation, a portion of me experienced the detached observation that Das had mentioned. It seemed as if a part of my consciousness were hovering near the ceiling, watching the entire exchange with a cool appraisal bordering on indifference. Another part of me wanted to laugh hysterically, to cry out, to turn the table over in raging disbelief and to flee from that vile darkness.

"That is my story," said Das. "What do you say, Mr. Luczak?"

"I say that your disease has driven you insane, Mr. Das."

"Yesss?"

"Or that you are quite sane but must play a role for someone."

Das said nothing, but the baleful eyes glanced quickly to the side.

"Another problem with the story," I said, amazed at the firmness of my own voice.

"What is that?"

"If your . . . if the body was discovered only last year, I doubt if there would be much to find. Not after almost seven years."

Das's head snapped up like a nightmare jack-in-the-box. There was a scraping sound in the curtained darkness.

"Oh? Who said that the discovery occurred last year, Mr. Luczak?"

My throat constricted. Without thinking, I began talking. "According to Mr. Muktanandaji, that was when the mythical resurrection took place."

A hot breeze stirred the flame and shadows danced across Das's ruined face. His terrible grin remained fixed. There was another stirring in the shadows.

"Ahhh," exhaled Das. His wrapped and mangled hand scraped across the table in an absent gesture. "Yesss, yesss. There are . . . from time to time . . . certain reenactments."

I leaned forward and let my hand fall next to the stone. My gaze searched out the human being in the leprous hulk across the table from me. My voice was earnest, urgent. "Why, Das? For Godssake, why? Why the Kapalikas? Why this epic obscenity about Kali returning to rule the world or whatever the shit it's about? You used to be a great poet. You sang songs of truth and innocence." My words sounded insipid to me but I knew no other way to say it.

Das leaned back heavily. His breath rattled through his open mouth and nostrils. *How long can someone live in this condition*? Where the flesh was not ravaged by the disease, the skin looked almost transparent, fragile as parchment. How long had it been since this man saw sunlight?

"There is a great beauty in the Goddess," he whispered.

"Beauty in death and corruption? Beauty in violence? Das, since when has a disciple of Tagore sung a hymn to violence?"

"Tagore was blind!" There was a new energy in the sibilant whisper. "Tagore could not see. Perhaps in his dying moments. Perhaps. If he had been able to then, he would have turned to *her*, Mr. Luczak. We all would turn to *her* when Death enters our night chamber and takes us by the hand."

"Fleeing to some sort of religion doesn't justify violence," I said. "It wouldn't justify the evil you sang of it—"

"*Evil*. Pahhh!" Das spat a gob of yellow phlegm on the floor. "You know nothing. Evil. There is no evil. There is no violence. There is only *power*. Power is the single, great organizing principle of the universe, Mr. Luczak. Power is the only *a priori* reality. All violence is an attempt to exercise power. Violence is power. Everything we fear, we fear because some force *exerts its power over us*. All of us seek freedom from such fear. All religions are attempts to achieve *power* over forces which might control us. But *She* is our only refuge, Mr. Luczak. Only the Devourer of Souls can grant us the *abhaya mudras* and remove all fear, for only She holds the ultimate power. She is power incarnate, a force beyond time or comprehension."

"That's obscene," I said. "It's a cheap excuse for cruelty."

"Cruelty?" Das laughed. It was the rattling of stones in an empty urn. "Cruelty? Surely, even a sentimental poet who prattles of eternal verities must know that what you call cruelty is the only reality which the universe recognizes. Life subsists on violence."

"I don't accept that."

"Oh?" Das blinked twice. Slowly. "You have never tasted the wine of power? You have never attempted violence?"

I hesitated. I could not tell him that most of my life had been one long exercise of control over my temper. My God, what were we talking about? What was I doing there?

"No," I said.

"Nonsense."

"It's true, Das. Oh, I've been in a few fights, but I've always tried to avoid violence." *I was nine, ten years old. Sarah was seven or eight. In the woods near the edge of the forest preserve. 'Take down your shorts. Now!'*

"It is not true. Everyone has tasted the blood wine of Kali."

"No. You're wrong." *Slapping her in the face. Once. Twice. The rush of tears and the slow compliance. My fingers leaving red marks on her thin arm.* "Only unimportant little incidents. Kid stuff."

"There are no unimportant cruelties," said Das.

"That's absurd." *The terrible, total excitement of it. Not just at the sight of her pale nakedness and the strange, sexual intensity of it. No, not just that. It was her total* helplessness. *Her submission. I could do anything I wanted to.*

"We will see."

Anything I wanted to.

Das rose laboriously. I pushed back my own chair.

"You will publish the poem?" His voice rasped and hissed like embers in a cooling fire.

"Perhaps not," I said. "Why don't you come with me, Das? You don't have to stay here. Come with me. Publish it yourself."

Once, when I was seventeen, an idiot cousin dared me to play Russian roulette with his father's revolver. The cousin put the single cartridge in. He spun the chamber for me. In a second of pure, mindless bravado I remember lifting the gun, putting the barrel to my temple, and squeezing the trigger. The hammer had fallen on an empty chamber then, but since that day I had refused to go near guns. Now, in the Calcutta darkness, I felt I had again lifted a barrel to my head for no good reason. The silence stretched.

"No. You must publish it. It isss important."

"Why? Can't you leave here? What can they do to you that they haven't already done? Come with me, Das."

Das's eyes partially closed, and the thing before me no longer looked human. A stench of grave soil came to me from its rags. There were undeniable sounds behind me in the blackness.

"I choose to stay here. But it is important that you bring the Song of Kali to your country."

"Why?" I said again.

Das's tongue was like a small, pink animal touching the

slick teeth and then withdrawing. "It is more than my final work. Consider it an announcement. A birth announcement. *Will you publish the poem?*"

I let ten heartbeats of silence bring me to the edge of some dark pit I did not understand. Then I bowed my head slightly. "Yes," I said. "It will be published. Not all of it, perhaps, but it will see print."

"Good," said the poet and turned to leave. Then he hesitated and turned back almost shyly. For the first time I heard a note of human longing in his voice. "There is . . . something else, Mr. Luczak."

"Yes?"

"It would mean you would have to return here."

The thought of reentering this crypt after once escaping it made my knees almost buckle. "What is it?"

He gestured vaguely at *Winter Spirits* still lying on the table. "I have little to read. They . . . the ones who care for my needs . . . are able to get me books occasionally when I specify titles. But often they bring back the wrong books. And I know so few of the new poets. Would you . . . could you possibly . . . a few books of your choice?"

The old man lurched forward three steps, and for a horrifying moment I thought he was going to grasp my hand in his two rotted ones. He stopped in mid-motion, but the raised and bandaged hands seemed even more touching in their imploring helplessness.

"Yes, I'll get some books for you." *But not come back here*, I thought. *I'll give some books to your Kapalika friends, but to hell with that* return *crap*. But before I could phrase the thoughts out loud, Das spoke again.

"I would especially love to read the work of that new American poet, Edwin Arlington Robinson," he rushed on quickly. "I have read only one new poem of his, 'Richard Cory,' but the ending is so beautiful, so perfectly applicable to my own situation, to my own ambitions, that I dream about it constantly. If you could bring such a work?"

I could only gape. *That new American poet*? Finally, not knowing what else to say, terrified of saying the wrong thing, I nodded. "Yes," I managed to get out. "I'll try."

The sad and twisted form turned and left the room. A second later so did I. The black curtains clung to me for a second as if restraining me, refusing to let me escape, but then I was free. Free!

Calcutta looked beautiful to me. Weak sunlight filtering through the clouds, crowds of people, the riot of afternoon traffic—I looked at it all with a joyous sense of relief that added a glow to the scene. Then I remembered Das's final comment and doubts assailed me. No, I would think about that later. For now I was *free*.

The two Kapalikas had been waiting at the bottom of the stairway. Their services as guides were needed for only a few minutes to lead me through the *chawl* to a main street where I managed to wave down a taxi. Before leaving me, one of them handed me a soiled card with the note *In front of Kalighat—9:00* scrawled on it. "This is where I'm to bring the books?" I asked the thinner man. His nod was both affirmation and farewell.

Then the black and yellow cab was poking through barely moving traffic and I spent ten minutes just reveling in my release from tension. *What a goddamn experience*! Morrow would never believe it. Already I found it hard to believe. Sitting there, probably surrounded by crazy Calcutta street thugs, talking to what was left of one of the world's great poets. *What a goddamn experience*!

This kind of story would never work for *Harper's*. The *National Enquirer*, perhaps, but not *Harper's*. I laughed out loud, and the sweaty little cabdriver turned in his seat to stare at the crazy American. I grinned and spent several minutes writing potential leads and weighting the story so it would have the proper dried and cynical attitude for Morrow. Too late I realized that I should have been noting my location, but by then we were miles from where I'd hailed the cab.

Finally I recognized the large buildings that meant we were near the center of the city. About two blocks from the hotel, I had the driver let me out in front of a dilapidated storefront with a large sign proclaiming MANNY'S BOOKSELLER. The interior was a maze of metal shelves and tall heaps of books, old, new, some thick with dust, most from English publishers.

It took me about thirty minutes to find eight books of good, recent poetry. There was no collection by Robinson, but a *Pocket Book of Modern Verse* had "Richard Cory" as well as "The Dark Hills" and "Walt Whitman." I turned the yellow paperback over in my hands and frowned at it. Could I have misunderstood Das's message? I thought not.

Deciding nothing then, I nonetheless spent several minutes choosing the last two books just on the basis of their size. As the bookseller was counting out my change in odd-shaped coins, I asked him where I could find a drugstore. He frowned and shook his head, but after several attempts I explained my needs. "Ah, yes, yes," he said. "A chemist's." He gave me directions to a shop between the bookstore and the hotel.

It was almost 6 P.M. when I got back to the Oberoi Grand. The Communist pickets were squatting along the curb, brewing tea over small over fires. I waved at them almost cheerily and reentered the air-conditioned security of another world.

I lay half dozing while Calcutta moved into evening. The buoyant excitement and relief had drained away to be replaced by a weight of exhaustion and indecision. I kept replaying the afternoon's encounter, trying in vain to lessen the incredible horror of Das's disfigurement. The longer I denied the images that flickered behind my closed eyelids, the more terrible their reality became.

". . . so beautiful, so perfectly applicable to my own situation, to my own ambitions, that I dream about it constantly."

I did not have to open the newly purchased paperback to know the poem of which Das had spoken.

"And Richard Cory, one calm summer night,
Went home and put a bullet through his head."

Simon and Garfunkel had made that particular image accessible to everyone in their song of the previous decade.

I dream about it constantly.

It was almost seven P.M. I changed my trousers, washed up, and went downstairs for a light dinner of curried rice and fried dough that Amrita had always called *poori* but that the menu referred to as *loochi*. With the meal I drank two cold quart bottles of Bombay beer and felt less depressed by the time I went back up to the room an hour later. As I came down the hall I thought I heard the room phone ringing, but by the time I'd fumbled out my key the sound had stopped.

The brown sack was where I had tossed it on the closet shelf. The .25-caliber automatic was smaller than I had remembered. Perhaps the very *toyness* of the little pistol helped me to determine what to do next.

I removed the package of razor blades and the bottle of glue from the chemist's sack. Then I tested three of the larger books for size, but only the hardback of Lawrence Durrell's poetry seemed right. I flinched before beginning; all of my life I've hated the thought of damaging a book.

It took me forty minutes of hacking away, always worried that I was going to slice a finger off, before I could say I was finished. The wastebasket was half filled with shredded paper. The interior of the book looked as if rats had chewed at it for years, but the little automatic fit perfectly in the space I had hollowed out.

Just seeing it there made my pulse pound. I continued to tell myself that I could always change my mind and throw the thing in an alley somewhere. Actually, the book would be a clever way to get it out of the hotel so I could toss it. Or so I told myself.

But I took the pistol out of its nest and gingerly pressed the loaded clip until it clicked and locked. I searched but could find no safety. Then I set the pistol back in the book and carefully glued the pages together at several points.

I dream about it constantly.

I shook my head and packed the books in the brown bag lettered MANNY'S BOOKSELLER. The Durrell went third from the bottom.

It was 8:50. I closed up the room and moved quickly down the hall. That was when the elevator doors opened and Amrita stepped out carrying Victoria in her arms.

Chapter Thirteen

"And midnight, bestial cries . . .
Who is enemy to whom, who—
In the ferocity of this false city?"
—Siddheswar Sen

"Bobby it was *dreadful*. The one o'clock flight was delayed until three. We sat there and sat there, and the air conditioning wasn't working much of the time. The stewardess said that it was a mechanical problem, but a Bombay businessman next to me said the pilot and the flight engineer were having some sort of feud. He said this had happened several times in the past few weeks. Then they brought the plane back to the terminal and we all had to get off. Victoria had spit up all over me and I didn't have time to change into the other blouse I'd packed in the carry-on bag. Oh, It was *dreadful*, Bobby."

"Uh-huh," I said and glanced at my watch. It was just 9:00.

Amrita was sitting on the bed, but I still stood by the open door. I could not believe that she and the baby were actually there. *Damn, damn, damn.* I had the urge to grab Amrita and shake her fiercely. I was dizzy with fatigue and confusion.

"Then they told us to board another flight to Delhi that stopped in Benares and Khajuraho. I would have just been able to make the Pan Am connection if it had left on time."

"But it didn't," I said tonelessly.

"Of *course* not. And our luggage was never transferred. Still, I was planning to take the seven-thirty flight to Bombay and fly BA to London, but the incoming flight from Bombay had to go to Madras because of a problem with the landing lights at the Calcutta airport. They rescheduled the flight for eleven but, Bobby, I was so *tired,* and Victoria had been crying for *hours*. . . ."

"I understand," I said.

"Oh, Bobby, I called and called but you weren't in. The manager promised to give you my message."

"He didn't," I said. "I saw him when I came in, but he didn't say anything."

"That *matyeryebyets,*" muttered Amrita. "He *promised.*" Amrita never indulged in cursing unless she could do so in the anonymity of another language. She knew that I didn't speak Russian. What she did not know was that this particular obscenity had been my Polish grandfather's favorite Russian word to describe all Russians.

"It doesn't matter," I said. *This changes everything.*

"I'm sorry, but all I could think about was taking a cold shower, being able to feed Victoria, and leaving with you tomorrow."

"Sure," I said. I went over and kissed her on the forehead. I could not remember seeing Amrita so upset before. "It's all right. We'll leave tomorrow morning." I looked at my watch again. It was 9:08. "I'll be right back."

"You have to leave?"

"Yeah, for a few minutes. I have to give these books to someone. I'll only be a little while, kiddo." I stood in the doorway. "Listen, make sure this is locked and put the chain bolt on, okay? Don't open the door for anyone but me. If the phone rings, let it ring. Don't answer it. All right?"

"But why? What—"

"Just do what I say, damn it. I'll be back in thirty minutes or so. Please, Amrita, just do what I ask. I'll explain later."

I turned to go then but stopped when I saw Victoria waving her arms and legs from the blanket where Amrita had been changing her. I crossed the room, swept the baby up in the air, and blew noises on her bare stomach. She was naked, soft, wiggling with joy. She grinned widely at me and reached for my nose with both pudgy hands. She smelled of Johnson & Johnson Baby Shampoo, and her skin was soft beyond imagining. I laid her back down and bicycled her legs with my hands. "Take care of your mom until I get back, okay, Little One?"

Victoria stopped her wiggling and stared at me solemnly.

I kissed her stomach again, touched Amrita on the cheek, and hurried out.

I never got to the Kalighat. I had just come out the front door of the hotel and was thinking about how to get rid of the Durrell book when the black Premiere pulled up next to me. The heavy man in khaki was driving. A stranger opened the backdoor.

"Get in, please, Mr. Luczak."

I stepped back and clutched the bag of books to my chest. "I . . . I was supposed to go . . . to meet someone at the Kalighat," I said stupidly.

"Get in, please."

I stood frozen for several seconds. Then I looked up and down the street. The hotel entrance was only twenty paces away. An affluent-looking young Indian couple laughed together under the awning while porters carried their luggage from a gray Mercedes.

"Here," I said. "This is what I promised him." I fold the top of the sack over and handed it to the man in the backseat.

He made no effort to take the books. "Please get in, Mr. Luczak."

"Why?"

The man sighed and rubbed at his nose. "The poet wishes to see you. It will be brief. He says you agreed to this."

The heavyset driver frowned and turned sideways in his seat as if to say something. The man in the back put a hand lightly on the other's wrist and spoke. "The poet has something he wishes to give you. Please get in, Mr. Luczak."

I was amazed to find myself bending to enter the vehicle. The door slammed and we accelerated into traffic. Into the Calcutta night.

Rain and flames. Highways, side streets, alleys, and muddy ruts past overgrown ruins. The glow of lanterns and reflected city lights. And through it all, I waited for the Kapalika to turn to me, to demand to inspect the books. I waited for the shouts and fists to follow.

We rode in silence. I held the sack of books on my lap and

kept my face to the window, although I remember seeing little detail except my own pale reflection staring back. Eventually we stopped before a high iron gate. Somewhere nearby, two tall brick chimneys poured flame into the night. This was not the way I had come before. A man in black came out of the drizzle and opened the gate to let us pass.

The headlights revealed empty brick buildings, railroad sidings, and a small mountain of dirt on which an abandoned truck lay half-buried in the weeds. When we finally stopped it was in front of a wide door illuminated by a yellow bulb. Insects threw themselves at the light.

"Get out, please."

There were doors and corridors. Two men in black carrying flashlights joined us. From somewhere there came the muted strum and crash of sitar and drums. At the top of a narrow staircase we stopped and the men in black spoke sharply to the driver. Then came the search.

One of the men took the sack of books. I stook passively while rough hands patted my sides, poked along my inner thighs, and ran quickly up and down my legs. The driver opened the package and took out the first three paperbacks. He flipped the pages almost angrily, tossed them back in, and removed a larger, hardback book. He showed it to the other three. It was not the Durrell anthology. The man in khaki tossed it back in, folded the sack, and handed the package to me without speaking.

I stood there and began to breathe again.

The Kapalika in black gestured with his flashlight and I followed him up another short staircase and then to the right down a narrow hallway. He held a door open, and I entered.

The room was no larger than the first one we had met in, but there were no curtains here. A kerosene lantern sat on a wooden shelf next to a porcelain cup, some wooden bowls, a few books, and a tiny bronze statue of the Buddha. Strange that the avatar of Kali should keep an image of Buddha near.

Das sat hunched and cross-legged on the floor near a low table. He was studying a slim book, but he looked up as I entered. The brighter light made his affliction all the more evident.

"Ah, Mr. Luczak."

"Mr. Das."

"You were kind to return."

I looked around the tiny room. An open doorway in the back led to darkness. From somewhere came the smell of incense. I could faintly hear the discordant strumming of a sitar.

"Those are the books?" asked Das and gestured clumsily with his heavily wrapped hands.

"Yes." I knelt on the wooden floor and set the package on the low table. An offering. The lantern hissed. The greenish-yellow light illuminate circles of flaking corruption on the poet's right cheek. Deep fissures in his scalp showed whitely against the darker skin. Mucus clogged Das's torn nostrils, and his breath whistled audibly over the hiss of the lantern.

"Ahh," sighed Das. He laid his hand almost reverently on the wrinkled paper. "Manny's Booksellers. Yes, I used to know him well, Mr. Luczak. Once, during the war, I sold Manny my collection of romantic poets when rent money was scarce. He set them aside until I could buy them back some years later." Das's large, liquid eyes turned up to look at me. Again I was all but overwhelmed by the knowledge of pain visible there. "You brought the Edwin Arlington Robinson?"

"Yes," I said. My voice trembled and I roughly cleared my

throat. "I'm not sure that I think as much of him as you do. You might reconsider. His 'Richard Cory' really is not worthy of a poet. It holds out no hope."

"Sometimes there is no hope," whispered Das.

"There's always some hope, Mr. Das."

"No, Mr. Luczak, there is not. Sometimes there is only pain. And acquiescence to pain. And, perhaps, defiance at the world which demands such pain."

"Defiance is a form of hope, is it not, sir?"

Das looked at me for a long minute. Then he glanced quickly toward the darkened back room and lifted the volume he had been reading. "This is for you, Mr. Luczak." He laid it on the table so that I would not have to take it from his hands.

It was an old book, thin, beautifully bound, with thick, heavy parchment pages. I ran my hand over the embossed fabric cover and opened it. The heavy pages had not yellowed or grown brittle with age. The spine had not stiffened. Everything about the thin volume spoke of craftsmanship and care.

Some of the poems were in Bengali, some in English. Those in English I recognized immediately. The flyleaf held a long inscription in Bengali, but the same hand had penned a final note in English: *For young Das, the most promising of my 'Chosen Eight.' Affectionately—* The signature would have been indecipherable had I not seen it very recently, behind glass, hastily scrawled beneath a Nobel Prize acceptance speech. *Rabindranath Tagore, March, 1939.*

"I can't accept this, sir."

Das only stared at me. The eyes were ancient beyond age, sad, yet lit with a purpose I had not seen before. He stared at me and I did not argue again.

A tremor went through the poet's body, and I realized what exertion it must take for him to speak, to concentrate. I rose to leave.

"No," whispered Das. "Closer."

I dropped to one knee. There was a smell that rose from the poor man's disintegrating flesh. My own skin crawled as I leaned over to hear better.

"Today," he rasped, "I spoke of power. All violence is power. *She* is such power. She knows no limits. Time means nothing to Her. Pain carries the sweet smell of sacrifice to Her. This is Her time. Her song knows no ending. Her time has come round once again, you see." He slipped into Bengali, then a smattering of French, then a torrent of Hindi. He was raving. His eyes were focused elsewhere, and the pained, sibilant rush of words went nowhere.

"Yes," I said sadly.

"Violence is power. Pain is power. It is Her time. Do you see? Do you see?" His voice rose to a shout. I wanted to hush him before the Kapalikas rushed in, but I could only stay there on one knee and listen. The lantern sputtered in rhythm to his agitated hissing. "The centre cannot hold. Mere anarchy is loosed upon the world! Her song has just begun . . ."

The old man leaned forward, dry breath wheezing up out of his damaged lungs. He seemed to come back to himself then. The wild, distracted look left his eyes to be replaced by a terrible weariness. The leprous hand stroked the stack of books on the table as if it were a cat. When he spoke, his voice was calm, almost conversational. "Know this, Mr. Luczak. This is the age of the unspeakable. But there are acts beyond the unspeakable."

I stared, but Das was not looking at me. He was not looking at anything in the room.

"*We* have always been capable of committing the unspeakable," he whispered. "*She* can commit the unthinkable. Now we are free to follow."

Das stopped. Saliva moistened his chin. I knew now that his mind had been damaged. The silence stretched out to several minutes. Finally he brought himself back by a great effort and focused his gaze on me. A rotting stump of a hand, wrapped in filthy, reeking rags, raised itself in a gentle benediction.

"Go. Go now. Go."

I was shaking violently when I stumbled out into the corridor. Flashlights bobbed through the darkness toward me. A rough hand took the Tagore volume, turned it over, handed it back. I clutched it in both hands and followed the circle of light down the maze of halls and stairways.

We were at the open door; I could see the car and smell the rain, when suddenly the shots rang out. Two sharp sounds, almost simultaneous, sounding flat and final in the dark.

The four men stopped, shouted back and forth in Bengali, and ran back up the stairs. For several seconds I was left alone at the open door. I stared blankly out into the dark and rain. I was numb, disbelieving, afraid to act, barely able to think. Then the heavy man in khaki ran back down the stairs, seized me by the shirtfront, and dragged me upstairs with the other running men.

The lantern still spilled its cold white light. Flashlight beams bobbed and converged. I was pushed forward, scraping through shoulders, past the circle of noise into a center of silence.

Das seemed to be resting his head on the table. The small

chromed pistol—gripped firmly in his left hand—was thrust obscenely into the bulging mouth. One eye was almost closed, while the other showed only the white and seemed to balloon out as if some great pressure were still building within the shattered skull. Already a pool of dark blood had accumulated in the steady flow from mouth, ears, and nostrils. The air was redolent with incense and cordite.

There were shouts. At least eight or nine men were in the room, more in the dark hall. One man was screaming. Another accidentally jabbed me in the chest as he swung his arms around. The man in khaki reached down and jerked the pistol from Das's clenched jaws, breaking a front tooth off as he did so. He waved the bloodied pistol and let out a high, thin wailing that might have been a prayer or a curse. More men shoved into the room.

This is not real. I felt almost nothing. There was a loud humming in my ears. The buffeting all around me was a distant, unrelated thing.

Another man entered. He was older, bald, and wearing a simple peasant's *dhoti*. The plainness of his appearance, however, was belied by the deference with which the crowd parted for him. He looked down on Das's body for a moment and then touched the leprous head gently, almost reverently, the way the poet had touched my gift of books. Then the man turned black eyes my direction and said something softly to the crowd.

Hands closed on my shirt and arms, and they took me away into the dark.

I sat in an empty room for an unknown time. There were sounds beyond the door. A small oil lamp gave me light. I sat on the floor and tried to think about Amrita and the baby but could not. I could concentrate on nothing. My head ached. After a while I picked up the book they had left me with and read some of Tagore's English poems.

Sometime later three men entered. One held out a small cup and saucer to me. I saw the steam rising form the dark tea.

"No, thank you," I said and returned to my reading.

The heavy man said, "Drink."

"No."

The man in khaki took my left hand and broke my little finger with an upward twist of his wrist. I screamed. The book dropped to the floor. I grabbed the injured hand and rocked back and forth in agony. The tea was offered again.

"Drink."

I took the cup and drank. The bitter tea scalded my tongue. I coughed and spluttered some out, but the three watched until I swallowed the rest. My little finger jutted backward almost comically, and there was a nerve of fire running up my wrist and arm to a point at the base of my neck.

Someone took the empty cup and two of them left. The heavy man smirked and patted me on the shoulder as one would a child. Then they left me alone with the bitter taste of tea and cowardice in my mouth.

I tried to tug the finger back into place, but even the act of touching it made me cry out and come close to fainting. Sweat poured from me and my skin turned cold and clammy. I picked up the book with my right hand, flipped to the page I had been reading, and tried to concentrate on a poem about a chance encounter on a train. I was still rocking slightly and crooning soft syllables of pain.

My throat burned from whatever had been in the tea. A few

minutes later the words on the page slid crazily to the left and ran together.

I tried to stand then, but the oil lamp chose that second to flare into blinding brilliance and then to fade to blackness.

Blackness. Pain and blackness.

The pain brought me out of my own comforting darkness into a less benign but no less absolute lack of light. I was lying on what felt like a cold stone floor. There was not the faintest gleam of light. I sat up and cried aloud as the pain coursed up my left arm. The ache throbbed more fiercely with each heartbeat.

I felt around with my right hand. Nothing. Cool stone and hot, moist air. My eyes did not adapt to the dark. The only time I had ever experienced darkness this total was one time spelunking in Missouri with friends when we had turned off all our carbide lamps. It was a claustrophobic, inward-pressing darkness. I moaned as a thought struck. *What if they have blinded me?*

But my eyelids felt normal enough to my hasty touch. There was no pain in my face, only the sickening dizziness that the tea had brought. *No, thank you,* I had said. I giggled, but stifled the ragged sounds while I could.

I began crawling, cradling my throbbing left hand to my chest. My fingers encountered a wall—smooth masonry or stone. Was I underground?

When I stood up, the dizziness grew worse. I leaned against the wall, pressing my cheek to the cool surface. A quick touch told me that they had left me dressed in my own clothes. I thought to search through my pockets. Shirt pockets held an airline receipt, the smaller of my two notebooks, a felt-tip pen, and flakes of clay from the stone I'd carried there earlier. Trouser pockets held my room key, wallet, coins, a slip of paper, and the book of matches Amrita had given me.

Matches!

I forced myself to hold the matchbook in my throbbing left hand while I struck a match, shielded it, lifted it.

The room was actually an alcove, three solid walls and a black curtain. *Déjà vu* rose up in me. I had time to lift back the edge of the curtain and to sense a larger darkness beyond before the match burned to my fingertips.

I waited, listening. Currents of air moved against my face. I dared not light another match in case someone was waiting in the larger room. Over the ragged sound of my own breathing I could hear a soft, susurrant undertone. The breathing of a giant. Or of a river.

Testing with my foot, I slid past the heavy cloth and into an immense, open space. I could see nothing, but it *felt* immense. The air seemed slightly cooler and moved to random currents, bringing to me the scent of incense and of something heavier, as rich and heavy as the smell of week-old garbage.

I took short steps, moved my right hand in front of me cautiously, and tried not to remember the images—filtered through the memory of sing-song English—which nonetheless rose to mind. Twenty-five steps brought me in contact with nothing. The Kapalikas could be back at any second. They could be there *now.* I began to run. I ran heedlessly in the dark, openmouthed, clutching my left hand to me.

Something struck me in the head. I saw pinwheel colors and fell, striking stone, falling again. I landed on my left hand and yelled in pain and shock. The matchbook slipped from my fingers. I kneeled and felt around wildly for it, ignoring the pain, expecting a second blow to descend at any second.

My right hand found the cardboard square. I was shaking so hard that it took three strikes to light the first match. My gaze followed the light upward.

I was kneeling at the base of the Kali idol. My head had struck her lower, outstretched hand. I blinked as blood trickled from my brow into my right eye.

I stood up despite the terrible dizziness. I would not kneel in front of that thing.

"Do you hear that, bitch?" I said loudly to the dark stone face four feet above me. "I'm not kneeling in front of you. Do you hear that?" The blank eyes were not even looking my way. The teeth and tongue were a child's comic book terror.

"Bitch," I said, and the match burned out. I stumbled off the low dais, away from the idol and into the black emptiness. Ten steps, and I stopped. There was no reason to feel around in the dark now. There was little time. I lit a match and held it until I could fumble out the airline receipt. My tiny torch threw a fifteen-foot circle of light when I held it aloft and looked around for a door, a window. I froze until the flaming paper scorched my hand.

The idol was gone.

The pedestal and dais where it had stood a second before were empty.

Something scraped and scrabbled beyond the fading light. There was movement to my left, and then I had to drop the burning paper and the darkness returned.

I struck another match. Its puny glow barely illuminated me. I pulled the spiral notebook from my safari shirt pocket, tore pages out with my teeth, and switched hands. The match died. Something made a sound not ten feet from me in the dark.

Another match. I spat out the crinkled pages, kneeled, and set the flame to them before the blue glow died. Light flared up from the tiny pyre.

The thing froze in mid-movement. It crouched on six limbs like some huge and hairless spider, but fingers groped and twitched at the end of some of its limbs. The neck arched, jutting the gaunt face toward me. Breasts hung down like eggs from an insect's belly.

You're not real.

Kali opened her mouth and hissed at me. Her jaw gaped wide. The crimson tongue slid out, five inches, ten inches; it unrolled like crimson, melting wax, until it touched the floor where it curled at the tip like a questing serpent and slid quickly across the cold stone toward me.

I screamed then. I screamed again and put the rest of my notebook to the flame. then I lifted the burning cardboard and stepped *toward* the hissing nightmare.

The tongue whipped sideways, barely missing my foot, and the apparition scrabbled backward on six bent limbs until it disappeared in the darkness beyond my flickering light. The notebook was already burning my fingers. I flung the dying brand in the direction of the scraping sounds and turned and ran the other way.

I ran full speed, seeing nothing, sensing nothing, arms pulled in, and if I hadn't struck another match while I ran I would have run headfirst into the waiting wall. I hit it anyway and screamed as the flame expired. I spun around while striking another match. Eyes gleamed coldly to my right. There was a sound a cat makes when vomiting.

I backed up against the wooden wall. If there had been a curtain of any sort, anything combustible, I would have torched it then. Better to die in the flaming brilliance of a burning building than to be alone in the dark with *it*.

I slid along the wall to my left, lighting match after match until only a few remained. The eyes were no longer visible. I felt boards, splinters, and nails against my injured hand but no door. No window. The scrabbling sounds were everywhere, cartilage scraping on stone and wood. The dizziness was much worse now and threatened to throw me to the floor.

There has to be an exit.

I stopped, lifted my curling match, took a breath, and ignited the rest of my matchbook. There, in the brief, bright flare, on the wall three feet above my head, were visible the outlines of a window. The panes were intact but painted black. The light faded as the dying flames nipped at my fingers.

Dropping the burning matchbook, I crouched and leaped. The window frame was inset, and my fingers found a grip. My legs battered against the smooth wall, trying to find leverage. Somehow I pulled myself to one elbow on the narrow sill, my cheek touching the blacked-out squares of glass. I balanced there, my arms shaking uncontrollably, preparing to break the painted glass with my forearm.

Something grabbed at my legs.

My forearm came down full weight on my broken finger, and in a second's instinctive arching I teetered backward, lost the precarious balance, and slid down the wall to sprawl on the hard floor.

The darkness was absolute.

I had risen to my knees when I felt the presence near me.

Four hands closed on me.

* * *

Four arms roughly lifted me and carried me.

One's spirit does not depart immediately after death, but, rather, watches the disposition of events much as a disinterested spectator might.

There were distant voices. A light shone through my eyelids and then was gone. Cool rain fell on my face and my arms.

Rain?

More voices, raised in argument now. Somewhere a tinny car engine started up, exhaust rattling. Gravel crunched under tires. My forehead ached, my left hand pulsed intolerably, and my nose itched.

This can't be what dead is.

The noise of a four-cylinder engine was very loud. I tried to look around, and discovered that my right eye would not open. It was caked shut with drying blood from the cut on my brow.

The idol's hand.

Through the slit of my left eye, I saw that I was being supported—half dragged—by the heavy man in khaki and another Kapalika. Several other men, including the bald one in white, were talking animatedly in the rain.

You can go back to sleep. No!

The rain, my aching hand, and an intolerable itch kept me from sliding down the dark chute into unconsciousness again. One of the men supporting me turned his face my way, and I quickly shut my eye—but not before I caught a glimpse of a green van, the driver's door dented, windowless in the back. A sick sense of recognition washed through me.

The men continued to argue, voices rising shrilly. I listened, and it was as if I suddenly had become proficient in Bengali. I knew without any doubt that they were discussing what to do with my body once they carried out the bald man's orders concerning me.

Finally, the man in khaki grunted, and he and another Kapalika carried me to the back of the van. The tops of my feet dragged across gravel. They let me fall forward into the airless interior. My head struck the side of the truck and struck again on the metal floorboards. I risked opening my eye long enough to see the heavy man and the other Kapalika climb in the back with me while another jumped into the front left passenger seat. The driver turned and asked something. The heavy man kicked me sharply in the side. The air rushed out of me but I did not stir. The Kapalika laughed and said something that began with "Nay."

That's two I owe you, you fat motherfucker.

The anger helped. The hot fire of it served to clear my mind and to quell the fog of terror that filled me. Still, as the van began to move and the sound of crunching gravel came to me through the metal against my ear, I could think of absolutely nothing to do. This was the point in a thousand movies I'd watched where the character overpowers his captors after a vicious fight.

I could not fight them.

I doubted if I could sit up without help. And not all of my weakness was because of whatever drug they had put in the tea. I hurt already. I didn't want them to hurt me anymore. My only possible weapon was to continue feigning unconsciousness and to pray that this would give me another few minutes before they hurt me again.

He broke my finger. I had never had a broken bone before. Not even as a child. It was something I had been vaguely proud of, like having a perfect attendance record in school.

Now this sweaty son of a bitch had broken my finger with no more thought or effort than I would take to turn the dial on a TV. It was this matter-of-fact callousness that convinced me that these men would not just dump me off somewhere to let me find my way back to the hotel.

All violence is an exercise in power, Mr. Luczak.

I would have begged them to let me go then if a greater fear had not held me in check. I was paralyzed by the dark uncertainty of what they would do next; but somewhere, just beneath the panicked scurry of my thoughts, was the realization that as long as they focused their anger on *me*, Amrita and Victoria would be left alone. So I said nothing, did nothing. Nothing except lie there in the hot darkness, smelling the dried shit and old vomit stink of the van's interior, listening to the banter and nostril-clearing sounds of the four Kapalikas, and praising each precious second that passed without further pain being inflicted.

The van shifted up through gears and moved at speed onto a paved section of street. Several times the high sound of the exhaust echoed back to us as if we were between buildings. Occasionally I could hear the blare of trucks, and once I sneaked a glance that showed reflected rectangles of headlights flitting along the van's inner wall. A second later the Kapalika in khaki said something to me in soft, sneering Bengali. My heart began to pound.

We stopped then. The brakes squealed, and the other Kapalika in the back with us shouted angrily as he was thrown forward. Our driver shouted a curse and palmed several sharp blasts on the horn. I could hear a shouted reply from outside. There was the crack of a whip followed by the angry bellow of an ox. Our driver screamed obscenities and leaned on the horn.

A minute later I heard the front van doors open as both the driver and the other Kapalika in front jumped out to continue shouting at whatever obstacle was in our way. The curses continued. The third Kapalika squeezed forward, jumped out, and joined the unseen argument. That left only the man in khaki in the van with me.

This is my chance.

Knowing that I had to act was not enough to make me act. I knew that I should make a dash for the open doors, strike out at the squatting man next to me. *Do something.* But although I somehow was convinced that this would be my last chance at surprise, my last chance to escape, I could not translate my thoughts into actions. Only lying there seemed to offer the guarantee of a few more minutes without confrontation. Without new pain. Without being killed.

Suddenly the rear doors exploded open. The heavy man, shoved violently from the side, fell clumsily to the floorboards. A hand gripped my arm and roughly pulled me to a sitting position. My legs flopped outside and I blinked in pain, my right eye twitching open against a crust of blood.

"Come! Stand! Hurry." It was Krishna's voice. It was Krishna's face looming over me, hair flying, sharp teeth exposed in a gleeful, maniacal grin. It was Krishna's thin right arm that braced me upright and supported me firmly when I almost fell forward onto my face.

"*Nahin!*" shouted the Kapalika and vaulted out of the back of the truck. He was twice as broad as Krishna and his face was distorted with fury. "*Mutė!*"

Krishna's left hand shot up, straight-armed, a crossing guard stopping traffic. The heel of his palm, rigid as a brick, went forward into the advancing man's face. The Kapalika's nose flattened like a pulped piece of fruit. He screamed then and arched backward, banging his head against the van's rear door, dropping to his knees, pitching forward. Still holding me upright with his right arm, Krishna brought his left leg up rapidly in a stiff arc that ended when his shin slammed into the heavy man's throat just under the hollow of the jaw.

There was a sound like thin plastic breaking, and the Kapalika's scream cut off abruptly.

"Come! Hurry!" Krishna pulled me along, tugging me upright as I teetered to one side. I shuffled as fast as I could, trying to find my balance on legs that felt as if they were full of Novocaine. I looked over my shoulder at the fallen man, at the van with all of its doors open like broken wings, and at the bullock cart beyond, blocking the intersection and the narrow street. The three Kapalikas stood frozen next to the cart. For several seconds they stared at us with stupefied expressions and then began running our way, shouting, waving their arms. One man already had what looked to be a long knife in his hand. The bullock cart creaked off into the darkness.

"Run!" shouted Krishna. My shirt ripped as he pulled me along. I almost fell then, waving my arms as I pitched forward, but he grabbed the back of my torn shirt and pulled me up.

We ran left into a pitch-black alley, left again into a courtyard bathed in lantern light. An old woman looked up in surprise as we came in through an open door. Krishna swept aside a curtain of beads and we leaped across sleeping forms on the floor of a dark room to go out a back way.

Shouts and screams rose behind us as we emerged into yet

another courtyard. The three Kapalikas exploded from the dark doorway just as we ducked into another, narrower gap between buildings. Garbage was ankle-deep there, and we bounced and splashed through it. Even there were the sheeted, silent figures, squatting, huddling from the water that still dripped from eaves and filled the low spots. Krishna actually jumped over the bony knees of one squatting form that looked to be more corpse than man.

I could not keep up with Krishna, and when we had to run up two flights of wooden stairs, I finally collapsed to my knees on a dark landing, gasping for breath. The Kapalikas shouted to one another in the courtyard below.

Krishna shoved me through an open door. There were a dozen people in the room, squatting near an open fire or huddled back against cracked wallboards. Part of the ceiling had collapsed into the center of the room, and broken masonry and plaster had made a small mound upon which they had built their fire. Smoke streaked the walls and sagging ceiling.

Krishna hissed a rapid sentence in which I thought I heard the word *Kali*. No one looked up at us. Deadened eyes continued to watch the low flames.

There were footsteps on the stairs. A man shouted. Krishna grabbed my elbow tightly and led me into a tiny room empty except for several bronze pots and a small statue of Ganesha. An open window gave out onto a narrow alley between the buildings.

Krishna stepped to the window and jumped. I stepped to the low sill and hesitated. The alley could not have been more that five feet wide. It was at least a twenty-foot drop to nothing but darkness. I could hear a squelching sound where Krishna had jumped but nothing else. I knew I couldn't leap into that lightless pit.

Suddenly I could hear the Kapalikas shouting at the entrance to the outer room. A woman screamed. I cradled my left hand and jumped.

The garbage must have been seven or eight feet deep where I landed. I went into it up to my thighs and fell sideways into something soft and vile. Rats squealed and scurried away along the walls. I could see nothing. My legs made soft, gasping sounds as I tried to wade forward in the narrow space. I began thrashing about in panic when I continued to sink above my waist in the yielding, putrid mass.

"Shhh." Krishna grabbed my shoulders and held me still. Above us, the faint rectangle of light was obscured as a man leaned out. He disappeared back into the room.

"Quickly!" Krishna seized my arm and we began wading down the reeking trench. I pressed off from a wall and tried to swim forward through the soft refuse. Our arms flailed at each other to gain leverage, but it was like wading through waist-deep mud.

Suddenly, behind us, someone held a flaming board out the window from which we'd jumped. The man deliberately dropped the brand into the muck of the alley. It bounced once and set some greasy rags to smoldering where it came to a stop. Krishna and I froze. We could not have been more than shadows amid the heaps of garbage all around us, but one of the Kapalikas pointed our way and shouted to the other two.

I don't know whether the man with the knife jumped or was pushed, but he screamed as he fell into the alley with us. The torch was beginning to sputter out in the dampness and human waste, but it and the burning rags gave enough light to show hundreds of furry, squirming forms—some as large as cats—hunching over the heaps of waste toward us as they fled the smoke.

My skin actually rippled in revulsion. I had not known that such a reaction was physically possible. Krishna leaped back the way we had come. The Kapalika rose like a diver coming to the surface of a pool. His arms flailed and steel glinted in his right hand. The fire was all but extinguished now, and Krishna was less than a shadow as he closed with the other man. Their grunts were barely audible over the rising screech of the fleeing rats. Fat, wet bodies touched my bare arms, and I vomited then, retching helplessly into piles of foul-smelling darkness.

The two Kapalikas above us leaned and strained to see, but the alley was in almost total darkness once again. I *thought* that I could see Krishna and the other man pivoting in awkward jerks, two clumsy dancers in slow motion. Sparks flew as the Kapalika's knife hand was slammed repeatedly into the brick wall. Then I *thought* I saw Krishna behind the other, pulling back long hair, forcing him face first into the yielding pit. I squinted in the darkness and thought I saw Krishna's knee in the Kapalikas arching back, forcing him deeper, deeper . . . but then Krishna was next to me, tugging me with him, wading with me away from the window.

The two Kapalikas disappeared from the dim rectangle above us. Our own movement was nightmarishly slow. One of us would become stuck and use the other's body as leverage to free himself.

I had waded most of the length of the alley when a sudden thought made me want to retch again. There was no light ahead of us. *What if we're going the wrong way, toward a brick wall, a dead end?*

We were not. Five more waded steps, and the alley turned sharply to the right and the level of trash diminished. Fifteen more steps and we were out.

We stumbled out onto a wet and empty street. Rats brushed by our ankles, hopping in their panic, and splashed off through rain-filled gutters. I looked left and right but could see no sign of the last two Kapalikas.

"Quickly, Mr. Luczak," hissed Krishna; and we ran across the street, moved quickly over tilted slabs of sidewalk, and blended into the dark shadows under sagging metal awnings. We ran from shop to shop. Occasionally there would be sleeping forms in the wet doorways, but no one called out; no one tried to stop us.

We turned down another street and then dodged through a short alley onto an even wider street where a truck was just disappearing from sight. There were streetlights here, and an electric glow came from numerous windows. Above us, a red flag flapped in the breeze. I could hear the sound of traffic on nearby streets.

We stopped for a minute in the dark doorway of a caged and shuttered store. We were both gasping, bent over from the pain of exertion, but Krishna's narrow face showed the gleeful, blood-sport mask of joy I had seen there that first night on the bus. He started to speak, took another breath, and straightened up.

"I will leave you now, Mr. Luczak," he said.

I stared at him. He steepled his fingers, bowed slightly, and turned to walk away. His sandals made soft sounds in the puddles.

"Wait!" I cried. He did not stop. "Just a minute. Hey!" He was almost lost to the shadows now.

I took a step forward into the pale circle of the streetlight. "Stop! *Sanjay,* stop!"

He stopped. Then he turned and took two slow steps in my direction. His long fingers seemed to twitch. "What did you say, Mr. Luczak?"

"Sanjay," I repeated, but it was more of a whisper this time. "I'm right, aren't I?"

He stood there, a basilisk with a wild corona of dark hair framing his terrible gaze. The smile appeared then and widened into something far worse than a shark's grimace. It was the grin of a hungry ghoul.

"I'm right, aren't I, *Sanjay*?" I paused to take a breath. I had no idea what to say next. But I had to say something—anything—to keep him at bay. "What's your game, Sanjay? What the fuck is going on?"

He did not move for several seconds; and I half expected a silent rush, long fingers reaching for my throat. Instead, he threw back his head an laughed. "Yes, yes, yes," he said. "There are many games, Mr. Luczak. *This* game is not yet over. Good-bye, Mr. Luczak."

He turned and trotted into the darkness.

Chapter 14

"Calcutta is a terrible stone in my heart"
—Sunil Gangopadhyay

If I had found a taxi sooner . . .

If I had gone straight to the hotel . . .

It took me the better part of an hour to get back to the hotel. At first I staggered from street to street, staying in the shadows, freezing when I saw anyone walking my direction. Once I jogged through an empty courtyard to get to a wider avenue from which came the sound of traffic.

A man lurched out of a shadowed doorway at me. I yelled, jumped back, and threw up my fists in an instinctive gesture. I screamed again when my little finger tried to bend with the rest of my left hand. The man—an old man in rags with a red bandana around his forehead—stumbled back in the act of saying "Baba" and let out his own scream of fear. The two of us left the courtyard in different directions.

I came out onto the avenue to see trucks passing, private cars swerving around cyclists, and, most welcome of all, a public bus moving slowly down the street. I banged on the side of the moving vehicle in my eagerness to board it. The driver stared as I dumped a pocketful of coins at him. Along with the required *paisas* there must have been several days' worth of his salary in the American money I dumped there.

The bus was crowded, and I squeezed through the standing passengers to find a position less visible from the street. There were no straps. I grabbed a metal bar and hung on to it as the swaying bus ground through gears and lurched from stop to stop.

For a while I fell into a half-dream state. The overload of the past few hours had left me drained of everything except the desire to stand there and *be safe*. Many blocks had passed before I realized that a wide space had been opened around me and that the other passengers were staring.

Haven't you ever seen an American before? I thought at them. Then I looked down at myself. My clothes were soaked and reeking from the unmentionable filth I had waded through. My shirt was ripped in at least two places and no one could have guessed that it had once been white. My bare arms were caked with scum and my right forearm was still redolent from my own vomit. The little finger on my left hand protruded at an impossible angle. From the way my brow and forehead felt, I had the beginning of a spectacular bruise there, and caked blood still adorned my brow, eyelid, and cheek. No doubt my hair and expression looked wilder than Krishna at his wildest.

"Hi," I said and gave a limp wave at the group. Women raised their saris over their faces, and the entire huddle pressed back until the driver shouted at them not to crowd him.

A thought occurred to me then. Where the hell was I? For all I knew, this might have been the nightly express to New Delhi. At the very least, the odds were great that I was going the wrong way.

"Does anyone here speak English?" I asked. The staring passengers pressed even farther away from me. I bent and peered out the barred windows. A few blocks passed before I saw the neon-lit facade of some sort of hotel or café. Several black and yellow cabs were parked out front.

"Hold it!" I called. "I'll get out here." I pressed through the quickly parting throng. The driver screeched to a halt in the middle of the street. There was no door to be opened. The crowd made way to let me pass.

I argued with the drivers for several minutes before I remembered that I still had my wallet. The three drivers had taken one look at me and decided that I was not worth their time. Then I remembered to take out my wallet and hold up a twenty-dollar bill. Suddenly the three were smiling, bowing, and opening their car doors for me. I settled into the first cab, said "Oberoi Grand," and closed my eyes. We roared away through rain-slick streets.

Several minutes later I realized that I was still wearing my watch. The dial was difficult to read, but when we passed a lighted intersection I could make it out. It said 11:28 . . . that was impossible! Only two hours since the car had brought me to Das? A lifetime had passed since then. I tapped the crystal, but the second hand continued pulsing steadily.

"Hurry!" I said to the driver.

"*Atcha*!" he called back happily. Neither of us had understood the other.

* * *

The assistant manager saw me enter the lobby and watched me with an expression of horror. He raised his hand. "Mr. Luczak!"

I waved at him and entered the elevator. I did not want to talk to him. The adrenalin and mindless euphoria were wearing away to be replaced by nausea, fatigue, and pain. I leaned against the wall of the elevator and held my left hand steady. What would I tell Amrita? My thoughts stirred sluggishly and I settled on a simple tale of being mugged. I would tell her the rest of the story someday. Perhaps.

It was midnight, but there were people in the hall. Our room door was open and it looked as if a party were going on. Then I saw the Sam Browne belts on the two policeman and the familiar beard and turban of Inspector Singh. *Amrita called the police. I said I'd be back in thirty minutes.*

Several people turned to watch me approach, and Inspector Singh stepped toward me. I began inventing details of the mugging—nothing serious enough to keep us in Calcutta an extra day!—and waved almost jauntily at the police. "Inspector! Who says there's never a policeman around when you need one?"

Singh said nothing. Then the scene registered on my exhausted mind. Other hotel guests were milling around, staring at the open door of our room. *The open door.*

I pushed past the Inspector and ran into the hotel room. I do not know what I expected to find, but my racing heart slowed as I saw Amrita sitting on the bed, speaking to an officer taking notes.

The relief made me sag back against the door. Everything was all right. Then Amrita looked at me; and in the pale, controlled calm of her absolutely expressionless face, I could see that everything was not all right after all. It might never be all right again.

"They've taken Victoria," she said. "They've stolen our baby."

"Why did you let her in? I *told* you not to let anyone in. Why did you let her in?" I had asked the same thing three times before. Amrita had answered three times. I sat with my back against the wall where I was slumped to the floor. My forearms rested on my raised knees and my broken finger jutted whitely. Amrita sat very straight on the edge of the bed, one hand lying primly atop the other. Inspector Singh sat nearby in a straight-backed chair, scrutinizing the both of us. The door to the hall was closed.

"She said she had brought the material back," said Amrita. "She wanted to exchange it. You and I were leaving in the morning."

"But . . . aw, Christ, kiddo—" I stopped and lowered my face.

"You didn't say not to talk to *her*, Bobby. I knew Kamakhya."

Inspector Singh cleared his throat. "Yet it was very late, Mrs. Luczak. Did this cause you any concern?"

"Yes," said Amrita and turned toward Singh. "I kept the chain hooked and asked her why she had come so late. She explained . . . she seemed embarrassed, Inspector . . . she explained that she had not been able to leave the house until her father was asleep. She said that she had called twice earlier."

"And had she, Mrs. Luczak?"

"The phone did ring twice, Inspector. Bobby had told me not to answer it. I didn't."

They both looked at me. I met Singh's gaze. I could not meet Amrita's.

"You are sure that you do not require medical assistance, Mr. Luczak? There is a doctor on call with this establishment."

"No. I'm sure." After the first few minutes, when Singh had asked what had happened to *me*, I had blurted out the entire story. It could not have been very coherent, but I omitted nothing but the fact that I had been the one who gave the pistol to Das. Inspector Singh had nodded and taken notes as if he heard such stories every evening.

It did not matter.

He turned back to Amrita. "I'm sorry to make you go back over this again, Mrs. Luczak, but can you estimate how long you were out of the room?"

Amrita trembled a bit through her icy control, and I could see the pit of hysteria and grief that lay under the surface. I wanted to go to her and take her in my arms. I did nothing.

"A minute, Inspector. Perhaps not that long. I was speaking to Kamakhya when suddenly I felt very dizzy. I excused myself, went into the bathroom to splash cold water on my face, and returned. Perhaps forty-five seconds."

"And the child?"

"Victoria . . . Victoria was asleep there. On the bed near the windows. We use . . . we use the pillows and cushion as a kind of . . . she likes to nestle, Inspector. She likes her head to be against something. And she won't roll off with the cushion there."

"Yes."

I pushed myself to my feet and walked to the foot of Amrita's bed. Anywhere as long as I didn't have to look at the other bed with it's empty circle of pillows and Victoria's blue and white blanket, still crumpled and moist where she had pulled it against her face in her sleep.

"You've heard all of this before, Inspector," I said. "When are you going to quit asking questions and get busy hunting for . . . for the person who has our baby?"

Singh looked at me with dark eyes. I remembered the pain in Das's gaze, and I understood a little better now that there might be no limit to hurting.

"We are searching, Mr. Luczak. The entire Metropolitan Police Force has been notified. No one in the hotel saw this woman leave. People on the street do not remember seeing such a person carrying a child or a bundle. I have sent a car to the address which Mrs. Luczak remembers from the sari shop. As you see, we have extended extra phone lines from the adjoining rooms so that we can receive communications while your line remains open."

"Remains open? Why?"

Singh glanced down, ran a thumb along the sharp crease of his trousers, and looked back. "For a ransom demand, Mr. Luczak. We must assume that there will be a ransom element to this kidnapping."

"Ah," I said and sat down heavily on the bed. The words had cut through me like sharp metal tabs that had to be swallowed. "I see. All right." I took Amrita's hand in mine. It was cold and limp. "But what about the Kapalikas?" I asked. "What if they're involved?"

Singh nodded. "We are checking into that, Mr. Luczak. You must remember that it is very late."

"But I gave you the description of the factory area where I met Das."

"Yes, and that may prove to be very helpful. But you should understand that there are scores of such places near the Hooghly in Old Calcutta. Hundreds, if you count warehouses and dock areas to the north. And all of them are private property. Many are owned by foreign interests. Are you sure, Mr. Luczak, that this place was near the river?"

"No. Not positive."

"And you remember no landmarks? No street names? No easily identifiable references?"

"No. Just the two chimneys. There was a slum—"

"Was there any sign that this was a permanent location for these men? Any sign of long-term habitation?"

I frowned. Other than Das's meager shelf of belongings, there had been no such sign. "There was the idol," I said at last. "They used the place as a temple. That idol couldn't be too easy to cart around."

"The idol that walked?" asked Singh. If there had been the slightest hint of sarcasm in his voice, I would have gone for him then, broken finger and everything.

"Yeah."

"And we do not *know* that they are involved, do we, Mr. Luczak?"

I cradled my hand and glared at him. "She's M. Das's niece, Inspector. She's bound to be involved somehow."

"No."

"What do you mean, 'no'?"

Singh took out a gold cigarette case. It was the first time that I had even seen anyone in real life tap a cigarette against a cigarette case before lighting up. "I mean, no, she is not M. Das's niece," he said.

Amrita gasped as if someone had slapped her. I stared.

"You said, Mrs. Luczak, that Miss Kamakhya Bahrati was the niece of the poet M. Das. The daughter of Das's younger sister, according to her own account. Is that correct?"

"Yes."

"M. Das had no sisters, Mrs. Luczak. At least, none who survived infancy. He had four living brothers, all farmers, all citizens of the same village in Bangladesh. You see, I have been case officer on the disappearance of Mr. M. Das for eight years. I am well acquainted with his circumstances. If you had mentioned being contacted by this woman when we spoke, Mr. Luczak, I could have informed you of this fact." Singh exhaled smoke and removed a shred of tobacco from his tongue.

The phone rang.

We all stared. It was one of the extra phones. Singh answered it. "Hā?" There was a long silence. "Shukriya," he said at last, and added, "Very good, sergeant."

"What is it?" I demanded.

Inspector Singh stubbed out his cigarette and stood. "There is little else we can do tonight, I am afraid. I will return in the morning. My men will be in the adjoining rooms through the night. Any call to your room will be monitored by an officer at the switchboard downstairs. That was my sergeant on the phone. The address Kamakhya Bahrati gave the shop was a false one, of course. She had returned to the shop to pick up the fabric in person. It took some time for my men to locate the street number she had given the store, since the address is in a location where there are few buildings." He hesitated then and looked at me. "The address she gave is a public laundry park," he said. "A laundry park and cremation grounds."

Amrita was by far the braver and the smarter of the two of us during the hours and days that followed. I might have remained sitting on the bed for hours after Singh left if Amrita had not taken charge, gotten me out of my reeking clothes, and set the broken finger as best she could using a small toothbrush holder as a splint. I threw up again when she tugged the finger into place, but there was nothing left to vomit and the dry heaves would have soon turned to sobs of fury and frustration if Amrita hadn't thrust me under the shower. The water was tepid and under-pressured, but wonderful. I stood there for half an hour, actually falling asleep for a while, allowing the flow of water to pound away memories and terrors. Only a fierce core of sorrow and confusion continued to burn through my fatigue as I dressed in clean cotton and joined Amrita for a silent vigil.

Tuesday morning arrived as we sat together watching the Calcutta sunrise throw a wan, gray light through the open curtains. Temple bells, trolley bells, vendors' cries, and random street sounds came to us with the first light. "She'll be all right," I would say at intervals. "I know she will, kid. She'll be all right."

Amrita said nothing.

At exactly 5:35 A.M., the telephone rang. It was the room phone. I lunged across the room at it.

"Hello?" I thought I could hear an extra hollowness to the line. It was as if I were talking into a cave in the earth.

"Hello? Hello? Mr. Luczak, hello?"

"Yes. Who is this?"

"Hello? This is Michael Leonard Chatterjee, Mr. Luczak."

"Yes?" *Are you the go-between? Are you involved, you bastard?*

"Mr. Luczak, the police came to my home during the night. They told me about the disappearance of your child."

"Yes?" If this was going to be just a sympathy call, I would hang up. But it was not a sympathy call.

"The police awoke me, Mr. Luczak. They awakened my family. They came to my *home*. They seem to think that I am somehow involved in this event. They interview me in the middle of the *night*, Mr. Luczak."

"Yeah? So?"

"I am calling to strongly protest this aspersion on my character and invasion of my privacy," said Chatterjee. His voice became higher and shriller as he began to shout. "You should not have given them my name, Mr. Luczak. I am a person of some stature in this community. I will not have such aspersions cast on my character, sir. You have no right."

"What?" It was all I could do to get the single syllable out.

"You have no *right*, sir. I warn you, any accusations you might make, any mention of my name, any involvement of the Writers' Union in your personal problems, Mr. Luczak, will result in legal action from my barrister. I am warning you, sir."

There was a hollow clunk as Chatterjee hung up. The line continued to hiss and crackle for several seconds, and then a second crash came as the policeman at the switchboard hung up. Amrita was standing next to me, but for a second I could not speak. I remained standing there, squeezing the receiver as if it were Chatterjee's neck, my rage reaching the point where blood vessels burst or tendons snap.

"What!" demanded Amrita, shaking my arm. I told her.

She nodded. Somehow the phone call vitalized her into action. First, using one of the extra lines, she called her aunt in New Delhi. Her aunt knew no one in Bengal, but she had friends who had friends in the *Lok Sabha*, one of the houses of government. Amrita simply told of the kidnapping and asked for help. I could not fathom what form that help could take, but the mere fact of Amrita's *acting* made me feel better.

Next she phoned her father's brother in Bombay. Her uncle also owned a construction company and was a man of some influence on the west coast of the subcontinent. Although he had been awakened from a sound sleep by a niece he had not heard from for a decade, he promised to get on the next plane to Calcutta. Amrita told him not to—not yet—but did ask him to contact any Bengal authorities who might help. He promised to do so and to keep in touch.

I sat listening to the elegant Hindi phrases and watched my wife as I would a stranger. When she later told me the substance of the calls, I felt the reassurance that a child knows when hearing adults confer with other adults over important matters.

Before Inspector Singh arrived at eight-thirty that morning, Amrita had called Calcutta's three main hospitals. No, no American children or light-skinned children fitting that description had been admitted overnight.

Then she called the morgue.

I could never have made that call. I could not have stood there as she did, back straight, voice steady, and inquired of some sleepy stranger as to whether the body of my child had been brought in during the dark Calcutta night.

The answer was no.

Only after she thanked him and hung up did I see the trembling begin in her legs and move up her body until her hands shook and she had to cover her face with them. I went to her then and took her in my arms. She did not release her tense control, not yet, but she bowed her head into the hollow of my neck and we rocked back and forth together, saying nothing, rocking together in the shared pain and ache of it.

Inspector Singh brought no news.

He sat and drank coffee with us around the small table in the room. Men in helmets came and went, delivering papers, receiving instructions.

Singh told us that security officials at the airport and train stations had been notified. Did we have a photograph of the child? I did. It was two months out of date. Victoria had much less hair then. Her face was less distinct. Beneath her dimpled legs I could see the orange blanket, a forgotten artifact of that distantly carefree Memorial Day picnic. I hated to give up the photograph.

Singh asked more questions, gave reassurances, and left us. A thin police sergeant poked his head in and reminded us in broken English that he would be next door. We nodded.

The day passed. Amrita had lunch brought up. Neither of us ate. Twice I took long showers, the door left open so that I could hear Amrita or the phone. My flesh still smelled of the previous night's foulness. I was so tired that I felt disconnected from my body. My thoughts circled around and around like a loop tape.

If I had not gone.

If I hadn't got in the car.

If I had returned sooner.

I turned off the water and slammed my fist into the tile.

By three P.M. Singh had returned with two other officers from the Metropolitan Force. One spoke no English. The other had somehow acquired a cockney accent. Their report was not helpful.

No one named M. T. Krishna was teaching at the University. Five instructors named Krishna had taught there during the past decade. Two had retired. Two were now in their mid or late fifties. One was a woman.

There was no record of any Krishna affiliated with the United States Education Foundation in India. Indeed, there was no USEFI office in Calcutta. The nearest branch was in Madras. Phone calls had been placed, but no one in Madras had any information about a Krishna or Sanjay. No one had been sent to meet us at the Calcutta airport. USEFI had no idea I was in the country.

There had been many students named Sanjay at Calcutta University. None contacted so far fit the description that I had given the police. Officers were working on it, but it might be several weeks before all of the currently registered Sanjays were contacted. It was, after all, a midterm holiday.

It *had* been confirmed that a Jayaprakesh Muktanandaji had been a student there, but he had not registered during the previous term. A waiter at the University Coffee House, however, had seen Muktanandaji there only two days ago.

"That's after I met him there," I said.

So it seemed. Muktanandaji had shown his waiter friend a rail ticket he had purchased. He said that he was going home to his village of Anguda. The waiter had not seen the young man since. Singh had telephoned the Commissioner in Jamshedpur, who would telegraph the provincial constable in Durgalapur. The constable would go to Anguda to find Muktanandaji and bring him back to Durgalapur for questioning. They should be hearing from him by late Wednesday.

"Tomorrow!"

"Yes, Mr. Luczak. It is a remote village."

There were many Bahrati families in the Calcutta phone book. None contacted had a daughter in her twenties with the name of Kamakhya. The name, after all, was quite unusual.

"How is that?" I asked.

"I will explain later," said Singh.

There had been contacts made with informers in the *goondas* underground. No useful information had been forthcoming, but overtures continued. Also, the police would be questioning members of the Beggars' Union.

My stomach turned over at those words. "What about the Kapalikas?" I asked.

"'Ow's that?" asked the other inspector.

Singh said something in Bengali and turned back to me. "You must understand, Mr. Luczak, that the Kapalika Society remains—technically—a myth."

"Bullshit," I said. "It was no myth that someone was going to kill me last night. It's no myth that our little girl is missing."

"No," said Singh. "But we have no hard evidence yet that the *thugees*, *goondas*, or the so-called Kapalikas are involved. It is also complicated by the fact that various criminal elements often call upon a corrupt, Tantric form of mysticism, frequently invoking local deities—in this case, Kali—in order to impress their initiates or to frighten the common people."

"Uh-huh," I said.

Amrita crossed her arms and looked at the three men. "So you have no real news for us?" she asked.

Singh glanced at the other two. "No progress, no."

Amrita nodded and picked up the phone. "Yes, hello, this is Room six-twelve. Would you please put through a call for me to the American Embassy in New Delhi? Yes. It is very important. Thank you."

The three men blinked. I saw them to the door while Amrita waited by the phone. In the hall, the other two officials moved away while I detained Singh for a moment. "Why is Kamakhya Bahrati's name so unusual?"

Singh stroked his mustache. "Kamakhya is . . . not a common name in Bengal."

"Why is that?"

"It is a religious name. An aspect of . . . of Parvati."

"Of Kali, you mean."

"Yes."

"So why isn't it common, Inspector? There are enough Ramas and Krishnas around."

"Yes," said Singh and flicked lint from his cuff. The steel bracelet on his wrist caught the light. "Yes, but the name Kamakhya, or its variant, Kamaksi, is associated with a particularly unattractive aspect of Kali once worshiped in the great temple at Assam. Some of their ceremonies were very unwholesome. The cult was outlawed some years ago. The temple is abandoned."

I nodded. I did not react to the news. I went back to the room and calmly waited for Amrita's call to be completed. And all the while the mad laughter built inside me and the screams of rage rattled their cage to be freed.

* * *

Around five P.M. on that endless day I went down to the lobby. A sense of claustrophobia had grown in me until I found it hard to breathe. But the lobby was no better. I bought a cigar in the gift shop; but the clerk kept glancing at me, and the sympathetic stare of the assistant manager approached resentment. I imagined that a Muslim couple in the lobby were whispering about me, and it was not my imagination when several waiters stepped out of the Garden Café to point and crane my way.

I hastily retreated to the sixth floor, jogging up the stairs to release energy. The English custom of calling the second floor the first gave me an extra flight of exercise. I was panting and sweating freely when I emerged into the hallway of our floor. Amrita was hurrying toward me.

"Something?" I asked.

"I just remembered something important," she said in a rush of breath.

"What's that?"

"Abe Bronstein! Krishna mentioned Abe Bronstein to us when we were leaving the airport that first night. Krishna *must* have some association with USEFI or *somebody*."

Amrita went to talk to the police sergeant in 614 while I had a call put through to the States. Even with the policeman expediting things at the switchboard, it was thirty minutes before they got an overseas line. Something in me came close to pulling apart when I heard the familiar growl from New York. "Bobby, good morning! Where the hell are you calling from? It sounds like you're calling from the moon on a cheap CB."

"Abe, listen. Listen, please." As quickly as I could, I told him about Victoria's disappearance.

"Aww, shit," moaned Abe. "Shit, shit, shit." Even through ten thousand miles of bad connection I could hear the deep pain in his voice.

"Listen, Abe, can you hear me? One of the suspects in this thing is a guy named Krishna . . . M. T. Krishna . . . but we think his real name is Sanjay something. He met us at the airport last Thursday. Can you hear me? Good. This Krishna said that he worked for USEFI . . . that's the American Education Foundation . . . yeah . . . and that he picked us up as a favor for his boss. Neither Amrita nor I can remember what he said his boss's name was. But he also mentioned *your* name, Abe. He specifically mentioned your name. Hello?"

"Shah," said Abe through the hollow echoes.

"What?"

"Shah. A. B. Shah. I cabled him right after you left for London and asked him to give you a hand if you needed it."

"Shah," I repeated, writing quickly. "Great. Where can we get hold of him, Abe? Is he in the Calcutta directory?"

"No, Bobby, he's not in Calcutta. Shah's an editor of the *Times of India*, but he also works as a cultural advisor for USEFI in New Delhi. I knew him several years ago when he taught at Columbia. I never heard of this Krishna son of a bitch."

"Thanks, Abe, you've been a lot of help."

"Damn, Bobby, I'm so *sorry*. How's Amrita holding up?"

"Beautifully. She's a rock, Abe."

"Ahhh. It'll be all right, Bobby. You gotta believe that. They'll get Victoria back for you. She'll be okay."

"Yeah."

"Let me know when things work out. I'll be at my mother's. You've got the number, right? Let me know if I can help. Aww, *damn*. It'll be all right, Bobby."

"Good-bye, Abe. Thanks."

Amrita had not only informed Singh, but was on the phone to the third of Calcutta's three large newspapers. She snapped out instructions in peremptory Hindi.

"We should have done this earlier," she said when she got off the phone. "Now they won't appear until tomorrow's editions." Amrita had taken out a half-page ad in each of the papers. Runners would pick up copies of the photograph we had loaned the police. There would be a $10,000 reward for any helpful information regarding the case; $50,000 for the safe return of Victoria or any information leading to her safe return, no questions asked.

"Jesus," I said stupidly, "where will we get fifty thousand dollars?"

Amrita looked out the window at the evening chaos on the street. "I would have offered twice as much," she said. "But that would have been almost a million rupees. This amount is more believable somehow, more exciting to the greedy."

I shook my head. I hadn't seemed able to think of anything. I quickly called Singh and gave him the information about Shah. He promised to follow up on it immediately.

I dozed for an hour or so. I hadn't meant to. One minute I was sitting in the chair near the window, watching the last of the gray eveing light fade, and the next minute my head snapped up and it was night outside with heavy rain banging at the glass. One of the police lines was ringing. Amrita came in from the hall, but I beat her to it.

"Mr. Luczak?" It was Inspector Singh. "I was able to get through to Mr. A. B. Shah at his home in New Delhi."

"And?"

"Indeed it was he who received your Mr. Bronstein's cable. Mr. Shah has great respect for your friend and immediately dispatched a Foundation subordinate of his, a young man named R. L. Dhavan, to travel here to offer his services to you as a guide and interpreter."

"Dispatched? From Delhi to Calcutta, you mean?"

"Exactly."

"So where is he?"

"That is what Mr. Shah was beginning to wonder. That is what we wondered. We took a very careful description of the gentleman's appearance and clothing when last seen."

"And?"

"And, Mr. Luczak, it seems that Mr. R. L. Dhavan has been with us all along. His body was found stuffed in a trunk at Howrah Station last Thursday afternoon."

There was a power failure shortly after ten P.M. The monsoon storm outside had entered some realm of ferocity beyond my experience. Lightning slashed the night every few seconds and did a better job of illuminating the room than did the two candles a porter had brought. The streets were flooded within minutes of the initial deluge, and the frightening downpour grew worse by the hour. No lights were visible up Chowringhee. I wondered how the squatting millions in their burlap huts and the hutless street people survived nights like this.

Victoria is out there somewhere.

I moaned out loud and paced the room. I picked up one

phone and then the other to call Singh. The phone lines were dead.

The assistant manager came up to explain to the sleepy policeman next door and to apologize to us. Thousands of phones in the area were out of order. He had sent a runner to the telephone company, but the offices were closed. No one knew when service might be resumed. Sometimes it took days.

When the clerk left, I removed our clothes from the closet and hung them on a shower rod in the bathroom.

"What are you doing?" asked Amrita. Her voice was slightly slurred. She had not slept in over forty hours. Her eyes were dark and weary.

I said nothing, but pulled out the heavy round wooden dowel that had served as a rod for hangers. It was almost four feet long and felt agreeably solid in my hands. I propped it behind a chair near the door. Outside, lightning crashed nearby and caught the flooded scene in a second's stroboscopic clarity.

At ten minutes after eleven, there was a heavy knock. Amrita startled awake in her chair while I stood and hefted the dowel. "Who is it?"

"Inspector Singh."

The Sikh wore a pith helmet and a dripping black raincoat. Two soaked policemen stood in the hall. "Mr. Luczak, we would like you to come with us on an important matter."

"Come where, Inspector?"

Singh shook water from his helmet. "To the Sassoon Morgue." At Amrita's involuntary intake of breath, he hurried on, "There has been a murder. A man."

"A man? Does this relate to whatshisname? Dhavan?"

Singh shrugged. Water fell to the carpet. "We do not know.

The . . . style of the murder has connotations of the *goondas*. The Kapalikas, if you will. We would like your help in identifying the body."

"Who do you think it is?"

Again the shrug. "Will you come, Mr. Luczak? My car is waiting."

"No," I said. "Absolutely not. I'm not leaving Amrita. Forget it."

"But for identification to be made . . ."

"Take a photograph, Inspector. Your department has a camera, doesn't it? If not I'll wait for close-ups in the morning paper. Calcuttans seem to enjoy viewing corpse photos the way we get a kick out of comic strips back in the States."

"Bobby!" said Amrita. Her voice was raw. We were both exhausted. "The Inspector is only trying to help."

"Yeah," I said. "Tough. I'm not leaving you again."

Amrita picked up her purse and umbrella. "I'll go too."

Both Singh and I looked at her.

"The phones are out," she said. "No one can call us. It's been twenty-four hours, and there has been no ransom demand. No contact of any kind. If this can help, let us do it *now*."

Lightning illuminated the boarded windows and the two rain-pelted stone lions left over from some earlier, more innocent era. The morgue entrance was reached by a rear drive that curved between dark, dripping buildings and heaps of garbage which were melting in the downpour. A crumpling overhang sheltered the broad doors to the Sassoon Morgue.

A man in a rumpled suit met us in an outer office. Even there, the air was thick with the high-school-biology scent of formaldehyde. Kerosene lanterns threw shadows behind filing cabinets and tall stacks of folders on every desk. The man steepled his fingers at me, bowed perfunctorily, and released a veritable tirade of Bengali at the dripping Inspector.

"He says that Mrs. Luczak can remain here," translated Singh. "We will be in the next room."

Amrita nodded and said, "He also said that the morgue needs an emergency generator, Inspector. He invited the politicians at City Hall to get off their asses and come down here to sniff the roses. Is that right? It was an idiom."

"That is correct," said Singh and surrendered a grim smile. He said something to the morgue official, and the little man blushed and led Singh and me through swinging doors and down a short, tiled hallway.

A hanging lantern showed an area which might have been Jack the Ripper's idea of an operating room. It was filthy. Papers, cups, and various detritus lay everywhere. Knives, scalpels, and bone saws were scattered across stained trays and tabletops. A huge dish of a light—inoperative now—and the gleaming steel table with open drains confirmed the purpose of the room. That and the body which lay exposed on the table.

"Ah," said the Inspector and stepped closer. He beckoned impatiently for me to join him. The morgue official lifted the lantern from its peg on the wall and hung it from the bar of the curved operating-room light. The swinging light threw swirls of patterns on the slick steel.

When I was a child my parents had invested in a set of *Compton's Pictured Encyclopedias*. My favorite section was the chapter on the human body. There were pages there of translucent overlays. You started with the whole body, skin and all, and as you flipped the delicate pages you descended farther into the mysteries of the body's crowded interior. Everything was neat, color-coded, and labeled for reference.

The body before me now was the second page—MUSCLES & TENDONS. From the neck down the skin had been flayed open and pulled back. It lay bunched under the corpse like a moist and wrinkled cape. But there was no neat labeling of muscles here, only a human being looking like raw meat, greasy fluids catching the light; thick, white fibers disappearing into raw, pink striations; and yellowish tendons stretched like bloody thongs.

Singh and the other man were looking at me. If they expected me to cry out or be sick they were to be disappointed. I cleared my throat. "You've already begun the autopsy?"

Singh translated the other's brief sentence. "No, Mr. Luczak. This was the way he came in two hours ago."

I reacted then. "Jesus! Why would anyone kill and then skin a human being?"

Singh shook his head. "He was not deceased when he was first seen. He was on Sudder Street. Screaming. Running, according to witnesses. He fell. Sometime later the screaming stopped. Eventually someone sent for a police wagon."

I took two involuntary steps back. I could hear my mother's voice echoing from the third-floor landing on Pulaski Street. *Robert Luczak, you come in here this minute before I skin you alive*. It was possible.

"Do you know him?" Singh asked impatiently. He gestured for more light. The corpse's head was thrown back, frozen in final agony by the grip of early *rigor mortis*.

"No," I said through gritted teeth. "Wait." I forced myself

to step into the tight circle of light. The face was untouched except for the distorted features. Recognition hit me like a fist.

"You *do* know him," said Singh.

"Yes." *I had said his name. Dear God, I had said his name when talking to Das.*

"It is Mr. Krishna?"

"No," I said and turned away from the bright table. *I had said his name.* "It's the glasses that are missing. He wears glasses. His name is Jayaprakesh Muktanandaji."

Amrita and I slept until nine A.M. We did not dream. The roar of rain through the open window obliterated dreams. Sometime around dawn, the electricity and air conditioning must have come on, but we were not aware of it.

At 11:00 Singh sent a car to bring us to police headquarters. Any phone call to the hotel would be transferred to us there. The police center was another dark and cavernous room in another dark and labyrinthine building. Great mounds of file folders and yellowing documents obscured the desks and almost hid the faceless men hunched over typewriters that looked to have been used in Queen Victoria's day. Amrita and I spent several hours going through huge books of photographs. After hundreds of women's faces, I began to wonder if I would recognize Kamakhya Bahrati if I saw her. *Yes, I would.*

There was only one discovery. After scrutinizing a dark and faded photograph of a heavy man in prison gray, I tentatively identified him as the Kapalika in khaki who had broken my finger.

"But you are not sure?" asked Singh.

"No. He was older, heavier, longer hair."

Singh grunted and gave the photograph and instructions to

someone. He never told me what the man's name was or why he had once been jailed. *The sound of brittle plastic breaking.*

By early afternoon we returned to the hotel and were amazed to find that there had been over a hundred calls to the police-line number we had given in the newspaper ads. None of the calls had yielded hard information. The few that reported seeing the child here or there were being followed up, but the sergeant was pessimistic. Most of the calls were from men or women willing to sell us an infant for the price of the reward.

I slammed the door and we lay on the bed together and waited.

The late hours of that Wednesday are largely lost to me. I remember images clearly, but they seem unrelated to one another. Some I cannot separate from the dreams that have haunted me since those days.

Sometime around eight P.M. I got up, kissed Amrita good-bye as she dozed, and left the hotel. The solution to everything had become quite clear to me suddenly. I would go out into Calcutta, find the Kapalikas, tell them that I was sorry, that I would do whatever they wanted, and then they would give our baby back. It was simple.

Failing that, I would find the goddess Kali and kill the bitch.

I remember walking for many blocks, but at some point I was riding in a cab, watching faces on the sidewalk, sure that the next one would be Kamakhya. Or Krishna. Or Das.

Then the cab was parked under a banyan tree, waiting, waiting while I climbed a sharp iron gate and loped, half crouching, up a flower-lined drive. The house was dark. I rattled shutters. I pounded on doors. "Chatterjee!" I screamed. The house was dark.

At another time I was walking on the river's edge. The Howrah Bridge loomed above me in that last twilight before true darkness. Paved streets gave way to muddy lanes and dark slums. Children danced around me. I threw them all of my change. I remember looking back once and no longer seeing the mob of children but several men following me. Their mouths moved, but I heard nothing. They made a half-circle and began approaching me cautiously, arms half raised.

"Kapalikas?" I said hopefully. I think I said it. "Are you Kapalikas? Kali? Kapalikas?"

They hesitated and glanced at one another for courage. I looked at their rags and their lean-hungry bodies—muscles wound tight with anticipation—and I knew they were not Kapalikas. Or *thugees*. Or *goondas*. Only poor, hungry men ready to kill for a foreigner's money.

"All right!" I cried then. I was grinning. I could not stop grinning, although I felt that something sharp was cutting a hole in me while I grinned. The past few days, the night, Victoria—everything was contracting into a tight knot of pure joy at this.

"All right!" I shouted. "Come on. Come on. Please." My arms opened wide. I would have embraced them. I would have hugged them close in a sweaty, locker-room embrace while I joyously ripped their taut throats out with my teeth.

I think I would have. I do not know. The men looked at one another, backed away, and disappeared in the shadowed lanes. I almost cried when they had gone.

I don't know whether it was before or after my encounter with the men that I was in a small, storefront temple. There was a clumsy statue of a kneeling black cow with a red and white necklace. Old men squatted and spat into the smoky dimness and stared in horror at me. An ancient scarecrow repeatedly pointed at my feet and gabbled at me. I think he wanted me to remove my shoes.

"Fuck that," I said in a reasonable tone. "That doesn't matter. Just tell them that they win, okay? Tell them that I'll do whatever they want. All right? I promise. I really promise. I swear to God. Scout's honor." I think I began crying then. At least I watched through a prism of tears as an old man with most of his front teeth missing grinned vacuously at me, patting me on the shoulder as he rocked back and forth on his skinny haunches.

There was a great wasteland of shacks and old tires lying in the rain, and I waded through the mud for miles toward the tall chimneys and open flames that cast a red hue over everything and which receded from me no matter how I struggled to close the distance. I believe that this was a real place. I do not know. It has been the landscape of my dreams for so long now.

It was in the first false light of dawn that I found the little girl. She was lying in the street—in the mud path that passed for a street there. She was no more than five. Her long black hair was tangled, and she was curled under a thin tan quilt still wet from the night's showers. Something in her unselfconscious commitment to sleep drew me to her. I dropped to one knee on the muddy path. People and bicycles were already beginning to move, swerving to avoid us in the narrow lane.

The girl's eyes were closed tightly, as though in concentration, and her mouth was slightly open. Her small fist was curled against her cheek. Soon she would have to wake, tend the fire, serve the men, care for the younger chidren, and face the end of a childhood she had barely known. Soon she would become the property of a man other than her father, and on that day she would receive the traditional Hindu blessing—"May you have eight sons." But for now she had only to sleep, her fist curled, her brown cheek against the soil, her eyes closed tightly against the morning light.

I shook my head then and looked around me. It was almost dawn. The air had been swept almost clean by the rain, and there was the painfully perfect smell of fresh blossoms and moist earth.

I clearly remember the rickshaw ride back to the hotel. Sounds and colors were so clear that they assaulted my senses. My mind was also clear. If anything had happened while I was gone . . . if Amrita had needed me . . .

It was just dawn, but Amrita met me in the hall. She was wringing her hands with joy, and there were tears in her eyes for the first time since it had all begun.

"Bobby, oh Bobby," she said. "Inspector Singh just called. He's coming to get us. He'll be here in a minute. They're taking us to the airport. They've found her, Bobby. They've found her."

We sped along the almost empty VIP Highway. Rich streams of horizontal light threw everything into bold relief, and the shadow of our car kept pace in the moist fields.

"You're sure she's all right?" I asked.

"Yes, yes," said Singh without turning around in the front seat. "We only received the call twenty-five minutes ago."

"You're sure it's Victoria?" asked Amrita. We were both leaning forward and resting our arms on the back of the front seat. Amrita's hands would unconsciously fold and refold the Kleenex she was holding.

"The security guard believes so," said Singh. "That is why he detained the couple going through with the baby. They do not know that they are being detained. The chief security officer told them that there was a slight irregularity in their travel visa. They believe they are waiting for an official to arrive to stamp their visas."

"Why not just arrest them?" I asked.

"For what crime?" asked Singh. "Until the child is positively identified, they are guilty of nothing except attempting to fly to London."

"Who spotted Victoria?" asked Amrita.

"The security guard I mentioned," said Singh and yawned. "He saw your advertisement in the newspaper." There was a faint hint of disapproval in Singh's deep voice.

I took Amrita's hand, and we watched the now familiar countryside roll by. Both of us were mentally trying to make the little car go faster. When a herdsman blocked the wet pavement with his sheep for a long moment, we both shouted at our driver to honk, to drive through. Then we were shifting up through gears, passing a rumbling cart piled high with cane, and alone in our left lane again. Gaudy trucks sped by to our right, headed into town, white-shirted men waving brown arms at us.

I forced myself to sit back and take several deep breaths. The richness of the sunrise would have been wondrous at any other time. Even the empty, scarred high-rises and lean-tos in the muddy fields seemed cleansed by the sun's benediction. Women carrying tall bronze pots threw ten-foot shadows in the verdant ditches.

"You're sure she's all right?" I asked again.

"We are almost there," said Singh.

We swept up the curved drive past black and yellow taxis with their rooftops diamonded by raindrops, their drivers sprawled sleeping across front seats. Our own car had not quite stopped when we flung open the doors.

"Which way?"

Singh came around the car pointing. We moved quickly into the terminal. Caught up in our impatient rush, Singh jogged around the sprawled and sheeted forms sleeping on the filthy tiled floor. "Here," he said, opening a scuffed door marked AUTHORIZED PERSONS ONLY in English as well as Bengali. An Untouchable woman squatted in the corridor, sweeping dirt and paper into a small dustpan. Fifteen steps took us to a large room broken up by partitions and counters. I could hear teletypes and typewriters clacking.

I saw them immediately, the Indian couple, huddled in a far corner; the young woman holding the baby to her chest. They were strangers, little more than children themselves. The man was short and shifty-eyed. Every few seconds he would raise his right hand to brush at his unsuccessful attempt at a mustache. The girl was even younger than the man and plain to the point of homeliness. The scarf she wore did not hide stringy hair nor the smudged crimson dot which marked the center of her forehead.

But as we stopped twenty feet from them, Amrita and I had eyes only for the heavily wrapped bundle the woman was rapidly rocking. The child's face was not visible. We could see only a pale hint of cheek.

We walked closer. A great ache began in my diaphragm and rose to my chest. I ignored it. Inspector Singh motioned to the uniformed security guard who had snapped to attention. The guard brusquely said something to the young man, who immediately rose from the bench and walked nervously to the counter. As he stood, the girl shifted to let him pass and we caught a glimpse of the baby's face in the thick folds of the shawl.

It was Victoria. Sleeping, pale almost to the point her skin glowed, but beyond any doubt it was Victoria.

Amrita let out a cry then, and everyone moved at once. The young man must have tried to bolt, because the security guard and another man from behind the counter rapidly pinned his arms back. The girl slid across the bench into the corner and clutched the baby to her breast while she began rocking quickly and babbling something that sounded like a nursery rhyme. Amrita, the Inspector, and I advanced quickly together as if to cut off any escape route the girl might consider, but she only turned her face to the green wall and began wailing more loudly.

Singh tried to restrain Amrita then, but she took three quick steps forward, pulled the woman's head back sharply by her hair, and removed Victoria from her grasp with a sweep of her left arm.

Everyone was shouting. For some reason I took several steps back as Amrita lifted our daughter high and began unwrapping her from the filthy purple shawl.

Amrita's first cry cut through the rest of the noise and reduced the room to silence. I continued backing up until I struck a counter. As Amrita's screams started, I turned away in slow motion and lowered my face and clenched fists to the cool countertop.

"Awww," I said. It was a soft noise and it came up out of

my earliest childhood. "Awww," I said. "Aww, no, please." I pressed my cheek tight against the countertop and struck my fists again my ears, but I could plainly hear when Amrita's cries turned to sobs.

I still have the report somewhere—the copy of the one Singh sent to Delhi. Like everything else in India, the paper is cheap and inferior. The type is so faint as to be almost transparent, a dull child's idea of a secret message. It doesn't matter. I do not need to see the report to recall its exact wording.

> 22.7.77 C.M.P.D./D.D.A.S.S. 2671067
>
> SECURITY GUARD JAGMOAN (YASHPAL, D.D.A. SEC. SERV. 1113) PROCESSED THE COUPLE IDENTIFIED BY PAPERS AS CHOWDURY, SUGATA AND DEVI, TRAVELING WITH INFANT TO LONDON, U.K., FOR PLEASURE, AT 04:28/21.7.77. SECURITY GUARD JAGMOAN DETAINED THE COUPLE AT CUSTOMS SECTION B-11 BECAUSE OF POSSIBLE RECOGNITION OF SAID INFANT AS MISSING AMERICAN LUCZAK INFANT, REPORTED KIDNAPPED ON 18.7.77 [RE: C.M.P.D. CASE NO. 117, dt, 18.7.77(S.R. 50/) SINGH.] INSPECTOR YASHWAN SINGH (C.M.P.D. 26774) AND LUCZAKS (ROBERT C. AND AMRITA D.) ARRIVED TO CONFIRM INFANT'S IDENTITY AT 05:41/21.7.77. INFANT WAS POSITIVELY IDENTIFIED AS VICTORIA CAROLYN LUCZAK b. 22.1.77. UPON FURTHER INSPECTION BY

CHILD'S MOTHER, IT WAS DISCOVERED THAT INFANT VICTORIA C. LUCZAK HAD BEEN DECEASED FOR SEVERAL HOURS. COUPLE IDENTIFIED AS SUGATA AND DEVI CHOWDURY SUBSEQUENTLY WERE PLACED UNDER ARREST AND TRANSPORTED TO C.M.P.D.H.Q. CHOWRINGHEE: SUSPICION OF CONSPIRACY TO KIDNAP, CONSPIRACY TO MURDER, AND ATTEMPTING TO TRANSPORT STOLEN GOODS ACROSS INTERNATIONAL BOUNDARIES. AUTOPSY REPORT [RE: LUCZAK—C.M.P.D./M.E. 2671067/21.7.77] CONFIRMED THAT THE LUCZAK INFANT HAD BEEN DECEASED FOR A PERIOD OF NO MORE THAN FIVE (5) HOURS AND NO LESS THAN TWO (2) HOURS AND THAT SAID INFANT'S BODY HAD BEEN USED AS A DEPOSITORY TO TRANSPORT STOLEN MERCHANDISE: LIST AND VALUE ESTIMATES APPENDED:

RUBIES (6)	RS. 1,115,000
SAPPHIRE (4)	RS. 762,000
OPALS (4)	RS. 136,000
AMETHYST (2)	RS. 742,000
TOURMALINE (5)	RS. 380,000

FURTHER DETAILS CONTACT SINGH (YASHWAN C.M.P.D. 26774). END REPORT.

Chapter Fifteen

"Calcutta Has Murdered Me"
—Kabita Sinha

Calcutta would not let us go. For two more days the city held us in its fetid grasp.

Amrita and I would not leave Victoria alone with them. Even during the police autopsy and the undertaker's preparations, we waited in nearby rooms.

Singh told us that we would have to remain in Calcutta for several weeks, at least until the hearings were completed. I told him we would not. Each of us gave a deposition to a bored-looking stenographic clerk.

The man from the American Embassy in New Delhi arrived. He was an officious little rabbit of a man named Don Warden. His idea of dealing with the unhelpful Indian bureaucrats was to apologize to them and explain to us how complicated we had made things by insisting on taking our child's body home so quickly.

On Saturday we rode to the airport for the final time. Warden, Amrita, and I were crowded into the backseat of a rented old Chevrolet. It was raining very hard, and the inside of the closed vehicle was hot and very humid. I did not notice. I had eyes only for the small white hospital van we were following. It did not use its emergency lights in the heavy traffic. There was no rush.

At the airport there was a final delay. An airport official came out with Warden. Both were shaking their heads.

"What's the matter?" I said.

The Indian official brushed at his soiled white shirt and snapped out several Hindustani phrases in an irritated tone.

"What?" I said.

Amrita translated. She was so exhausted that she did not raise her head and her voice was almost inaudible. "He says that the coffin we paid for cannot be loaded on the aircraft," she said wearily. "The metal airline coffin is here, but the necessary papers for the transfer of . . . of the body . . . were not signed by the proper authorities. He says that we can go to the city hall on Monday to get the necessary papers."

I stood up. "Warden?" I said.

The embassy man shrugged. "We have to respect their laws and cultural values," he said. "I've thought all along that it would be much easier if you would agree to having the body cremated here in India."

Kali is the goddess of all cremation grounds.

"Come here," I said. I led the two men back through the doors into the office next to the room where Victoria's body lay. The Indian official looked bored and impatient. I took Warden by the arm and led him to one corner of the room.

"Mr. Warden," I said quietly, "I am going to go into the next room and transfer my daughter's body to the required coffin. If you come into the room or interfere with me in any way, I will kill you. Do you understand?"

Warden blinked several times and nodded. I walked over to the official and explained things to him. I did so quietly, my fingers gently touching his chest as I talked, but he looked into my eyes and something he saw there kept him silent and immobile when I finished speaking and walked through the swinging doors into the dimly lit room where Victoria waited.

The room was long and almost empty except for some stacks of boxes and unclaimed luggage. At one end of the room, already opened on a counter next to a conveyor belt of metal rollers, was the steel airline coffin. At the far end of the room, on a bench next to the loading platform, was the gray casket we had purchased in Calcutta. I walked over to it and, without hesitating, unsealed the casket.

On the night Victoria was born, there was one part of the prepared ritual that I had been nervous about for weeks. I had known that the Exeter Hospital encouraged the new fathers to carry the newborn infants from the delivery room to the nursery next door for the obligatory weighing and measuring prior to returning the baby to the mother in the recovery room. I had worried about this for some time. I was afraid I might drop her. It was a silly reaction, but even after the excitement and exhilaration of the birth, I found my heart pounding with nervousness when the doctor lifted Victoria off Amrita's stomach and asked if I would like to carry my little girl down the hall. I remember nodding, smiling, and feeling terrified. I remember cupping her tiny head, lifting the still-damp-from-birth little form against my chest and shoulder and making the thirty-step trip from the delivery room to the nursery with a growing confidence and joy. It was as if Victoria was helping me. I remember grinning stupidly at the sudden and total realization that *I was carrying my child*. It remains the happiest memory of my life.

This time I felt no nervousness. I gently raised my daughter, cupped her head, held her against my chest and shoulder as I had so many times before, and made the thirty-step walk to the steel airline coffin with its small bed of white silk.

The plane was delayed several times before takeoff. Amrita and I sat holding hands during the ninety-minute wait, and when the big 747 did finally begin its take-off roll, we did not look toward the windows. Our thoughts were on the small transport coffin we had watched being loaded earlier. We did not talk as the plane climbed toward cruising altitude. We did not look out as clouds obscured the last view of Calcutta. We took our baby and we went home.

Chapter 16

"Surely some revelation is at hand;"
—William Butler Yeats

Victoria's funeral was on Tuesday, July 26, 1977. She was buried in the small Catholic cemetery on the hill overlooking Exeter.

The tiny white casket seemed radiant in the bright sunlight. I did not look at it. During the brief graveside service, I stared at a patch of blue sky just above Father Darcy's head. Through a break in the trees I could see a brick tower on one of the Academy's old buildings. Once a group of pigeons circled and wheeled through the shield of summer sky. Just before the end of the service there came a chorus of children's shouts and laughter, suddenly muted as they saw our group, and Amrita and I turned together to watch a pack of youngsters pedaling furiously as they approached the long, effortless grade down to the town.

* * *

Amrita planned to return to teaching at the university in the fall. I did nothing. Three days after we returned, she cleaned out Victoria's room and eventually turned it into a sewing room. She never worked in there and I never went in at all.

When I finally threw out some of the clothes that I'd brought back from Calcutta, I thought to go through the pockets of the torn and stained safari shirt I'd worn the night I'd brought the book to Das. The book of matches was not in any of the pockets. I nodded then, satisfied, but a second later I found my small notebook in another pocket. Perhaps I had both notebooks with me that night.

Abe Bronstein came up for a day in late October. He had been at the funeral, but we had not spoken beyond the necessary rituals of condolence. I had spoken to him one other time—a late, incoherent phonecall after I'd been drinking. Abe had listened for the better part of an hour and then said softly, "Go to bed, Bobby. Go to sleep."

On this Sunday in October we sat in the living room over white wine and discussed the problems of keeping *Other Voices* going and the chances of Carter's new energy program solving the gas shortages. Amrita nodded politely, smiled occasionally, and was a thousand miles away the entire time.

Abe suggested that we go for a walk in the woods behind the house. I blinked. Abe hated exercise of any kind. On this beautiful autumn day he was wearing the same gray, rumpled suit, thin tie, and black wingtipped shoes that he always wore.

"Sure," I said without any enthusiasm, and he and I set off down the trail toward the pond.

The forest was in full glory. The trail was cushioned with chrome-yellow elm leaves, and every turn confronted us with the flaming reds of maple and sumac. A row of hawthorn offered us both thorns and tiny, autumn apples. A paper birch lunged white against a perfect blue sky. Abe took a half-smoked stogie out of his coat pocket and slogged along, head down, chewing absentmindedly.

We had made two-thirds of the mile-and-a-half circuit and were approaching the crest of the small hill that overlooked the road when Abe sat down on a fallen birch and began methodically emptying his shoes of dirt and twigs. I sat nearby and looked back toward the pond we had circled near the inlet.

"You still have the Das manuscript?" he asked suddenly.

"Yes." If he asked next to use it in *Other Voices*—agreement or no agreement—our friendship would be at an end.

"Hmmm." Abe cleared his throat and spat. "*Harper's* give you any shit about not doing the article?"

"No." I heard a woodpecker pounding somewhere beyond the road. "I returned the advance. They insisted on still picking up the travel expenses. Morrow's not with them anymore, you know."

"Yeah." Abe lit the cigar. The smell fit perfectly with the autumn crispness. "Decide yet what you're gonna do with the fucking poem?"

"No."

"Don't publish it, Bobby. Anywhere. Anytime." He threw the still smoking match into a pile of leaves. I retrieved it and squeezed it between my fingers.

"No," I said. We were silent for awhile. A cool breeze came up and moved brittle leaves against each other. Far off to the north a squirrel was loudly scolding a trespasser.

"Did you know I lost most of my family in the Holocaust, Bobby?" Abe asked suddenly, not looking at me.

"No. I didn't know that."

"Yeah. Momma got out because she and Jan were in London on their way to visit me. Jan went back to try to get Moshe, Mutti, and the rest out. Never saw them again."

I said nothing. Abe exhaled cigar smoke against the blue sky. "I mention this, Bobby, because afterwards everything seems so *inevitable*, you know what I mean? You keep thinking you could have changed it but you didn't—like you forgot to do something, then everything happened like clockwork. You know what I mean?"

"Yes."

"Well, it *isn't* inevitable, Bobby. It's just plain fucking bad luck, is all. It's no one's fault. No one's except the mean bastards that feed off that shit."

I sat without speaking for a long time. Leaves spiralled down around us, adding their sad beauty to the carpet already there. "I don't know, Abe," I said at last. My throat hurt almost too much to go on. "I did *everything* wrong. Taking them there. Not leaving when I saw how crazy things were. Not making sure their plane got off okay. And I don't understand any of it. Who was responsible? Who *were* they? Krishna? What did the Kamakhya woman have to gain . . . How does she fit in? Most of all, why did I make the goddamned stupid mistake of taking Das that gun when—"

"Two shots," said Abe.

"What?"

"You told me that night you called that you heard two shots."

"Yeah, well, it was an automatic."

"So what? You think maybe when you blow your brains out you shoot again just to make sure? Eh?"

"What are you driving at, Abe?"

"*You* didn't kill Das, Bobby. *Das* didn't kill Das. One of the friendly Kapalika fellows maybe had a reason to set things up that way, eh? Your buddy Krishna . . . Sanjay . . . whatever the fuck his name was—maybe he wanted to be Poet Laureate for a little while."

"Why—" I stopped and watched a seagull pivot on a thermal several hundred feet above us. "But what did *Victoria* have to do with any of it? Oh, God, Abe . . . how could hurting her help anyone? I don't understand any of it."

Abe rose and spat again. Chips of bark clung to his suit. "Let's go, huh, Bobby? I got to get the bus back to Boston to get the damn train."

I started to lead the way down the hill, but Abe grabbed my arm. He was looking hard at me. "Bobby, you've got to know one thing. You don't have to understand. You *won't* understand. You won't forget, either. Don't think you will . . . you won't. But you got to keep going. You hear me? Day by day, maybe, but you got to keep going. Otherwise the fuckers win. We can't let them do that, Bobby. You understand me?"

I nodded and turned quickly to follow the faint trail.

On November 2 I received a short letter from Inspector Singh. It informed me that the male suspect, Sugata Chowdury, would not be standing trial. During his detention in Hooghly Prison Chowdury had "met with foul play." Specifically, someone had stuffed a towel down his throat while he slept. The woman identified as Devi Chowdury was expected to come to trial within the month. Singh promised to keep me informed. I never heard from him again.

In mid-November, shortly after the first heavy snowfall of that bitter winter, I reread Das's manuscript, including the final hundred pages that I had not finished in Calcutta. Das has been correct in his succinct summary: it was a birth announcement. To get the gist of it I would recommend Yeats' "The Second Coming." Yeats was a better poet.

It occurred to me then that my problem with deciding what to do with Das's manuscript was oddly similar to the problem the Parsees have in disposing of their dead. The Parsees, a dwindling minority in India, hold earth, air, fire, and water all as sacred and do not wish to pollute them with the bodies of their dead. Their solution is ingenious. Years ago Amrita had described to me the Tower of Silence in a Bombay park, above which circle the vultures in patient spirals.

I refused to burn the manuscript because I did not want the smoke rising like a sacrificial offering to that dark thing I sensed waiting just beyond the fragile walls of my sanity.

In the end, my solution was more prosaic than the Tower of Silence. I shredded the several hundred pages by hand—smelling the stink of Calcutta rising from the paper—and then stuffed the shredded strips in a Glad Bag to which I added some rotting vegetables to discourage scroungers. I drove several miles to a large dump and watched as the black bag bounced down a steep ravine of garbage to settle out of sight in a pool of foul muck.

Driving back, I knew that ridding myself of the manuscript had not stopped the Song of Kali from echoing in my mind.

Amrita and I continued to inhabit the same house. We suffered advice and continued sympathy from our friends, but we saw other people less and less as the harsh winter progressed. We also saw less and less of each other.

Amrita had decided to finish up her Ph.D. work, and she set into her schedule of early rising, teaching, library work, grading papers in the evening, more research, and early to bed. I rose very late and was often gone for dinner and much of the evening. When Amrita gave up the study about ten P.M., I would take possession of it and read until the early hours of the morning. I read everything during those sunless months—Spengler, Ross McDonald, Malcolm Lowry, Hegel, Stanley Elkin, Bruce Catton, Ian Fleming, and Sinclair Lewis. I read classics I'd had on my shelves unread for decades, and I brought home best-sellers from Safeway. I read everything.

In February a friend offered me a temporary teaching position at a small college north of Boston, and I took it. At first I commuted each day, but soon I took a small furnished apartment near the campus and went back to Exeter only on weekends. Frequently I did not return even then.

Amrita and I never talked about Calcutta. We did not mention Victoria's name. Amrita was retreating into a world of number theory and Boolean Algebra. It seemed to be a comfortable world for her: a world in which rules were abided by and truth tables could be logically determined. I was left outside with nothing but my unwieldy tools of language and the unfixable, nonsensical machine of reality.

I was at the college for four months and might not have

returned to Exeter if a friend had not called to tell me that Amrita had been hospitalized. Doctors diagnosed her problem as acute pneumonia complicated by exhaustion. She was hospitalized for eight days and too weak to get out of bed at home for a week after that. I stayed home during that time, and in the small acts of nursing I was beginning to feel echoes of our earlier tenderness; but then she announced that she felt better, she returned to her computer work in mid-June, and I went back to my apartment. I felt irresolute and lost, as if some huge, dark hole was opening wider in me, sucking me down.

I bought the Luger that June.

Roy Bennet, a taciturn little biology professor I'd met at the college, had invited me to his gun club in April. For years I had supported gun-control laws and hated the idea of handguns, but by the end of that school year I was spending most Saturdays on the firing range with Bennet. Even the children there seemed proficient at the two-handed, wide-legged firing stance that I knew only from the movies. When someone had to retrieve a target, everyone politely broke their weapons open and stepped back from the firing line with a smile. Many of the targets were in the shape of human bodies.

When I suggested that I would like to buy my own gun, Roy smiled with the quiet joy of a successful missionary and suggested that a .22-caliber target pistol would be good to start with. I nodded agreement, and the next day spent a small fortune for a vintage 7.65mm Luger. The woman who sold it said that the automatic had been her late husband's pride and joy. She included a handsome carrying case in the price.

I never mastered the preferred two-handed stance, but

became reasonably proficient at putting holes in the target at twenty yards. I had no idea what the others were thinking or feeling as they plinked away on those long-shadowed evenings, but each time I raised that oiled and balanced instrument I felt the power of its pent-up energy course through me like a shot of strong whiskey. The slow, careful squeezing, the deafening report, and the blow of the recoil along my stiffened arm created something akin to ecstasy in me.

I brought the Luger back to Exeter with me one weekend after Amrita's recovery. She came downstairs late one night and found me turning the freshly oiled and loaded weapon over and over in my hands. She said nothing, but looked at me for a long moment before going back upstairs. Neither of us mentioned it in the morning.

"There's a new book out in India. Quite the rage. An epic poem, I believe. All about Kali, one of their tutelary goddesses," said the book salesman.

I had come down to New York for a party at Doubleday, attracted more by the offer of free drinks than by anything else. I was on the balcony and debating whether to get my fourth Scotch when I heard the salesman talking to two distributors. I went over and took him by the arm, led him to a far corner of the balcony. The man had just returned from a trade fair in New Delhi. He did not know who I was. I explained that I was a poet interested in contemporary Indian writing.

"Yes, well, I'm afraid I can't tell you much about this book," he said. "I mentioned it because it seemed such a damned unlikely thing to be selling so well over there. Just a long poem, really. I guess it's taken the Indian intellectuals by storm. We wouldn't be interested, of course. Poetry never sells here, much less if it's—"

"What's the title?" I asked.

"It's funny, but I did remember that," he said. "*Kalisambvha* or *Kalisavba* or something like that. I remembered it because I used to work with a girl named Kelly Summers and I noticed the—"

"Who's the author?"

"Author? I'm sorry, I don't recall that. I only remember the book because the publisher had this huge display but no real graphics, you know? Just this big pile of books there. I kept seeing the blue cover in all the bookstores in the Delhi hotels. Have you ever been to India?"

"Das?"

"What?"

"Was the author's name Das?" I said.

"No, it wasn't Das," he said. "At least I don't think so. Something Indian and hard to pronounce, I think."

"Was his first name Sanjay?" I asked.

"Sorry, I have no idea," said the salesman. He was becoming irritated. "Look, does it make that much difference?"

"No," I said, "it doesn't make any difference." I left him and went to lean on the balcony railing. I was still there two hours later when the moon rose over the serrated teeth of the city.

I received the photograph in mid-July.

Even before I saw the postmark I knew the letter was from India. The smell of the country rose from the flimsy envelope.

It was postmarked Calcutta. I stood at the end of our drive under the leaves of the big birch tree and opened the envelope.

I saw the note on the back of the photograph first. It said *Das is alive*, nothing more. The photo was in black and white, grainy; the people in the foreground were almost washed out by a poorly used flash while the people in the near background were mere silhouettes. Das, however, was immediately recognizable. His face was scabbed and the nose was distorted, but the leprosy was not nearly so obvious as when I had met him. He was wearing a white shirt, and his hand was extended as if he were making a point to students.

The eight men in the photo were all seated on cushions around a low table. The flash showed paint peeling from a wall behind Das and a few dirty cups on the table. Two other men's faces were clearly illuminated, but I did not know them. My eyes went to a silhouette of a man seated on Das's right. It was too dark to make out facial features, but there was enough profile for me to see the predatory beak of a nose and the hair standing out like a black nimbus.

There was nothing in the envelope except the photograph.

Das is alive. What was I supposed to make of that? That M. Das had been resurrected yet another time by his bitch goddess? I looked at the photo again and stood tapping it against my fingers. There was no way of telling when the picture had been taken. Was the figure in the shadows Krishna? There was something about the hunched-forward aggressiveness of the head and body that made me want to say it was.

Das is alive.

I turned away from the driveway and walked into the woods. Underbrush grabbed at my ankles. There was a tilting, spinning emptiness inside me that threatened to open into a black chasm. I knew that once the darkness opened, there would be no hope of my escaping it.

A quarter of a mile from the house, near where the stream widened into a marshy area, I knelt and tore the photograph into tiny pieces. Then I rolled a large rock over and sprinkled the pieces onto the matted, faded ground there before rolling the rock back in place.

While walking home I retained the image of moist white things burrowing frantically to avoid the light.

Amrita came into the room that night while I was packing. "We need to talk," she said.

"When I get back," I said.

"Where are you going, Bobby?"

"New York," I said. "Just for a couple of days." I put another shirt over the place where I had packed away the Luger and 64 cartridges.

"It's important that we talk," said Amrita. Her hand touched my arm.

I pulled away and zipped closed my black suitcase. "When I get back," I said.

I left my car at home, took a train to Boston, caught a cab to Logan International, and boarded a ten P.M. TWA flight to Frankfurt with connections to Calcutta.

Chapter Seventeen

"*And what rough beast, its hour come round at last, Slouches toward Bethlehem to be born*?"

—William Butler Yeats

The sun rose as we were approaching the English coast, but even with the sunlight falling across my legs I felt trapped in a night that would not end. I was shivering violently, acutely aware that I was strapped into a fragile, pressurized tube suspended thousands of feet above the sea. Worse that that was a growing inward pressure that I first attributed to a claustrophobic reaction but then realized was something else altogether. There was a vertiginous tilting within me, like the first solid stirrings of some powerful homunculus.

I sat gripping the armrests and watching the silent mouthings of characters on a movie screen while Europe passed beneath us. I thought of Tagore's last moments. Meals arrived and were dutifully eaten. Late in the day I tried to sleep. And all the while the hollowness and dizziness grew stronger and there was the constant sound of insect wings in my ears. Repeatedly I would be on the verge of sleep, only to snap awake to the sound of distant, mocking laughter. Eventually I gave up the attempt to sleep.

I forced myself to join the other passengers during the refueling stop in Tehran. The pilot had announced the temperature outside as being 33 degrees, and only when the terrible heat and humidity struck me did I realize that it had been given in degrees Celsius.

It was late, sometime before midnight, but the hot air stank of waiting violence. Pictures of the Shah were everywhere in the echoing, brightly lit barn of a terminal, and security men and soldiers roamed around with their sidearms drawn for no apparent reason. Muslim women cloaked in black *chadors* glided like wraiths through the green fluorescent emptiness. Old men slept on the floor or knelt on their dark prayer rugs amid cigarette butts and cellophane wrappers while nearby an American boy of about six—blond hair and red-striped shirt incongruous among dark hues, crouched behind a chair and raked the customs counter with automatic fire from his toy M-16.

The PA system announced that our flight would be re-boarding in fifteen minutes. I stumbled past an old man in a red scarf and found myself in the public restrooms. It was very dark in there, the only light reflected from a single bulb outside the entrance. Dark shapes moved through the gloom. For a second I wondered if I had inadvertently entered the women's side and was seeing *chadors* in the darkness, but then I heard deep voices speaking in guttural syllables. There was also the sound of water dripping. At that second the dizziness struck me worse than before, and I crouched over one of the Asian toilets and vomited, continuing to spasm long after I had rid myself of the last of the airline meals.

I collapsed sideways and lay full-length on the cool tile floor. The emptiness inside me was almost complete now. I trembled as sweat poured from me and mixed with the salt of my tears. The incessant insect noise had risen to a crescendo so that I could hear distinct voices. The Song of Kali was very loud. I realized that already I had crossed the borders into her new domain.

In a few minutes I rose in the darkness, cleaned myself as well as I could at the only sink, and walked quickly into the green light to joint the others lining up for the flight to Calcutta.

We came out of the clouds, circled once, and landed at Calcutta's Dum-Dum Airport at 3:10 A.M. I joined the line descending the staircase to the wet tarmac. The city seemed to be on fire. The orange light turned back by the low monsoon clouds, the red beacons reflected in countless puddles, and the blaze of spotlights from beyond the terminal added to the illusion. I could hear no sound but the chanting chorus of shrill voices as I stumbled along with the others toward the customs shed.

A year before, Amrita, Victoria, and I had spent more than an hour going through customs in Bombay. This time I was through in less than five minutes. I had not the slightest anxiety that they would open my luggage. The little man in soiled khaki chalked an X on my suitcase directly over the outside compartment where I had hidden the Luger and ammunition, and then I was in the main terminal, walking toward the outside doors.

Someone will be here to meet me. Probably Krishna-Sanjay. He will tell me where to find the Kamakhya bitch before he dies.

It was almost three-thirty in the morning but the crowd was no less intense than the other times I had been in the airport. People shouted and shoved in the sick light from sputtering fluorescent strips, but I could barely hear the noise as I stepped over Kipling's "sheeted dead" while making little effort to avoid treading on the sleeping forms. I let the crowd move me. My arms and legs felt anesthetized, jerking along as if I had become a poorly handled marionette. I closed my eyes to listen to the Song and to feel the energy from the weapon only inches from my right hand.

Chatterjee and Gupta also will have to die. However small their complicity, they will have to die.

I stumbled along with the crowd like a man caught in a terrible windstorm. The noise and smell and pressure from the jostling mob joined perfectly with the growing emptiness within me to form a dark flower unfolding in my mind. The laughter was very loud now. Behind my closed eyelids I could see Her visage rising above the gray towers of the dying city, hear Her voice leading the rising chant, see Her arms moving to the beat of the terrible dance.

When you open you eyes you will see someone you know. You do not have to wait. Let it begin here.

I forced my eyes to stay shut, but gripping the suitcase with both hands I raised it to my chest. I could feel the crowd moving me forward with them toward the open doors. Screams of porters and the sewer-sweet smells of Calcutta came in clearly now. I felt my right hand begin unzipping the outside compartment of the suitcase where I had packed the loaded gun.

Let it begin here.

With my eyes still closed I saw the next few minutes opening before me like the waiting doors, like the maw of the great beast that was the city, and I could sense the dark flower opening wide inside me and then the lifting of the oiled perfection of the Luger and then the sacrament will commence, and then the power will flow up my arm and into me and through me and out of me in coughs of flame in the night, and the running forms will fall and I will reload with the satisfying *snick* of the new magazine sliding into place and the pain and the power will flow from me and the running forms will fall and flesh will fly from flesh from the impact and the flames of chimneys will light the sky and by their red hue I will find my way through the streets and lanes and alleys and I will find Victoria, in time this time, find Victoria in time, and I will kill those who took her from me and kill those who get in my way and kill everyone who—

Let it begin now.

"No!" I screamed and opened my eyes. My scream quelled the Song for only a second or two but in that time I pulled my hand out of the open suitcase compartment and shoved violently to my left. The doors were only ten paces in front of me and the crowd surged relentlessly toward them, the current of their progress faster now, more concentrated. Through the doors I caught a glimpse of a man in a white shirt standing by a small blue-and-white bus. The man's hair rose like spikes of dark electricity.

"No!" I used the suitcase as a battering ram to fight my way to the wall. A tall man in the crowd shoved me and I struck him in the chest until he let me pass. I was only three steps from the open doors now, and the movement of the crowd pulled me along as surely as an explosion of air into a vacuum.

Let it begin now.

"No!" I do not know if I shouted aloud. I threw myself forward, shoved against the crowd like a man wading chest-deep in a river, and with my left hand grasped the bar of an unmarked side door leading into the off-limits section of the terminal. Somehow I managed to hold onto the suitcase while human forms battered against me, fingers and arms accidentally striking my face in the melee.

I pushed through the door and ran, my suitcase banging against my right leg, surprised airport workers stepping aside as I passed. The Song roared louder than ever before, bringing enough pain to make me squeeze my eyes shut.

Let it begin here. Let it begin now.

I stopped in mid-stride, struck the wall, and stumbled backward with the force of the compulsion. My arms and legs twitched and thrashed as if I was in the midst of an epileptic seizure. I took two steps back toward the terminal.

"Fuck you!" I screamed—I think I screamed—and managed to stumble sideways against a wall that was a door, and then I was on my hands and knees in a long, dark room.

The door closed and there was silence. True silence. I was alone. The room was long and dimly lit, empty except for a few unclaimed stacks of luggage, some boxes, and trunks. I sat down on the cement floor and looked around with a rising shock of recognition. I looked to my right and saw the battered counter where the airline casket had waited.

The Song had stopped.

For several minutes I sat on the floor and panted. The emptiness in me was almost a pleasant thing now—an absence of something black and poisonous.

I closed my eyes. I remembered holding Victoria the night she was born, the other times, the milk and baby smell of her, and the thirty-step walk from the delivery room to the nursery.

Without opening my eyes I gripped the handle of my suitcase and—rising now—flung it as far as I could across the long room. It bounced off a dusty shelf and crashed out of sight into a heap of boxes.

I left the room, walked twenty steps down an empty corridor, emerged into the terminal ten paces from the only occupied ticket counter, and bought a ticket for the next flight out.

There were no delays. The Lufthansa flight to Munich held only ten other passengers when it lifted off the runway twenty minutes later. I did not even think about looking out to catch a last glimpse of Calcutta. I was asleep before the landing gear retracted.

I landed in New York the next afternoon and caught a Delta 727 to Logan International in Boston. There the last of my nervous energy left me and I could not keep my voice from cracking as I called Amrita and asked her for a ride.

By the time she got there in the red Pinto, I was shaking all over and not completely aware of my surroundings. She wanted to take me to a hospital, but I slumped deep into the black vinyl seat and said, "Drive. Please drive."

We headed north on I-95 with the evening sun throwing long shadows across the median. The fields were wet from a recent rainstorm. My teeth were chattering almost uncontrollably, but I insisted on talking. Amrita drove in silence, occasionally glancing at me with those deep, sad eyes. She did not interrupt me even when I began to babble.

"I realized that it was exactly what they wanted me to do. What *She* wanted me to do," I said as we approached the state line. "I don't know why. Maybe She wanted me to take his place the way he took Das's. Or maybe Krishna saved me because he knew they would bring me back someday for some other insanity. I don't know. I don't *care*. Do you see what's really important?"

Amrita looked at me and said nothing. Evening light turned her tan skin gold.

"I've been blaming myself every day, knowing that I'll go on blaming myself until I die. I thought it was my fault. It *was* my fault. Now I know you've been blaming yourself."

"If I hadn't let her in—" began Amrita.

"Yes!" I said. It was almost a shout. "I know. But we have to stop that. If we don't go beyond that, we'll not only destroy each other and ourselves, we'll destroy what the three of us *meant*. We'll be part of the darkness."

Amrita pulled into a rest stop near the Salisbury Plains exit. She took her hands off the wheel. We sat in silence for several minutes.

"I miss Victoria," I said. It was the first time I had said our child's name to her since Calcutta. "I miss our baby. I miss Victoria."

Her head came over against my chest. I could barely understand her through the muffling of my shirt and the beginning of her own tears. Then it was clear.

"So do I, Bobby," she said. "I miss Victoria too."

We held each other as the trucks moved by in a rush of wind and noise and the last of the rush-hour traffic filled the lanes with sunbaked colors and the sound of tires on pavement.

Chapter 18

"Considering that, all hatred driven hence,
The soul recovers radical innocence
And learns at last that it is self-delighting,
Self-appeasing, self-affrighting,
And that its own sweet will is Heaven's will;
She can, though every face should scowl
And every windy quarter howl
Or every bellows burst, be happy still."
—William Butler Yeats
A PRAYER FOR MY DAUGHTER

We live in Colorado now. In the spring of 1982 I was invited out to do a modest workshop at a mountain college here and I went back East only long enough to get Amrita. Our subsequent visit has turned into a reasonably permanent residence. We've leased the house in Exeter, furnishings and all, but the eight paintings are hanging here against the rough wood of the cabin and the little Jamie Wyeth oil sketch we purchased in 1973 comes closest to catching the rich play of light we see out the window. That quality of light obsessed us our first few months here, and both Amrita and I have—sheepishly at first—tried oil painting.

The college facilities here are primitive by Boston standards, our salaries are low; but the house we're living in was once a ranger's cabin, and from our large window we can see snowy peaks over a hundred miles to the north. The light is so sharp and clear that it borders on being painful.

We wear jeans most of the time, and Amrita has learned how to handle the four-wheel-drive Bronco in mud and snow. We miss the ocean. Even more, we miss some of our friends and the benefits of coastal civilization. Our nearest town now is eight miles down the mountain from the campus and its boasts only 7,000 people at the height of the summer influx. The fanciest restaurant is called *la Cocina*, and our other dining choices are the Pizza Hut, Nora's Breakfast Nook, Gary's Grill, and the 24-hour truck stop on the Interstate. In the summer Amrita and I give a lot of our business to the Tastee Freez. The town library is operating out of an AirStream trailer until the new Civic Center is built. Denver is almost three hours away, and both mountain passes are closed for days at a time in winter.

But the air seems espcially clean here, and we feel somehow lighter in the morning, as if the altitude includes a dispensation from some of the gravity that inflicts its imperative on the rest of the world. And the quality of daylight here is more than a pleasant phenomenon, it is a form of clarity to us. A clarity which heals.

* * *

Abe Bronstein died last autumn. He had just finished work on the Winter Issue, the one that included a short piece by Ann Beattie, when he suffered a massive coronary while walking to the subway.

Amrita and I flew back for his funeral. Afterwards, over coffee with other mourners in the small townhouse he had shared with his mother, the old woman beckoned for Amrita and me to join her in Abe's room.

The small bedroom was made even smaller by the floor-to-ceiling bookshelves that filled the better part of three walls. Mrs. Bronstein was eighty-six and seemed too frail to hold herself erect as she sat there on the edge of the bed. The room smelled of Abe's brand of cigars and of leather bookbindings.

"Here, please," said the old woman. Her hand was surprisingly steady as she handed me the small envelope. "Abraham left instructions for you to have this, Robert." Her throaty voice must once have been beautifully exciting. Now, as it measured out the words in the precise diction of an acquired language, it was merely beautiful. "Abraham said that I was to deliver this to you personally—even, as he put it, if I had to walk to Colorado to find you."

At any other time, the image of this frail old woman hitchhiking across the prairie would have brought a smile from me. Now I nodded and opened the letter.

> "Bobby— April 9, 1983
>
> If you're reading this letter, then neither one of us is terribly thrilled about recent events. I've just come from my doctor. While he didn't tell me not to buy any long-playing records, he didn't try to sell me any long-term certificates either.

I hope that you (and Amrita?) didn't have to drop anything important. That is, if there *could* be anything important going on out there in that godforsaken wilderness you're calling home as of this writing.

I recently revised my will. Right now I'm sitting in the park near my old friend the Mad Hatter, enjoying a panatela, and watching some girls in halter tops and shorts tyring to convince themselves that it's really spring. It's a warm day but not so warm that it keeps their goosebumps from showing.

If Momma hasn't told you all yet, my new will leaves everything to her. Everything, that is, except the original Proust editions; the authors' correspondence files in my safety-deposit box; and the rights, titles, modest bank account, and executive editorship of *Other Voices*. These go to you, Bobby.

Now wait a minute. I don't want to be accused of hanging an albatross around your carefree Polish neck. Feel free to dispose of the magazine as you see fit. If you'd prefer that some other responsible party continue it—fine. I've given you full power of attorney for any such arrangement.

Bobby, just remember what we wanted the magazine to be. Don't unload it on some fucking conglomerate that wants a tax write-off and who'll hire some schmuck who can't tell good prose from day-old piss. If you have to put the magazine to sleep rather than lower its standards, that's all right by me.

If, on the other hand, you decide to keep it

going—*good*. You'll be surprised how portable a magazine like *Voices* can be. Take it out to wherever the hell it is that you live. (Miller was going to raise the rent on us anyway.) If you do give it a go, don't spend time worrying about continuing "Abe's old editorial policy." Abe didn't have any editorial policy! Just print the good stuff, Roberto. Follow your instincts.

One thing, though. Not all of the best writing has to be *Naked Lunch Regurgitated*. A lot of the stuff coming in will depress the hell out of you. If it's good, it deserves to be printed, but there's still room for writing that holds out some hope for humanity. At least I think there is. You know better than I, Bobby. You've been closer to the flames and managed to return.

Got to go. There's a cop been eyeing me here and I think he's appraised me correctly as a Dirty Old Man.

You can read this to Momma—she won't rest until you do—but leave out the "day-old piss" and the "fucking" before "conglomerate," Okay? Your first editing chore.

My love to Amrita.

—Abe"

Abe was right. The magazine was quite portable. The college was thrilled to have *Other Voices* originating from its P.O. box, and they obligingly cut back my teaching time to two sections with no cut in pay. I suspect that they would pay me for *no* teaching if my presence would keep Amrita in their math department. For her part, Amrita is pleased by the easy access to the college computer terminal that shares time with some monster Cray computer in Denver. She recently made the comment—"This place is pretty up to date." While on her way to the math building, she obviously has not noticed the quonset-hut dormitories, cinderblock buildings, and minuscule library.

I find it reasonably easy to edit an Eastern literary journal from the top of a Colorado mountain, although I do have to make five or six trips a year to confer with printers and to visit with some of the writers and sponsors. Amrita has become involved with the publication and has shown surprising strength as a reader. She says that her training in language and mathematics has given her a sense of symbolic balance—whatever the hell that means. But it has been at Amrita's urging that I've tried to include more Western writers including Joanne Greenberg and the Cowboy Poet of Creed.

The results have been encouraging. Subscriptions have gone up recently, we've established several shelfsale outlets, and our old readership appears to be remaining loyal. We shall see.

I have written no poetry. Not since Calcutta.

The Song of Kali never quite goes away. It is a background sound to me like discordant music from a poorly tuned radio station.

I still dream of crossing muddy wastes with gray-wrapped bodies underfoot while distant chimneys send up flames to lick at low clouds.

Some nights the wind comes up and I rise and go to the front window of the cabin and look into the blackness and hear the scrabbling of six limbs on the rocks outside. I wait, then, but the gaunt face with its hungry mouth and its thirsting eyes stays just back in the darkness, held away by . . . by what? I do not know.

But the Song of Kali still is sung.

Recently, not far from us here, an older woman and her grown daughter, both self-described "good Christians," baked her grandson in the oven to drive out the demons that made him cry in the evening.

One of my students here is distantly related to the California high school student who recently raped and murdered his girlfriend and then brought fourteen of his friends to view the body over a three-day period. One boy dropped a brick on the corpse to make sure she was dead. None of the kids thought to mention it to the authorities.

One of the new printers I met at Adamsons in New York last month was Siem Ry, a 42-year-old refugee from Phnom Penh. He had owned his own printing company there and was able to bribe his way into Thailand and to the U.S. a few years ago. He worked his way up in Adamsons after starting over as a printer's devil. Over a few drinks, Ry told me about the forced evacuation of the city and the eight-day forced march which killed his parents. He quietly told me about the labor camp that claimed his wife, and about the morning he awoke to find that his three children had been taken to an "education-labor camp" in a distant part of the country. Ry described a field he stumbled into while escaping. He said that human skulls were piled three-and four-feet deep across half an acre in one place.

The Age of Kali has begun.

* * *

I went down to the mobile-home library last week and read up on the so-called Black Hole of Calcutta. It had been only a phrase to me until then. The historical details were not relevent to much of anything. Essentially, the Black Hole was just an airless room crammed full of too many people during one of the sporadic rebellions in the 1800's.

But the phrase still haunts me. I've developed a theory about Calcutta, although theory is too dignified a word for such an intuitive opinion.

I think that there are black holes in reality. Black holes in the human spirit. And actual places where, because of density or misery or sheer human perversity, the fabric of things just comes apart and that black core in us swallows all the rest.

I read the papers, I look around, and I have a sinking feeling that these black holes are growing larger, more common, feeding on their own vile appetite. They are not restricted to strange cities in distant countries.

Without telling Amrita any of this, I asked her recently about astronomical black holes. She gave a long explanation, much of it based on the work of a man named Stephen Hawking, much of it technical, most of it indecipherable to me. But a couple of things she mentioned interested me. First, she said that it *did* look as if light and other captured energies might be able to escape astronomical black holes after all. I forget the details of her explanation, but the impression I got was that although it was impossible to climb out of a black hole, energy might "tunnel out" into another place and time. Second, she said that even if all the matter and energy in the universe were gobbled up by black holes, it would only ensure that the mass came together into another Big Bang that would start what she called a Fresh New Universe with new laws, new forms, and blazing new galaxies of light.

Maybe. I sit on a mountaintop and weave weak metaphors, all the while remembering a pale hint of cheek in a dirty shawl. Sometimes I touch the palm of my hand in an attempt to recall the sensation the last time I cupped Victoria's head in my hand. *Take care of your mom until I get back, okay, Little One*?

And the wind rises outside and the stars shake in the chill of night.

Amrita is pregnant. She hasn't told me yet, but I know that she confirmed it with her doctor two days ago. I think she's worried about what my reaction will be. She needn't be.

A month ago, just before school started again in September, Amrita and I took the Bronco up to the end of an old mining road and then backpacked about three miles along the ridgeline. There was no sound except for the breeze through the pines below us. The valleys there were either never inhabited or abandoned when the old mines played out. We explored a few of the old diggings and then crossed another ridge to where we could see snow-topped peaks extending away in all directions, to and beyond the curve of the planet. We paused to watch a hawk circle silently on high thermals half a mile above us.

That night we camped near a high lake, a small, perfect circle of painfully cold snowmelt. The half-moon rose about midnight and cast a pale brilliance on the surrounding peaks. Patches of snow caught the moonlight on the rocky slope near us.

Amrita and I made love that night. It was not the first time since Calcutta, but it was the first time we were able to forget everything except each another. Afterward, Amrita fell asleep with her head on my chest while I lay there and watched the Perseid meteors cut their way across the August night sky. I counted twenty-eight before I fell asleep.

Amrita is thirty-eight, almost thirty-nine. I'm sure that her doctor will recommend amniocentesis. I'm going to urge her not to go through that. Amniocentesis is helpful primarily if the parents are willing to abort the fetus if there are genetic problems. I don't think we are. I also feel—feel very strongly—that there will be no problems.

It might be best if we were to have a boy this time, but it will be fine either way. There will be painful recollections with a baby in the house, but it will be less painful than the hurt we've shared so long now.

I still believe that some places are too wicked to be suffered. Occasionally, I dream of nuclear mushroom clouds rising above a city and human figures dancing against the flaming pyre that once was Calcutta.

Somewhere there are dark choruses ready to proclaim the Age of Kali. I am sure of this. As sure as I am that there will always be servants to do Her bidding.

All violence is power, Mr. Luczak.

Our child will be born is the spring. I want him or her to know all of the pleasures of hillsides under clear skies, of hot chocolate on a winter's morning, and of laughter on a grassy Saturday afternoon in summer. I want our child to hear the friendly voices of good books and the even-friendlier silences in the company of good people.

* * *

I have not written any poetry in years, but recently I bought a large, well-bound book of blank pages and I've written in it every day. It is not poetry. It is not for publication. It is a story—a series of stories, actually—about the adventures of a group of unlikely friends. There is a talking cat, a fearless and precocious mouse, a gallant but lonely centaur, and a vainglorious eagle who is afraid to fly. It is a story about courage and friendship and small quests to interesting places. It is a bedtime storybook.

The Song of Kali is with us. It has been with us for a very long time. Its chorus grows and grows and grows.

But there are other voices to be heard. There are other songs to be sung.